THE CALL OF MAGIC

THE CALL OF MAGIC

THEODORE BELCASTRO

Other Novels by the Author

Honour Bound
Raven's Masquerade

Coming Soon...

Blood & Wine
Fiction & Fables (Short Story Collection)

A Note From the Author

It's a generally accepted truth that there are two certainties in life: death, and the absolute necessity of a sensible jumper in a British summer. A third, less well-advertised certainty, is that every good story needs a sturdy beginning, and not one that's been run through a third-rate editing package and spat out onto cheap paper.

But before we get to our tale of proper, actual magic, a brief word on the *other* kind. The common, mundane, yet staggeringly effective magic that allows certain organisations—often with names suggesting ancient Greek aspiration or perhaps just an overpriced sports shoe—to convince people that paying a princely sum is the only path to literary success. This is a dark, cynical magic that involves convincing talented, hopeful writers that a press release nobody reads (in the form of a singular social media post), a distribution method indistinguishable from leaving a box of books next to a postbox, and a contract that would make a tax collector weep with envy, is somehow a good deal.

It's a terrible, disheartening thing to watch a noble manuscript, brim-full of potential and genuine heart, get stripped of its dignity, its earnings, and its future by such an endeavour. Many a magnificent tale has ended up tethered to a "publishing house" with the promotional capabilities of a damp sock, all the while knowing that reclaiming the rights is often as easy as digging one's way out of a expensive, bureaucratic hole.

However, the magic in this book is rather more fearsome and fierier than the petty, contractual kind. It's about a young woman whose destiny, much like a good novel, was always meant to be free and independent. She finds herself called to an adventure where success is earned through courage and wit, not through a ridiculously high invoice for *enhanced platform promotion*.

Welcome to *The Call of Magic*. Where the only contract that matters is the one between the reader and the story.

I

A Green Moon and a
Paper Sword

Isla Morrigan moved along the narrow ledges of Falls
Creek's mountainsides, her fiery-red curls falling in wet
hanks around her shoulders. High winds blew, they howled
through stone and crevice. Clouds from an ebbing storm bore
down, obscuring the horizon of a new era, and the sea's spray
sent foamy suds into her pale cheeks.

Rounding a row of time-worn, stone teeth, Isla couldn't
bring herself to look down into the swell, although she heard
it lash against the rocks beneath her. Instead, damp skin
glowing magnificently in the scarce moonlight, she equipped
her longbow. Isla needed to find that lycan before the millen-
nial lunar eclipse. Before the celebrations.

Wrinkling her nose, Isla checked on Leif and glimpsed the two moons through the swift-moving nimbi above him. The eclipse was nigh.

Arriving at the alcove, a cavity within the central incisor, Isla ushered her bespectacled brother closer. Testing her drawstring as he arrived at her side, she gestured to the left and to their intended destination; she evaluated Leif's agitation as he took the lead at her insistence.

Isla pointed to his recurve bow, and he equipped it.

Steady your aim, they notched arrows together, *breathe*.

Leif's position was insecure. His slick and skinny fingers slipping on the drawstring. Legs too close together, a weak back, and an inbreath that lacked exhale. Isla beheld the incertitude blaze beyond those sullied spectacles and within his silver-grey eyes.

An arrow twanged and ricocheted from a rock, another shot past a willow, and the last one buried its tip within a carcass. Burgundy, coagulated blood splattered near a stunned Leif's feet, who'd yet to let loose a single shaft.

"Don't think while drawn, it only weakens your aim," said Isla as she retrieved her arrows. "Sheathe your weapon."

The willow branches whipped amid a breeze, while an irritable droning surrounded and penetrated the alcove. Mosquitoes and flies darted for the other remains that'd lay rigid in a muck of their own making which stained their charcoal-coloured coats.

A small number of wolves were slain; though, none of them were large enough to be mistaken for their lycan kingpin. He'd abandoned them as prey to the mountaintop's devilish crows. He'd betrayed his pack to escape.

Unknotting her locks, Isla brushed her lengthy curls behind an ear and swung her travelling bag around. Bypassing Velyn, a toy dragon, she retrieved a dagger. Eagerly slicing into the carcass ahead of her, she promptly raised a brow and toyed with the blood between her fingers.

"Leif, did you bring the bait?"

"Bait?" He cocked his head to the side. "I... well, I've bread and water?"

"Alongside parchment and a pencil, of course," said Isla, sliding the dagger into her sleeve and exhaling through her nose. "Had every hunter of this beast been as ill-equipped as yourself, there's no wonder why they failed."

"Isla, nobody has searched for our quarry since Father."

"Exactly."

Arms akimbo, Isla assessed the alcove.

But instead of discerning a clue to their target's whereabouts, she'd focused on her older brother as he'd bit his thumb and thought. An ill-at-ease countenance wrinkling his brow. It was expected, given the day and the anniversary's significance, but there was something more beyond that. Something that'd deeply troubled him.

A shadow loomed, cast by the eclipsing moons, and it'd advanced across the alcove – swathing Leif in its tenebrous embrace. Following its progression, Isla looked beyond the onslaught where stockpiles and bonfires erupted aflame around the town. The feast had begun.

Shit! Isla kicked at dirt. *Even if it'd been here – even if I'd killed it – they'd be too drunk to care.*

Thick plumes of wayfaring smoke lingered on the town's skyline, obscuring the glowing cyan and fuchsia neolyt.

Despite of their distance from the wonky, black buildings of Falls Creek, the glow of nightlife illuminated the alcove's rock pool and critters within it: salamanders which required no extra help to brighten the area.

Carried through the willow's droopy branches, however, was neither light nor shadow but an implacable and feminine voice which'd said, *"Seud alqamir alkadhari. Amjad waeadu basahr."* And as the voice dissipated as easily as it'd came, a bizarre, emerald light from the eclipse parted clouds and shone brighter than the neolyt ever could.

Leif hadn't reacted; he was frozen in place. His countenance contorted in an everlasting regard of malaise. Yet Isla had, and she'd spotted their prey standing proudly on his hind legs, glaring – not at the peculiar occultation, but at her.

Quietude prevailed within the alcove, and not even the distant beat of a mazurka was present.

This was it. Her moment to strike.

Advancing into the stench of wet dog, an arrow notched, the reality she'd stood within rippled and tore apart. Colour disintegrated into finite pebbles, and again into tiny granules of sand, before being consumed by a melancholic blackness.

Blinking at the daunting anomaly that'd absorbed her entirely, Isla had entered an environment where she was alone and miles away from both her quarry and sibling.

Her brother had vanished, the carcasses were gone, and she was alone. Isla searched for an answer to where she'd ended up – blinking again and again to emulate the sudden ability to alternate her habitat. And she received a response: the wind soughing a deviant tune.

In the low vale, Isla wanted to flee and seek the high ground – to take the advantage against a surprise attack from the lycan, had it plotted against her in some unforeseen way. Frozen in place by questions flooding her mind worse than last year's deluge, however, Isla's feet wouldn't budge.

Shakily, she instead reached into her bag for her toy dragon.

Stroking its honey-coloured wooden spine, she inhaled and pictured herself in the Varangian Guard's archaic armour.

I'm okay, she assured, feeling a strange calling within. A voiceless calling, whose want she understood: power. *Probably hit my head and don't remember coming here.*

A rustle startled her, the lofty crops that formed a canopy intimidated her, and Isla thrust the toy back within her bag. Exhaling, she beheld the emerald light accentuate the western hills in a bright and guiding silhouette through a gap in the foliage.

But a green eclipse was unnatural.

When the people of Falls Creek spoke about eclipses, their colour remained the same: golden. Leif's monetary woes and her want to kill Father's elusive quarry thus seemed insignificant to the questions presented to her – to all. Why and how?

Another inbreath, a look around, and she nodded. Isla knew where she was, thus the answers to those questions had to wait.

The road led to a pathway which dipped past the eastern slope and framed several bristling pine trees before reaching the only forest in the crater where Falls Creek was situated.

It led home.

Losing the advantage, floored by curiosity, and becoming the hunted, Isla decided to return to the hunt another day. A day where both her mind and the sky were clear of aberrations – real or imagined.

From the little she could see of the illuminated skyline above town, on her return home, Isla noticed the usual light pollution's absence. Nothing but the twinkling stars were discerned aloft Falls Creek's loftiest building: the bordello. Mana had ceased to be that night.

How and why, she couldn't tell for certain, but wondered if the greenness of the moon had anything to do with it.

A low growl, muffled in the rustling leaves, resonated.

Isla re-equipped her longbow. Another growl, a footfall, and the slither of rocks tutting through grass; the panting of a dehydrated tongue. An arrow notched.

Isla's wrists swelled, as did her fingers that kept the drawstring taut – exactly what she'd scorned Leif for doing earlier. Back aching, pulled from her constant tension, she cursed beneath her breath. Angry at herself for suggesting the hunt; angry at Leif for uncharacteristically agreeing to it.

The grass hissed, closer this time. Moonlight dwindled behind flora, rapidly diminishing her view. A howl sounded from behind! Isla let the drawstring loose, scraping against her cheek and forearm.

A thud sounded on a gust and Isla pursued it without review, nearing the forest with every step. But the arrow had dug up nothing aside from dirt and snapped when hitting a rock.

Disheartened by the lack of dead lycan, a collection of aromas presented themselves to her: dirt, grass, and the scent of burning timber freshly doused by drizzling rain with a hint of cinnamon. No wet dog. Although the pleasant scents were soon overwhelmed by the distinct stench of sweaty armour.

Recalling the smell on Father and his clients, Isla spotted a quartet of cloaked individuals cut through the low-hanging leaves and moss and head into the forest.

Canine yelping demanded her attention and two fingers on the drawstring. But there was nothing to attack.

Returning to watch the group, they were already gone.

Isla wanted to go home. To recentre. Far too many things were demanding her attention, and she'd been drawn to them all as though attention deficient. She'd struggled with it at the best of times, while reading mostly, but it was a death sentence on the hunt.

A sentence she'd rather leave unwritten.

***

The iciness of pre-dawn settled in.

Kyojin snored, and owls hooted. The parted moons' revitalised silver light obscured by a canopy no longer belonging to crops, but criss-crossing boughs whose leaves were amber and orange. Thus, presented with a distinct lack of green light to drench the arable landscapes ahead of her, Isla puzzled over what she'd previously heard concerning green moons.

First, she thought of Leif's fables because it had to do with him – yet Father continued to come to mind, too. Then it hit her.

There was an argument, she vaulted over a felled tree. The fateful morning of Father and Mother's departure. Green moons and... something.

Carrying neither compass nor map and relying on experience to lead her home to their cottage on the town's outskirts, Isla trekked onward beneath the understorey. She bypassed the snarls of exotic creatures, and even the sun-kissed stony remains of the Amity Era's goblin army jutting out from dried riverbed filled with a funky cloud.

Plashes reverberated, and Isla's boots became wet with the red mud of Falls Creek's thaumaturgical soil. A different path than the one she knew. Though, and looking back, Isla swore that it was the right way.

Cold and hungry, she soon happened on scattered and disarranged travertine which she decided to keep to. However, they were rotted and riddled with greenery sprouting from every nook and cranny – topsoil unevenly covering what little of them were visible.

Isla continued along the path until arriving at a glade.

The ground looked dried and tattooed as if something had once belonged, but no leaves dressed the rectangular shape.

"Relax," a faint voice sounded. "We found this place, after all."

Retreating from the openness and behind a jagged stump, Isla peered around to see something or someone.

A sparkle, and a glimpse of an image, something like a painting, rippled through the air comparable to a portal from one of Leif's books. The shape of a small house. Branches sprouted from the chimney as etiolated leaves decorated the roof. The wood itself, broken and shabby. It rippled and warped, disproportioned and ugly, until popping into reality without a sound.

Isla hastily crouched below a window where a bough had grown through. Wrinkling her nose, she dug through her bag to clasp Velyn and stroke the dragon's spine. The voices became louder as a thinning, encircling fog lifted from the shack.

Peeking through the dirtied glass, she saw that the interior was overrun with weeds and the chimney puffed black smoke without igniting the conifer that sat amid the soot. She also spotted the same ominously cloaked quartet standing to the left of the fireplace.

Closer than before, Isla was able to discern a womanly fig-ure wield a peculiarly coiled staff, two men with their swords drawn, and one with his arms folded authoritatively. There was also a scrawny trio, separated and to the right. Those three wore leather coats laced with furs, and judging by their inconsistent lamellar armour Isla surmised their position as mercenaries.

Although contrasting, both groups wore the same polished, black-obsidian vambrace. All aside from the staff-wielder.

Isla shuffled closer, kneeling on a cluster of twigs. In unison, they bowed and snapped, and the staff-wielder turned to the window, revealing stone skin, and screwed up her nose.

Isla fell to her stomach, panting and praying that she was unsighted, however unlikely.

There was a sense of knowing in that quick glimpse.

Fresh fog then descended with a pop.

Isla rolled sideways, scurried on both hands and knees, and hugged the shack's exterior.

Knowing she shouldn't look; knowing the risk outweighed the reward... insatiable curiosity won her over. Brushing away twigs and leaves, she again peeked inside to observe the two men sheath their weapons.

Amid more muffled conversations, Isla could barely make out what was said but took note of words which bore emphasis: commandant, lieutenants, Ludwig, Enchantress, and Spellforge.

The latter name resonating with her as she tightened her grip on her toy, its wings singed and searing.

Presuming that the trio's tallest man was Ludwig, and the quartet were the lieutenants, commandant, and Enchantress, Isla pieced together the scenario. The potential commandant had ordered the lieutenant to his left to pay Ludwig, judging by the overspilling purse which he was greedily cupping.

"Within, you'll find more than what we'd initially offered," said the left-hand lieutenant as the fog dissipated again; the staff-wielder's stance faltering. "However, the extra isn't a bonus. It's there because we require something else from you and your brothers... a more demanding task. See, we require your skills of forgery."

"No, don't look to the Enchantress," said the right-hand lieutenant. "She's at her wit's end teaching us the art of makutus. So, forging the quarantine passes with magic is out of the question. Do this for us, and you'll be handsomely rewarded."

Ludwig nodded, seemingly without any qualms.

"Good. Now, sign your contract and leave us. We've business with the Conduit," said the right-hand lieutenant.

Following an exchange of handshakes, the Enchantress turned to the window, snarled, and in a blinding spectacle of strobing luminescence made the shack evanesce.

Alone and squinting at the empty glade, Isla miserably rose.

"Eavesdropping, are we?" A long staff of phosphorescing parchment materialised from nearby foliage, clasped by a bejewelled hand.

In response, Isla swung her bag, deposited her toy, and equipped her bow in a swift movement – her breathing in pace with a rhythm long ago taught to her. Lacking the time to notch an arrow, however, Isla broke her bow against her would-be-attacker's weapon in a swing.

The parchment disappeared and reappeared with swift crunches of origami. A butterfly fluttered beside her head, the phosphorescence remaining throughout its folded body.

Apparently unfazed, beckoning the butterfly to an open palm and stepping over what remained of her weapon, the man of six-foot-three revealed himself to her. Partially, at least. Amaranth-coloured attire akin to a priest's though crudely modified and frayed at the bottom; uncanny scars; a hood covering most of his face, aside from a freshly-shaven chin; and lastly, a distinct scent.

A mix between alcohol and an almond-esque fragrance – similar to the old tree's bark in town. It was rich and exotic, but when mixed with the alcohol was repulsive.

Although she could glimpse neither his lips nor his eyes, which were veiled beneath the hood's darkness, she comprehended his aversion to look at her. Keeping his head tilted and off-centre, sometimes even looking at his or her feet.

Pivoting, Isla attempted to run; legs moving apace as her heart pounded. Although where she'd expected to reach a kyojin's woody calf by that point, she remained in place – feet kicking at dirt, yet immovable.

"I'll make this quick." He clicked his tongue and retrieved a worn and ugly flask. "I pose no threat – not in my current state, anyhow – and thus I'll appreciate it if you'd lend me an ear and listen."

"What?" Isla was rotated and released from whatever hold was on her. "Are you with the others?"

"Had I been there'd be no use conversing with you."

He uneasily swayed and lost his footing, but before he could fall the butterfly had unfolded and re-folded itself in a matter of seconds – elongated and a staff once again. Catching himself on the rigid parchment, he winked, hiccupped, and quaffed whatever potent intoxicant was within that flask.

"You're a drunk."

Stipulating agreement with a gesture of hands, he glanced through a rift in the canopy, and towards the skies above. In doing so, his hood fell a little from his forehead, revealing ice-blue irises. The man wasn't ugly. Moreover, his demeanour didn't suit those strong cheekbones and ghastly scars that spread up his neck alongside those on his arms.

"The Emerald Eclipse, as I imagine you to know, isn't a natural occurrence," he said. "Every millennium both moons have been full and goldenly eclipsed at the stroke of midnight. What changed?"

"W-well, I can't say for certain..." Isla scowled, searching the tattooed soil beside them with desperate eyes. "In fact, I don't know."

"Then know this..." The wind howled as he took a swig. "The mundane life that this Realm has endured subsequent to the Purge, is now over."

"Over?" Allowed to retreat, Isla willingly – subconsciously – kept herself in place. "What're you on about? Who're you?"

A murder of crows took flight, his staff unfolded and re-folded; it twisted in the palm of his hand to create a sword unlike any other. A parchment sword with a whetted blade. In response, Isla jerked her wrist outward and revealed the dagger from her sleeve. Visibly undaunted by her threat, however, he found the stump and trained his gaze on it.

With a step closer to try and investigate his countenance, he held up a finger to Isla, wagged it side to side, and sniffed the air.

"Wet dog," she heard him whisper.

Ash enveloped the duo as a fire erupted between them. Shielding herself from the blaze, she noticed that it was her hands that were aflame. Flailing her arms wildly, the fire followed, yet didn't scorch her as it should've; her dagger burnt – it melted.

The pointed tips of her ears, which protruded from her hair, became hot. Throwing herself to the ground, with no better option in mind, Isla buried her hands beneath the cold, red dirt.

The fire extinguished, her dagger was ruined, the scarred man dematerialised, and Isla heard more canine yelping.

Turning back, she noticed a glittered dust ahead of the abnormal stump she'd used for cover. Haphazardly felled by industry, a jagged surface remained atop it. A weapon in the right hands. Viscous liquid pooled at the base, and the yelping sounded nearer – ahead of her.

Focusing, she glimpsed a lycan's body affixed to the sharp timber which'd impaled him; bit-by-bit becoming what he once was. A human. Beginning with his limbs, his lacerated torso, and then head. A single laceration, but a deep and precise one.

II

The Origami Oracle

Falls Creek's library was chilly and had a mouldy, stale aroma. Its roof was sunken in the middle, the windows hadn't been opened since its construction, and the bookshelves weren't aligned in an orderly fashion.

Despite its faults, however, Leif adored the place. Books were everything to him. Dreams and fantasy being better than remaining in the crooked town of Falls Creek. Yet, as he translated his fourth passage that afternoon, he was preoccupied with the idea of Isla's disappearance from the alcove – questioned the possibility.

Massaging the spine of a leather-bound treasure next to him before running a finger along the calligraphed title's silver-inlay: *A Druid's Guide to Healing*, he set down his pencil and spectacles.

Gently, Leif opened the book, glancing over the fact that it was a first edition, fourth print, and with slight foxing on the pages.

How did she disappear?

The work was engaging, chiefly the part regarding the treatment of a myocardial contusion, but Leif envied the brittle-paged tome which his fiancée Estrid Alberg was handling opposite him. A piece titled: *The Enthronement of Daeva.*

Could she have disappeared?

The grandfather clock chimed and the kindled logs aside it sizzled. Estrid stirred and smiled at him, seemingly pleased that he'd at least glanced at the gift she'd bought him. An attempt to draw his mind away from the anniversary of his parents' deaths.

Leif, with a sigh, returned the smile and closed *A Druid's Guide to Healing*, taking up his pencil and spectacles.

Attention roaming, it was ultimately fixated on a neat pile of books and scrolls beside him. A pile that seemed to grow larger each day. The thought of translating another piece on the Amity Era or transliterating a phrase in another religious text into Common, didn't aid in his waning attentiveness.

The books and scriptures of Falls Creek were becoming stale, and no matter how many times Leif pleaded for new additions to assist in both work and pleasure, he was denied. If he'd better texts at his disposal, he could translate quicker and more accurately – expanding to more dialects and languages like the notoriously difficult Sandscript. But the answer was always the same: imperial pay-cuts.

"Leif," the librarian called, her nose still buried in the pages of her umpteenth book. "Come and collect your wages."

Closing his notebook and locking the electrum clasp, Leif rose, placed his gift into his bag, and dawdled over to his boss. In tow, Estrid had left *The Enthronement of Daeva* on an end-table.

"A silver and four coppers." The usāgi librarian slid them across her cluttered desk as her tall, furry, pierced ears flopped. "Sorry, Leif."

With a deep, audible breath and a half-smile, Leif accepted his dinero and elbowed his way through the bent bookshelves, water damaged from last year's deluge, and outside into the streets of eventide.

Glaring into the palm of his hand, he spat, "Barely enough for a week's rations. How am I meant to support Isla's dreams with this?"

Splodges of darkness overcame the vibrant streets, as Leif envisioned that stygian nothingness seeping in. Splodges that represented the hopelessness he'd felt. Estrid mostly tried and failed to rectify that feeling, but she tried again by revealing *A Druid's Guide* from Leif's bag and holding it ahead of him.

"A healer's wage outweighs a passion for literature, my love."

Heard too many times over many dinners and late nights, Leif brushed her away and pocketed his pay. Glaring at his hands – hands which Estrid's patients endlessly praised – he pocketed those, too.

"At least let me help you." She pushed the book back into his bag. "Aivor and I've dinero to spare, if you'd only—"

"Estrid, please... I must *try*."

For Mother, he wanted to be the man she'd envisioned him to be. For Isla, he needed to be. But Estrid was right, and he knew that. The wage he'd earned from working at the library was nothing, and yet it'd meant more to him knowing that his mother would be smiling down on him – proud of the fact that he pursued the one passion they shared. Literature.

"All right." Estrid lay a hand on his shoulder. "Then, for now, how about you regale me with the old stories of Drengr and Seidr?"

"Knights and magic, you mean." He allowed the tenseness in his muscles to ebb. "Now, that I can do."

Estrid clasped Leif's forearm with both hands, rested her head on his shoulder, and sighed. The heels of their shoes clopped as they walked along the black-hematite cobblestone, beneath the fizzing neolyt which illuminated the moisture-laden streets and distinguished the hungry rat from the stale turd.

More than a few of Estrid's patients waved and hollered, and some even thanked Falls Creek's resident healer by purchasing her a bouquet or a box of brandy-filled chocolates. And Leif would watch on in silence as she typically denied the gifts and continued in stride towards the old tree. The Searwood.

When nearing the third colourfully lit signboard that evening, advertising the latest fashion out of Poirdeaux: the top hat, Leif spotted an idiosyncratic man leaning against the bordello's drums and vats. Admiring a piece of parchment which bore more foxing than a first-edition novel, he was dressed in an altered amaranth-coloured djellaba with an embroidered, golden design down the centre. And in a town like Falls Creek, such a man stood out.

Evidently to Leif alone, as Estrid took no notice.

Admiring the stars together, Leif held Estrid closer as she snuggled into his arm. The calling of hawkers from the bazaar reverberated throughout the narrow alleys to their left while the hammering of anvils did so to their right. The latter: a sound which continued to haunt Leif. Memories of an absent and cruel father whose skill of metallurgy and verbal assertions remained ingrained.

Who was that man in amaranth?

"Leif, there's still something I don't understand about Daeva," she said. "A fair number of works that aren't *The Enthronement of Daeva* state that she was wrongfully banished from our world, right?"

Passing the overhanging signs aside tightly packed, wall-to-wall buildings, they walked the sloping, twisting roads. Ducking beneath two low-hanging awnings of an aristocratic apartment complex, they stepped over a collection of luggage, and continued en route for the sea breeze.

"I wouldn't say *wrongfully*, but it's true that she was banished by... Well, I can't remember his name." Leif watched Estrid's open-toed boots. "A foolish necromancer with foolish ambitions, Mother would say."

"Mm-hmm. So, what're your thoughts on her ascension? I know her return to our world is improbable, but how do *you* think Daeva'll do it?"

Leif's fingers intertwined before separating to massage his knuckles. "It'll occur if there's strong enough magic to allow it."

"And can we as Laics do anything to stop that?"

"Sure. We can keep faith that the Purge did its job." Leif gently caressed Estrid's ebony skin with the tips of his fingers.

As the terrain evolved from cobblestones to pebbles and sand, Leif knew that they'd arrived at the Searwood without even lifting his head. It was the clashing of metal that made him do so, and he watched as the thickset and gigantic Aivor's blade slashed at Isla's.

Rather than the latest combination of both rapier and stiletto, Isla opted to use a claymore and shield to emulate the Varangian Guard's outmoded style. And he knew she'd do so in the hopes of one day being chosen by the Empress to ingest the sacred, silver blood of the first men and be inducted into the secretive fraternity of knights: dreaming that future ever since visiting Coventry with Father.

Dissimilar to Aivor, however, who'd blown Isla a kiss. Screwing up her nose, as Leif predicted she'd do, she discarded her shield bedecked with the Morrigan leviathan, and lunged.

Her favourite weapon, Seeker neither quivered, bent, nor unwillingly swayed: the platinum Father had folded into the meteorite being why. The repeatedly folded metal sustained neither nick nor dent from Aivor's impressive strikes. The rippling effect, provided by the folding, a weapon in and of itself when Isla would angle the light into her opponent's eyes.

A similar effect occurred with the etchings that depicted a leviathan locked in combat with a wriggling kraken.

The combatants approached, closing the gap between them, and brandishing their weapons – mirroring each other's gestures almost perfectly. Aivor bounded forward and slashed at Isla's bicep, breathing solely through his nose, but she deftly parried and manoeuvred to the side. Aivor's blade twanged against the pebbles instead.

Isla slashed left, diagonally, and from above – effortlessly, carelessly. Her balance was off. Aivor, taking advantage of his opponent's vulnerability, bent his knee in a passata sotto. Isla parried, attempted a riposte, failed, and retreated several paces.

Nearing, frowning, Leif saw the tips of Isla's ears turn red. Her emerald eyes giving the impression of sparking in fury, and yet she was holding back – mentally preoccupied, almost – evident by her lack of etiquette and preciseness. The wind gathered beneath formerly fiery-red curls – a recently dyed or otherwise streak of ashen dividing her hair – and blew it in and around her face.

Why isn't she feinting at Aivor's abdomen? He's open? Leif bit his thumb. *Is it that damned eclipse's fault? Where did she go that night?*

"How's she doing?" asked Estrid.

Releasing his thumb from his gap-toothed bite, Leif's shoulders drooped, and he came into a lean against his companion.

"To be honest, I've no idea. She's barely spoken a word to me since we entered the Industrial Era."

Instead of feinting, Isla keenly observed Aivor's footwork. He'd practiced his pirouettes in Rimathea, undoubtedly, a watered-down and somewhat barbaric take on a Poirdelais' technique. The footsteps which had dried in the mud were neither scattered in circles nor did they overlap. Aivor stepped precisely where he needed to, a foot behind the other and on attacking shifted the weight onto his toes before pouncing left.

The Danse Macabre.

Leif had seen it enough times to recognise it.

As twilight waned and the westward sun dwindled, sporadically shining from behind meandering clouds, Aivor flourished and shifted his foot – disarming Isla and grabbing Seeker's hilt. A new move, a simple move, yet effective. A move Leif believed even he could do.

Sheathing the weapons, Aivor picked a petunia which'd sprouted through some rocks beside Isla's dirty and bare feet. She'd neither spar nor fight with shoes on.

Grinning, Leif and Estrid turned around and came to face Falls Creek's Searwood. The declaration of love comparable to all Aivor's previous vows and gifts. Thus, Leif's curiosity of disappearing acts and green moons endured to him studying the Searwood ahead of him.

He wondered if Coventry's, the first to plant its roots, looked as sad before its death.

A colossal tree and a last of its kind, a notion which grieved him. In its prime, it would've possessed greener leaves and firmer boughs than any mortal man could comprehend. Yet, and amid its waning years, its nakedness brought a sadness to all who looked at it.

Its droopiness was further harshened by the rotting blackness from bough to branch, to root; and at the trunk's centre, a perfect hole was situated where a Searwood's heart once dwelt. Falls Creek's thaumaturgical soil became its life support, but even that wasn't enough. It failed the tree, as it'd failed the two who were buried beneath it. A set of graves which Leif refused to look at.

He felt ill. An abnormal feeling in his heart that twisted and gnawed yet wasn't his own. Thus, Leif half-turned to furtively observe the declaration of love over his shoulder.

He looked to Isla.

Aivor had revealed an envelope from the breast pocket of his sleeveless, outmoded gambeson. A bar of chocolate, too.

"It's a song." He'd cracked his knuckles, a nervous twitch.

"About me?" She accepted the envelope. "Let me guess: judging by the feel of parchment... length of the envelope... yep, it must be! It's about green moons and my emerald eyes, right?"

They shared a laugh.

"A bar of chocolate too, hey?"

"No!" Aivor exclaimed and pulled away. "Sorry. It's... it's my dinner. I'm playing my mandolin at the bordello tonight, see? Had no time to pack anything else."

Stunned at the idea of Aivor ever eating chocolate, let alone touching anything sweet, Leif watched Isla toy with the parchment. As one, they both looked in the direction of the bordello.

"Strange," said Estrid.

"What's that?" Leif turned and noticed that she too was watching.

"He's been increasingly tense of late. But when I ask him if everything's all right, he assures me it is. And I believe him. Plus, I know when he's lying. Looks up and to the right like a toddler."

"Isla's the same. Yet she worries me, Estrid." He crossed his arms. "Do you see it in her eyes?"

"I see it. But whatever that is, it's been there since your mother and father's deaths, just... less so."

"Yeah, maybe," he said. "I just can't wrap my head around how she'd disappeared that night."

"It was a strange night for everyone. I, for one, couldn't sleep knowing that you, of all people, were out hunting."

"Jokes aside, nobody we know reported lost siblings."

Estrid redirected her intent look towards him, a scowl wrinkling her forehead. "Come off it, Leif."

"Mm." He reached for his chest and massaged it, noticing his sister subtly do the same. "All right."

The strange feeling in his heart had intensified, and it was nothing like he'd read about in *A Druid's Guide*, nor anything seen when aiding Estrid with her patients. An alien gnawing that felt to twist his arteries and strain them before releasing and pumping something through his veins that either elated or depressed him. At that moment, it was the latter.

The feeling as equally intense as Isla's scowl.

She and Aivor strode by, whispering and hissing. Strange for the pair of them. From behind, Leif assessed the tightness in Isla's shoulders. Boots in one hand and the envelope clasped in the other: its edges singed by some sort of heat.

Leif and Estrid followed them through the cobblestoned streets of Falls Creek, its nightlife accentuating hawker stalls and Amity Era architecture.

Ahead, a logging crew had left their haul outside the bordello and beside a cartful of hewed hematite, sickening Leif to the core. A quarter of the forest had already been felled to fuel the flintlock factories, killing several kyojins – and an unidentified logger impaled on a jagged stump – in the process.

All due to a trade deal.

Shivering at the postulation of progression, and losing Estrid amid unbalanced alcoholics, Leif moved onward.

As he rounded the corner, he came face-to-face with a man of six-foot-three dressed in an artlessly customised and hooded djellaba. Its priestly, traditional sleeves were haphazardly cut and what'd remained had frayed. It displayed his scarred arms, a loose-fitting brown belt, and matching brown boots that were so worn the right sole was loose.

It was same man from earlier, folding the same piece of parchment into a shape.

"Old attire there, friend," said Leif, unable to hold his tongue, but receiving nothing but a smirk in response. "Are you lost?"

"Evidently, the poor man." Estrid reappeared at Leif's left, grabbing a hold of his hand before evaluating the djellaba, "Okay... Might've stepped out from the Amity Era."

"When the Imperium was just that and companies weren't even an idea in the cleverest of minds, right?" said the stranger, admiring the origami unicorn he'd created. "A fine era free of scientists and their mana. A simpler time."

Leif and Estrid froze, their mouths agape.

Ogling him further, they observed his wrists and fingers which possessed silver and platinum jewellery of various quality and from numerous regions of the Realm – a ring in his right nostril and a dangling hobgoblin totem in his left earlobe. Moreover, the crude and hieroglyphic scarring that spread around most of his bronzed skin had glowed as the ne-olyt above his head flickered.

When a newfound silence uncomfortably prevailed, Leif heard an out-of-sight Isla holler his and Estrid's name.

"Run along now, you wouldn't want to lose your friends on a night like tonight." He smirked again, revealing his pearly-white teeth and the scent of alcohol on his breath.

Doing as they were told, the stranger watched on until Leif lost sight of him completely. And yet when entering another district, Leif glanced over his shoulder, and again when they'd crossed a road. Reminiscence drew him to do so; a recollection of pictures and words written long ago, and yet names and events were lost on him.

The stranger had reminded him of someone. Fixated on the bordello's contemporary irimoya roof and chigi finials that stood out like a sore thumb, he couldn't get him out of his head.

Again, he asked himself: *How in the world did Isla disappear? And who was that man in amaranth?*

III

Mana à Trois

Isla caught a whiff of rancid offal. Discarded by the butcher, it wafted through Falls Creek and was carried towards the Morrigan cottage on the outskirts of town. Usually, it'd be overcome by the creek that flowed at the foot of the surrounding mountains which carried a strange, mossy, and pleasant scent. But that night the offal was particularly potent.

Amid it, and that strange calling to power that remained with her, Isla looked at her hand where a singed Velyn sat in waiting. Her wooden eyes glaring back at her beholder.

Aivor's hiding something, she thought, hastily jogging through the conjoined alleyways, barely touched by moonlight's silver streaks. *He'd not lay a finger on anything sugary, not since his seventeenth birthday.*

At the apartment complex's low-hanging awnings, she climbed and inhaled deeply when reaching the rooftop. From that height, she could see the bordello standing straight and tall in the distance.

The voiceless calling stirred within, and, aligning with her wants, encouraged her pursuit of Aivor. They wanted the same thing, Isla and this strangeness that guided her without words. Nonsensical, yet so was the fact that her hands were once aflame with no burns to prove it.

Thoughts about the shack returned – memories of the scarred man, the stone-skinned woman, and the commandant. A deal was struck. *Does it have anything to do with Aivor?*

"That green moon was an optical illusion," said an old voice from below, bringing her back into the moment. "Caused by a refraction of light in the atmosphere. A mirage, they say."

"Nah," said another, "heard it was a far-off sea's reflection. A green sea, mind."

Peering into the distance, her head pounding against the weight of numerous questions, Isla realised where she would've rather been: a dishevelled and abandoned church on Falls Creek's shoreline that was situated near her parents' graves.

Gargoyles still discernible, and the holy symbol affixed to the finials. A symbol Isla once worshipped. Years had passed. The old, strawberry-coloured wood and mortar had collapsed, and only the belfry and steeples remained.

A bygone era, Isla stroked Velyn's spine and pocketed her. *Let's get this over with in time for dinner.*

With rushed breaths to psych herself up, Isla ran towards the bordello, rooftiles breaking and coming loose underfoot, concentration ahead and unfaltering. She sprinted on the balls of her feet – sprung – and leapt with her toes.

Pouncing over the complex's courtyard, Isla caught an apartment's damp windowsill. Recalling her lessons in parkour with Leif, she clasped it with both hands and raised her knee against the drainpipe to her right. A move he'd taught her.

What Leif lacked in swordplay and courage he made up for with his ability to climb and translate.

Straddling it, Isla rode the cool blackness downward.

Arriving at the bordello's five-storey tall entrance, Isla snuck in; avoiding the drunkards that stumbled over the threshold. Surrounded by women whose faces were plastered in foreign makeup to make their peepers bigger and lips thicker, men whose bellies were bigger than their brains, and dinero that jingle jangled.

Tables were upturned, chairs broken, and the bar's stools were held together by termite-riddled wood and rusted, bent nails.

Inspecting one and all in the hope to spot Aivor and his mandolin, she instead saw a familiar man whose forehead and curly fringe were lying in a puddle of ale, a firm grip on a tankard. A thin salt-and-pepper moustache, days-old stubble on his chin, and hair shaved on all sides where hieroglyphic scars were.

The scarred man.

Opposite him, and behind the bar, was Aivor.

"Bastard," she hissed through her teeth. "And a liar, too."

Checking the neolyt above them, Isla watched as streams of light – like particles floating in a ray of sunshine – fed into the scarred man. The neolyt flickered, and the mana that gave it light was fading. She'd never seen anything like it.

Raising his head and pouting at Aivor, Isla glimpsed more burgundy scarring on the stranger; clearly discernible beneath the bar's neolyt. It spread equivalently to vines that had inscribed hieroglyphs along their pathing, twirling and engraving. And, amid the neolyt that flickered, the burgundy turned golden and glowed from his skin – bronzed by the sun.

"Your chocolate." Aivor tapped it with his finger.

Instead of moving in, she'd decided to sit and wait. To eavesdrop and see why he'd lied to her. And she watched the moustachioed man shrug, straighten his thin, platinum diadem with an empty prong setting affixed to the front where a gem ought to be, and proceed to mimic an origami unicorn prancing along the countertop en route for the chocolate.

"Look, I'm glad to see you, Basem," Aivor halted the prancing with a hand, "but all I'd required was your written permission to send the girl to Spellforge. However, now that you're here, take her home to where you both belong and train her. You must!"

Basem and Spellforge? Her legs became jelly and her knees had buckled. *The old tales! Spellforge was mentioned in the shack.*

"Must I?" Basem croaked, fiddling with his nose ring.

"There's no doubt in my mind that Isla can feel a change within her. I know it. I can see it and sense it. You can, too. She witnessed the eclipse, and now it's happening."

Light-headedness struck when hearing her name. *Are they after me? This feeling within me, and what I saw at the shack... Could it be? Magic?* She caught herself on a gambler's table, scattering the chips and dinero that were haphazardly strewn across it.

"Well," Basem tutted, "I'd told you to keep her inside, didn't I? But you didn't. So, I'd approached her – warned her – when the occultation of the two moons caused the Calling. I've done my part."

"Inside or not, you know that the Emerald Eclipse's power would've found her." Aivor unwrapped the chocolate and handed it to Basem. "Please, she needs training, and you're the only one that can do it. It's not safe for her to come into her powers any other way."

Basem took a bite of the treat. "Safe or not, I simply can't train her. I'll botch it and lose her like I had my daughter. No. She can either teach herself, being who and *what* she is, I'm sure she's capable; or you can repress it."

What am I? Isla inched a little closer, her fingers numb from how tightly she'd squeezed them into a fist.

"I can't." She heard the pleading in Aivor's voice. "A Mystic without magic is useless in the face of the Calling."

"Then forget about it, Alberg. These things tend to sort themselves out, anyway. If not, I'll return and cast *Alnisyan* on her."

"The Calling doesn't just go away," said Aivor. "It can't be left to chance, nor to a spell which lacks a decent success rate. Heck, you said it yourself that the mysterious Enchantress is here in search of the Conduit. She aims to fulfil the Dyadic Prophecy, as should you."

I've heard that term before... Conduit. Isla thought, shivering in the metaphoric darkness that enshrouded her. *Is that what I am?*

As she lingered, trying her best to unfurl her fingers from a clenched fist, Basem finished his chocolate and attempted to stand. Proving too difficult a task, however, he clicked his fingers – almost dimming the neolyt completely – and transformed that unicorn into the same phosphorescing staff Isla remembered him with.

"Where are you going?"

"Home, Aivor Alberg. To Spellforge where I can drown my sorrows."

"Wait!" Isla forced herself to stand on shaky legs, pleading to an attentive room that'd quietened from its previously raucous atmosphere. "I... do I get a say in any of this?"

Basem's eyebrows fluttered as he caught himself on his staff and tottered forward, a hand reaching for Isla. But as if something within him ground to a halt, she'd noticed that he withheld himself.

"You've your mother's eyes," he said as tears welled.

Standing there, feeling her heartbeat increase in pace with her rushed breathing, Isla noticed the same streams from the neolyt that'd entered Basem's body enter her.

She felt the mana that powered their modern Realm enrich her bloodstream; felt it awakening unknown dormant things – melding that voiceless calling with her own inner monologue. It was growing and stirring. The Calling, as Aivor and Basem had named it. She didn't know how. She didn't even understand mana, as most people hadn't – but it felt amazing. Invigorating!

Holding up a clammy hand, Isla admired the licks of contained flames dance and encircle her forefinger and singe her fiery-red curls. Looking around her, more streams from the overhanging mana-lamps were entering her chest.

"Amazing," she said.

A pop then drew them to the bar as the neolyt combusted! But where glass was expected to fall, none had. No shards descended, nor landed within drinks; they neither cut patrons nor sliced into the bordello's whores. Everything – including the motes – was suspended. Everything. Even her audience.

It'd taken Isla a moment, between noticing her hands extended ahead of her – fingers splayed – and the flames wither into wispy smoke, that it was her doing. That the rush which'd jolted her body and made her feel lightheaded was her using magic.

Isla had casted.

Realising, however, that the two conspirators were unfrozen, a feeling of betrayal oozed into every memory and thought before the idea of shock could even materialise. Icy tears of rage trickled down her flustered and red cheeks because of it. She didn't want to be there any more. Not with them. Schemers and sneaks.

Aivor tried to approach her, stepping around Basem, but Isla reached for Velyn – for the spine – and ran.

Behind, she heard the bordello's frequenters gasp as the glass fell and shattered. Time had resumed. The establishment darkened, the streets were robbed of colour provided by signboards, and all mana had expired like it had that other night.

As she sprinted, frightening stray cats and leaping over the homeless, Isla heard her name called from the lips of a living legend. An aenyr. A quasi-mythological man. But not from Aivor's... and that hurt.

Footfalls belonging to old, worn boots continued from over her shoulder – crashing and cursing too when he'd collided with a storefront. Still, Isla ran as fast as her legs could take her, exiting the main town and nearing the old church.

The sea breeze encircled as she hid behind a steeple and panted, caressing her flustered cheeks in a salty, flavoursome mist. She stroked Velyn's spine again and watched the six-foot-three aenyr approach.

Basem encroached on her haven, and Isla removed her boots and socks.

A stern right hook knocked her pursuer backward and caused him to trip – losing his origami staff. A jab at his straight nose, a sweep of the feet, and she'd managed to take him to the ground. Following him and tangling her limbs around her opponent's, Isla snatched Basem's arm and thrust her pelvis upward and against the elbow. An eerie crack reverberated alongside an ear-piercing squeal.

"That's for leaving me alone that night, without an explanation for any of this!"

Rolling away, Basem distanced himself insofar as he could, folding his injured arm within his dishevelled djellaba.

"Tell me what happened back there!" she demanded. "How did I drain all that mana?"

"Because mana is magic, and magic is mana," said Basem, breathlessly.

"You lie."

Closing the gap between them, Isla's athletic legs dug through the dirt. With a pounce, her foot connected with Basem's jaw in an upward kick. But before he could fall, she dug her fingers into his shoulders and brought her knee upward once, twice, thrice, and once again.

Cockily, she kept him there – looking deep within his two piercing, ice-blue eyes. They were strange to her, his irises, as Isla perceived them to be oddly familiar with a resonating warmth that massaged her heart and searched her countenance lovingly.

He threw a punch and blackness overtook her vision as she stumbled backward. Blindingly throwing her fist forward, Isla was caught by Basem's foot that'd knocked her away. Winded, she recovered her vision in time to resume her stance.

"You may have your mother's looks," he summoned an origami thrush to land atop his shoulder, "but your ignorance besmirches that image."

"Shut up!"

As a crowd gathered, whispering and murmuring about magic, Basem retreated to the shoreline and knelt beside the wavelets. Remaining in her stance, Isla saw that the water was an anomalous colour before a glow of magenta gradually wrapped around Basem's fractured arm and evaporated into a cloud of discoloured steam.

He rose, and Isla remained readied.

In a blink, however, he was gone and in another he'd reappeared. Like that other night, although her environment remained the same. Out of sight, Isla felt his presence beyond her right shoulder; smelt the overwhelming stink of alcohol. She wanted to attack, felt that it was the only option, but something within her forced her to refrain from such actions.

Curiosity.

Looking ahead and spotting Aivor arrive on the shore, puffed and frantic, the thrush emerged next to Isla's head with a buzz that resonated from deep within the parchment bird. Aivor turned away.

"*Alnisyan,*" Basem whispered.

Isla's world spun, blackness overcame all, and she entered an amphitheatre of dread and dreams.

Beneath black skies which lacked starlight, and moons that'd yet to emerge, Isla awoke to spot an anomaly which traversed the high and dark blackness and enshrouded her in fear and hopelessness. Something large, winged, scaly, and wriggling.

A dragon. The swooping sounds reverberated, and its breath alit the landscape with flame.

But... dragons haven't been seen in years!

It dove to attack, and she vaulted over a raised mound which sat south of a dried watering hole. The black soil beneath her feet becoming sticky with splodges of red and sporadic, but long, greenswards – the terrain attempting to hold her in place as it moaned and groaned. Wispy hands reaching out to grab a hold of her ankles and shins.

The realm of her mind was twisted and ghoulish.

Breathless and afraid, Isla leapt from cover and sprinted to the hole, only to find it not dried but full of a slick and opaque substance. Observing her reflection within the oleaginous matter, visible when the molten tore through the sky, a charred corpse rose from it. Crude runes were inscribed on his imposing chest, nails pierced both hands and feet, ash fell about him, and smoke whipped upward.

Isla's chest tightened, her eyes swelled, and she turned to flee, finding the same corpse ahead of her: clean, alive, and tawny-skinned. Father was resurrected as thunder clapped and blue lightning slithered across the endless sky.

Bypassing his daughter in long strides, Father revealed Seeker from its scabbard affixed to his muscular back and brandished it before the beast that pursued her.

The dragon dove, its exalted amaranth colour coruscating in sequences from head to tail – elongated talons extended ahead of its body, reaching for its quarry. Isla dove to the right, barely avoiding the attack, and entered her father's tall shadow.

Father lunged with the blade – the fluidity of his movements a thing of beauty – and he brought Seeker down.

Dust obscured her view and anxiety gripped her heart, rhythmically strangling the beat to bring her further to her knees. Her fear had overcome her ferocity, and a doubt replaced assurance. The power she'd reverenced on Falls Creek's beach, a distant memory in the black and stormy expanse as the dragon sought to devour her.

Thereafter, she'd glimpsed a glisten – hope in Isla's eyes, but truly a blade in the queer reality. A blade forged of meteorite, to be exact. A smile accompanied it, her father's smile. A smile she'd missed more than anything in the world.

Father had returned, bringing with him all that she'd momentarily lost. The dragon was dead. She was whole again.

Hearing the crash of wavelets against a mostly-pebbled beach, Isla stirred. Feeling the finite grains of sand sift through her fingers, tangible and not mythical, she realised that the townsfolk had all left her there. Alone.

Although the real world, her fate was no less cruel.

Each one of them afraid of her, she didn't doubt that they'd all demand her head on a pike as was the custom during the Purge. It was their nature, after all.

Mana is magic, and magic is mana, she thought. *If only they knew. Hypocrites, the lot of them.*

Feeling Velyn sitting hotly in her palm, she'd remembered. Remembered all that the spell had tried forcing her to forget.

Isla remembered that she was late for dinner.

IV

◈

Prophecy by Pyre

That night, as a brisk wind sifted through an ajar window of their cottage, Leif daydreamt of himself in the Archives. Dreamt of being surrounded by unbiased and unaltered non-fiction which numbered above the thousands; shelves that towered over anything Falls Creek offered.

Archives that were once accessible to all, including Mystics who'd go there to study texts and translate pieces untranslatable without the Archive's works. Chiefly, the Sandscript language. Since the Purge, the Varangian Guard have hidden that knowledge from all outsiders.

Questions, however, had distracted him from those dreams. Questions pertaining to his sister who was once again missing.

Skewering a cold pea on his fork, Leif heeded the pile of books he'd brought home for Isla to read. Not one was opened, and yet she found use for *Histories and Hearsay*: a coaster for an unwashed mug.

Dropping the fork and pea, Leif rounded the table to the opposite side that'd doubled as his workstation. Perhaps a little work would help put his mind at ease. Hunching over, he checked the clock, scrutinised it, before assessing the meagre door. It'd been hours since she'd set out.

Endeavouring to ignore that fact, Leif stared at his recent translations. Pensively, he'd watched each letter fuse into nothing more than gibberish splayed across his page. It was useless.

Replacing a sheet of folded parchment between his pages, a reminder of certain words he couldn't commit entirely to memory, he wandered over to the window. Biting his thumb, he searched the dark, outlying street for signs of his sister's whereabouts. Again, it was useless.

So, he moved deeper into their bijou cottage. Continuing down the short hall that bore three doors – two to his right, and one on the left – and an opulent mirror.

Twisting the left-hand handle, Leif peeked inside and assessed the room, cringing at the creak from the unused hinges. All that was within was as it were two years ago – a simpler period free of monetary shortcomings and disappearing sisters.

Leif beheld the gryphon mural above the bedhead and his parents' portraits. Mother's necklace that she was buried with forever shimmering beyond a painter's matte brushstrokes, while an absence of melanin in her once-red hair made her appear albino as it had in life.

Releasing the handle with a sigh, he shifted closer towards the mirror. Leif didn't know why he did, as he'd despised his reflection. Leaning closer, he cringed at his aquiline nose and tawny skin before a rigid feeling overwhelmed him, and a harsh reflection portrayed him as he was in Father's eyes.

He trembled, remembering the despotic words spoken on departure: a declaration of cowardice when green moons arise. And then it hit him. Green moons.

Leif sprinted to Isla's pile of books, removed the unwashed mug, and frantically dusted the cover of *Histories and Hearsay*. With trembling fingers, he'd flicked through the pages and marked his intended one with a triumphant tap.

It read:

An eclipse, although identified as sacred, can also be a sign of turmoil if anything other than its natural golden illuminated the night. Rumour states that if an eclipse was ever to be emerald again, it'll signify the beginning of the Dyadic Prophecy and a new era of...

"Of what?" Leif scrunched the page's corner as he attempted to read through the coffee-stained passage.

Thoughts bashed their way to the forefront of his mind – ideas, more like – of where and when he's read about an Emerald Eclipse and Dyadic Prophecy. But there were so many books, and so many, many words and names. After commencing work for the librarian, he barely had space in his head to remember himself much less hearsay and predictions.

"Eclipse, eclipse, eclipse." Leif continued to bite his thumb.

Clicking his fingers, he ran back down the hall into Isla's room on the right and dove for her nightstand. Fumbling through her overfilled and messy drawers, he dismissed the gifts from Aivor before identifying the worn, black leather cover to *The Holy Writ*.

Flicking through, he found and read:

Although debated by many, we believe the first lunar eclipse was emerald in colour. A sign of magic's arrival. And as spoken from a Sage, the Dyadic Prophecy foresees the summoning of another. Another Emerald Eclipse that'll mark a new beginning. A new era.

"Magic," he whispered, spectacles sliding down his nose. "A new era of magic... The sign was summoned, and thus it'll be."

Isla's disappearance into thin air... was magic.

Leif trembled again, calling to mind the djellaba-wearing stranger. His palms were slick with sweat, and his heart was racing quicker than an assassin's sprinting footfalls.

Flicking through the tome, at first aimlessly before evolving into intention, Leif hawkishly discovered the sought passage. Translated and transliterated last year, the name had eluded him – but in the accompanying picture was where he'd seen that odd man before.

Five aenyr siblings, all in robes, as was the fashion amid Mystics. Each with an azurite gem placed in sturdy prong settings belonging to unique pieces of jewellery, and a single, black-bladed weapon wielded by a chestnut-haired woman. Each bearing a phoenix crest over the heart.

But it was the man in the middle, a man in amaranth, that Leif scrutinised. The man outside the bordello.

He gulped, running a finger over the painted diadem. The paint itself phosphorescing like a makutu from tales; like the neolyt of city streets. He knew who he was.

With a quivering hand, Leif flipped the page and admired more artwork. Two portraits: an indistinct ashen-haired woman, who'd reminded him of Mother, and a rather ordinary looking man. A drop of silver blood above them both intertwined together at the top before evolving into the same phoenix crest from before. The subtitles of Harbinger and Conduit below a calligraphed: Dyad.

Silver blood, Leif stroked his clean-shaven chin. *The blood of the first men. Special blood. Mixed with an aenyr's to create the Dyad.*

The front door slammed open and shut, startling Leif, followed by a bone-weary groan. He ran towards it.

Arriving in the kitchen to see his sister for the first time in hours, he collapsed on the table.

"Isla, I've so much to tell you! Where were you? Never mind!" The rate that he'd breathed quickened after every word. "The eclipse was a sign – the call of magic! Somebody is going to re-surface magic!"

She addressed him with a vacant stare before focusing on her palms that seemed far redder than usual. Isla then sniffed at the cold dinner in an inscrutable countenance and by-passed Leif before halting at her door with an inbreath.

He reached out to her shivering arm but was promptly slapped away by scorching-hot fingers and a bestial snarl. Smelling singed flesh, Leif spotted a burn in the shape of four fingers on his forearm; the surrounding hair nothing but small, burnt buds.

"Sorry," said Isla before quickly pulling him into her room.

Leif backed away and tore a lengthy piece of fabric from the bottom of his tunic to dress his forearm.

With that alone, the sting had declined, and the stench had lessened.

"Give me a minute."

He did.

"Okay." She grabbed at him, but Leif eluded her and followed instead. They sat beside each other on the bed, and Isla brushed aside *The Holy Writ*. "I'm sorry I was late."

"S-sorry? Dinner be damned, did you not hear—?"

"I heard, damn it! I'm... I'm trying to tell you something."

Glaring into her eyes that lacked any spark, he kept his mouth shut and leant in. The old springs in her mattress creaking.

Isla explained what she could. Thereafter, the two exchanged knowledge that ranged from Basem, magic, her disappearance, the Dyadic Prophecy, the dragon in her dreamscape, and Isla furthering it with allegations concerning mana. It was the most she'd spoken to him in a while.

They cried, they argued, and then Isla mentioned that she was the Conduit.

"N-no, that's not possible. The Conduit is meant to be a male. I saw it before in *The Holy Writ*. It's the Harbinger, his equal, who's a woman." He saw her deflate, and as she bowed her head, he realised that the ashen had spread further into her red hair. "Isla, you're special – you've always been. And I can wager that the Enchantress let you live that night in the forest for a purpose. Whether her own, or another's."

"Either way, she's after the Conduit. And I've a feeling she'll come for it tonight. I... I know it."

Running his fingers along his burn, Leif nodded. "Somehow... I do, too. A feeling within your heart, right?"

"Mm-hmm. Different from what the Calling feels like. But strange, nonetheless." Glaring at her feet, swaying in an unsteady manner, Isla uttered, "Quickly, remind me of the prophecy."

Keeping her upright with a firm hand, Leif took up *The Holy Writ*. Its leather seemed colder.

"I still can't believe this is happening." He cleared his throat. "The Dyadic Prophecy outlines two figures, two equals: the Harbinger and the Conduit. When united as one, they'll bring about a new era. Another era of magic. To achieve this, the Conduit must..." his chest tightened, "...

must willingly sacrifice their life while the Harbinger casts the spell. It must be so to achieve their united goal."

A tight chest evolved into terror as smoke was conjured at his feet. Tracing its origin, where it soon became thicker, Isla's palms sparked aflame before ceasing and emitting smoke instead. Her eyes were closed, and she was in a sort of trance-like state. And no matter how drastically Leif shook her or called her name, she didn't wake.

"They're here," she uttered in a ghastly manner, stroking Velyn. "They've come."

His heart raced, and his breath caught in his throat. Leif reached for her face and brushed his knuckles against her warm cheek. A very warm cheek. This wasn't like Isla – this wasn't like his sister at all.

Spasmodic wildfire outfluxed from Isla's palms as she sharply squealed, burning everything at unnatural speeds.

But not the toy.

Leif threw himself away from her, grabbing for Seeker's scabbard. The furnishings quickly turned to ash as brimstone crept up the walls, gradually blackening the ironwood. Although remaining in her trance, Leif noticed that Isla would glance at the window – through it – with closed eyes. Approaching it on unsteady legs, his palm slick with sweat on the claymore's hilt, he beheld a small group led by a woman in a dark, hooded robe and a coiled staff in her stony hand.

His exhale stuttered into a whimper. The smoke choked him.

We need to get out of here.

"Isla!" Leif clapped his hands before her nose and garnered no response. "Isla, you need to go. You need to flee! Isla, hear me!"

In a panic, he reached for her heart and placed his palm flatly against her chest. With an inbreath, he closed his eyes, and spoke to her – through her – to whichever part of her he could reach.

"*I don't want to leave you,*" she said. "*I can't lose you, too.*"

Leif awoke in a void of blackness, surrounded by nothing but his and Isla's voices and words. Alphabets, runic and otherwise, floated above their heads – their words translated and transliterated into numerous languages he's seen before. Magic.

"*Please,*" he spoke with his mind, and not his mouth. "*I can buy you time, but only a little.*" He winced as the real-world window exploded, feeling its shards scrape against him. "*Please, for me. Let me be a man. Flee, and don't ever look back.*"

"*But they're not after me.*"

Isla appeared in a room of smoke and cinder. They'd returned to the real world – to Isla's bedroom aflame. But she was frozen, her eyes sunken and irises almost colourless.

It was in the palm of her hand where they both regarded her scorched dragon toy.

The surrounding smoke was drawn to it, fringing her fingers, slithering along the creases of her palm, and even reaching upward towards her forearm and bicep. A dense smoke, which bore magenta sparkles throughout alongside a spectacular and controlled lightning, took shape around Velyn.

As quickly as it'd been drawn, the smoke was dispersed with a simple blow from Isla.

Within that palm, where a toy once sat, was a living creature whose scales reflected the approaching fire and whose small stature resembled the fae from Rimathea's southern forests.

"Whether they're after you or not, they know you know something. I think that's why they're here." Leif lifted a trembling forefinger and stroked the small dragon's belly. "Isla, look at me. I won't let any harm befall you. Take this... faedragon and flee. Flee."

The siblings' gazes entangled as they lingered in a lonely, yet content, silence. Isla then pushed Seeker against Leif's chest and nodded.

"For protection," she said and grabbed her travelling bag.

Thanking her with a half-smile and feeling sick to the stomach, Leif knew what he had to do.

Together, they fled the room.

Seizing his partially burnt bag as they bypassed his workstation, Leif felt for *A Druid's Guide to Healing* and watched his recurve bow reduce to kindle alongside his burning work and books.

Emerging from the opaque smoke into a cool zephyr that'd stunk of ruination, Leif watched Aivor and Estrid sprint towards them. Before reaching the cottage, however, the Albergs were flung backward by the staff-wielding woman, who'd thereafter turned to the Morrigans.

Leif felt her unseen eyes bore into him and destroy what little confidence he'd mustered in himself, as though the cosmos' entire focus was given to him entirely in that moment. No longer able to sense any presence aside from his own, he held his breath.

"Come forth." A long, ugly finger was pointed at him. "We can't dwell here any longer, Conduit. We've work to do!"

The flames spread. They neared town and engulfed a farmer's crops. The wailing and moaning of all which burned shook Leif to his core. Yet not as much as when he was called *that.*

"No," he said and backed away. The word *sacrifice* haunting his waking mind. "You've got the wrong guy."

Leif felt Isla's hand loosen in his own as she tried to pull away from his stern grip. Her palms were hot, and from the corner of his eye he could see her frown; the tips of her ears becoming red.

The Enchantress' stone skin became visible in the spreading flames that'd already reached the town, and she extended her hideous hand. As she twisted it, she exposed a terrific piece of glowing jewellery that'd darkened her left ring finger. It appeared rotted, blackened by a force unknown to Leif.

She cackled amid the outlying, combusting houses that were feeble at the feet of Isla's empowered wildfire; their occupants squealing alongside the old wood that burnt.

The two men beyond the stone-skinned Mystic, equipped with a black-obsidian vambrace, took an unconscious Estrid into their arms and tore at her clothes whilst Aivor lay prone.

Out cold with a boot against his cheek, Aivor's nose was buried within the red topsoil. His strength had betrayed him and lost itself in the dirt he'd writhed in.

The Enchantress snarled, and Leif conceded to the fact that the vile look on her already twisted countenance would send shivers down the spine of even the most confident knights.

"Run." He turned to Isla. "Run to wherever, and don't look back. Don't look back."

Planting a wet kiss on his cheek, Isla squeezed his hand and let go. But Leif could tell there was something off – felt it again through whatever bond they bore. She was jealous.

The Enchantress allowed for her departure, and Leif watched his sister weave through the crowds of panicking townsfolk; some that were evacuating and those that chose to stay and fight the flames. Most distancing themselves from Isla, spitting at her and cursing.

Her outburst in the bordello. They know what she is, thought Leif as his blood ran cold and he reached for Seeker's hilt.

Looking back at his destroyed home, the pluming smoke blended into the blackness of night and obscured the skyline. The cottage's roof cracked and moaned – barely hanging on.

A signboard in the distance fell, its mana-lamps exploding one-by-one, and he drew his father's sword. Its balance was remarkable, and yet he didn't know how to wield it; its magnificence wasted on him.

The Enchantress approached, her men didn't. Preoccupied with a restrained Estrid, whose breasts were exposed to the brisk wind – a boot still pressed against Aivor's face.

The cottage's roof collapsed in a great bang and burnt the ground between Leif and his would-be abductor. Seizing the opportunity, he retreated from her. Vaulting over debris and towards a collapsed, burnt tree, Leif acted on instinct alone.

I'll draw their attention. He saw the Enchantress through the flames. *I'll make them chase me.*

"You dare to turn your back on me?" Her voice boomed with an air of inquisitiveness. "Acidic chaos, smokeless flames, drink deep the soul of my enemy!"

Lifting her staff and pointing it, she cast green embers that'd evolved into acidic skulls which pursued and attacked Leif who'd dove behind the cover he'd sought. A cocktail of acid and fire.

Against the charred bark, he glared at Seeker. Prayed that if he looked at the sword for long enough, if he gripped it tighter, that a wave of confidence would wash over him like the heroes of yore. But for the life of him, he couldn't force himself to budge. He could run on rooftops, yet he couldn't fight.

You coward, he chastised himself, punching his knee and peering.

"Doubt somebody so lily-livered is the Conduit, Enchantress," said one of the two. "Want us to gut him like we'd his mother, instead?"

"No! Wound him, if you must, but don't kill him." She broke her staff over her knee in a terrific blast of light. "I need him alive."

Heartbeat slowing to a faint thud, Leif's world spun. Mother's killers. In sickness, he'd lurched and choked on a cascade of vomit. Crossbow bolts were a volleyed, piercing the wood in a rain of death. One or two collapsed a weak spot and another flew beyond the bark to graze Leif's burnt forearm.

Screaming at his wound, vomit gushed through his mouth and nose, choking him and bulging his eyes as he struggled to breathe.

A bombardment of bolts flew overhead in a deluge that'd blocked out the glow of fire. Vision impaired by smoke, tears, and dirtied spectacles, Leif slipped and fell as he'd attempted to move on and flee. To escape!

Another volley, followed by tinkering and murmuring.

His enemies were reloading.

Stirring to his knees, Leif held Seeker close to his chest and carefully but hurriedly planned his escape route. Nevertheless, his arm refused any weight on it. So, he crawled through the mud, vomit, blood, and ash – he humiliated himself to survive.

"He's not here," he'd heard said, "and it's too dark to track him. We'll only be wasting munitions."

"Excuses! Find that boy, or you'll die as mortals!"

Dropping behind a fence line when he heard movement stir, Leif beheld the Enchantress reveal a piece of basalt from her pocket and run a salivating tongue against it.

Reaching the ruins of the Morrigan cottage, mere metres from Aivor and Estrid, his bloodied hand went for Seeker's hilt again. With the Enchantress' back turned to him, he perceived a chance to save them from their dismal fate. But Estrid had awoken, and her pleading eyes found what'd become of the Morrigan cottage. With them, she'd encouraged Leif to look above.

What'd remained was about to collapse in finality, and through that finality burn them all to cinder. He saw no other way, and in his panic foresaw no light at the tunnel's end for any of them if he'd stayed. Estrid saw that, too.

She smiled at him, and those transfixing eyes motioned towards the town's exit. Mouthing a final exchange of lovefelt words that were unheard, but known truly and deeply, Leif wept anew. Like the twinkle at pre-dawn on the horizon of a new day, his colourful romance with his beloved Estrid had glinted across his mind's eye. A life and love shared ruined in a heartbeat.

With a pleading look and tearful eyes, Leif sprinted away from the only woman he'd adored more than life itself, that wasn't his mother or sister, and in the direction of the zigzagging pathway that led out of Falls Creek.

On departure, the cottage collapsed. The Enchantress roared, and yet Leif held faith that the Albergs survived.

He needed to. To survive another day. For Mother. For vengeance.

Momentary shortcomings seemed such a miniscule worry then. In fact, on his observance of Falls Creek's ruination, those worries were all but extinct. A fleeting memory overwhelmed by a profound sense of dread.

Droves of refugees fled too, and he awaited the best moment to join them. A break in their disorganised retreat led by the Comte and an armoured man with a black-obsidian vambrace atop a barouche. Woven into a tapestry of fear and flesh with nothing but a bag on his back, and sword in hand, Leif carried onward – not taking his eyes off the barouche – until the smell of smoke and ruin was behind him.

On the outskirts and road to Deacon, whispers had already reached his ear of a Mystic's wildfire that'd ruined all in its wake. How Isla Morrigan was responsible.

V

Secrets of the Searwood

Isla followed a pathway highlighted by scarce and temporary lampposts in place of missing mana-lamps. The nimbi and lingering smoke obscuring the sun, scarcely permitting natural illumination to peek through, as ahead of her the rain pitter-pattered on wet pebbles and sand which'd failed to mix with the burgundy sap that'd wept from the Searwood.

Isla sought to flee from Falls Creek, yet couldn't, and she knew that the Calling was responsible. It wanted her to go to the Searwood – to the grounds where she'd train.

Grounds barely recognisable, as Falls Creek had devolved into nothing but smoking ruins. The rainfall dousing what little wildfire remained and thrived on unmoistened wood. The smell was horrendous, too. An infusion of burning flesh, hair, and crops; the three abreast a coalescence of sewage and floodwater – the latter arriving with a belated downpour.

The town was destroyed, the Albergs were missing, and the townsfolk either wanted Isla dead or were frightened to death by the mere thought of her.

Avoiding the vigilance of murderous survivors that swore black and blue that they'd have her head, Isla held her breath. She didn't want Basem's company, not in the slightest, but his kind's immortality would've come in handy, as she'd crept by the butcher and his cleavers akimbo.

Grabbing a discarded tarp beside the librarian's calcined remains, she threw it over her head and shoulders before ducking behind a charred cartful of hewed hematite and continued. The dilapidated church by the Searwood appearing unimpaired juxtaposed to the ruins.

Near the tree's unsettling aura, away from the townspeople, Isla looked at her palms that glistened beneath the sporadic rays and tried her best to summon something at will. To cast. She clicked her fingers, clapped her hands, stamped her feet, and even tried praying to whichever divine would hear her.

Nothing. She could do nothing.

The cause of fire, death, and grief thus played on her conscience as her boots squelched. Particularly the fact that she'd abandoned the Albergs, regardless of Aivor's secret keeping; that she should've stayed with Leif.

The Conduit, she stroked Velyn's scaly spine, disheartened by her impotent attempts at magic. *I hope he's okay.*

Vines at her dirtied feet actively slithered around the Searwood's aura; an aura unseen but heard when close – a bizarreness that'd toast most peoples' skin and boil others, which is why a distance was kept. A magical circumference that the elements couldn't penetrate.

Despite how wet Isla was, the blackened tree wasn't. Rain evaporated before ever reaching the old bark.

Velyn, surmounting Isla's shoulder, squawked in what she presumed to be an attempt to draw her away from that splendid enigma. But the Calling spoke of better things, again aligning with her wants, and blocking out anything the honey-coloured faedragon attempted to do.

Isla threw off the tarp. *You can do this.*

The aura grew intense on approach. So much so that it felt to melt skin and boil blood, yet she continued onward. A foot forward, her boots grazed exposed roots, Isla ducked to avoid a low-hanging bough, and then the heat expired.

Clicking her fingers again, she watched a flame come alive between forefinger and thumb.

It'd accepted her.

Inches from the Searwood, Isla reached for its black bark. Her slender, alabaster-white fingers zapped by the current running through it. Like mana, in a sense, she drew it into her bloodstream without knowing how or why; and like the bordello's mana, it'd felt amazing.

Mana is magic, and magic is mana, she smiled as Velyn receded into her travelling bag.

Isla caressed the Searwood's bark en route for the burgundy sap. Sure enough, it'd looked and felt like a tree but smelt of almond.

"That's it, then?" she said to it, and received nothing in return but what'd already amazed. "That's it."

Jerking her hand with the intention of letting go, a spark, bright and hissing, singed a singular green leaf that'd sprouted between her fingertips. Cautiously watching it, and struggling to swallow, Isla waited. For what, she couldn't say for certain, but she waited. Her nerves then seized absolute control of her body, jolting her head backward as she overheard continually whispered warnings urging her to hold on – to not let go no matter what. To never let go!

Had she wanted to, Isla couldn't. The Searwood had taken over – the current coursing through her differently than before. Intensely searching her. Reading her. A brightness overwhelmed her vision, a scope of whiteness accompanied by a sharp and high-pitched squall, and she was transported – or felt to be.

Hovering aloft Falls Creek like a raven in flight, she felt lighter... as though a spirit and not herself. Not wholly. Leif had read to her about these phenomena: an out-of-body experience.

Soaring through the air, she overlooked familiar and arable land. It was Rimathea, or more specifically: the Duchy of Gwynedd. And it was above an island, sequestered and splendid in its own way, where she heard a voice. Clear and defined... familiar.

"The Emerald Eclipse has been summoned, Isla." A figure materialised through the rising smoke of Falls Creek. *"Magic MUST re-surface, and you'll be the champion to do it."*

"Who're you?" A hovering Isla shielded herself from the sun's glare. "Show yourself!"

"You're asking the wrong questions and demanding where you should be listening." The figure was womanly in shape. *"But to ease your mind, I'll answer. I'm a Searwood, a last of my kind."*

"I... I'm speaking to a tree?"

"You must seek the Codex, our divine's own work." Slowly, the woman became more defined amid the clouds – ashen hair visible. *"With it, you'll re-surface what this land has lacked for far too long. And it is here, below your feet, where you'll find it."*

Isla squinted, the wayfaring smoke obscuring her location.

"Where's here? Help me!"

Through the plumes, the Searwood's projected image became clear. Ashen hair, skin so pale it looked identical to pearl, a signature necklace, and features so parallel to Isla's own that she thought she'd looked in a mirror had the image not been taller. Her pointy ears, that were missing on burial, had also returned in this new form.

"Mother?"

The image grinned, *"I've assumed your mother's image as she was kind to me, and thus I reflect such kindness on you, child. Do not fear me, only listen to what I've to say. Seek the Codex and re-surface magic. Such a task falls to you, and it MUST be accomplished, Isla. You must do this for all Mystics throughout the Realm. You mustn't fail."*

"And you expect me to do it alone?"

"*Alone? No. Seek the Key to the Undercroft, a man of six-foot-three. Without the Key, not even you can accomplish this task. Find the Key. Find the Codex. One can't be obtained without the other.*"

"The Key?" Isla glared down at Gwynedd, into the smoke that plumed from her hometown. "Six-foot... you mean Basem, don't you? Don't you?"

The image of Mother didn't answer and instead said, "*The Dyad mustn't fail. Years we've awaited, through the existences of too many Harbingers and Conduits born apart.*"

Her lips were frozen, unable to respond. Suspended and powerless to freely escape. Isla's world was shattered when learning that she wasn't the Conduit the Enchantress sought, a peculiar emotion when everything around was burning, but that elation had returned. Not the Conduit, but the Harbinger.

Isla had a purpose, and she chose to fulfil it.

With that assertion, she felt a forceful gust creep up behind her, like a predator at its prey; and when the image of Mother disappeared, she allowed it to carry her towards Falls Creek's far-off twin crater. The Searwood hadn't finished with her. There, she heard a laugh – not from the Searwood – reverberate the red mountaintops, and she was shown a basalt stele, one of few, somewhere within the scarlet dwellings.

Isla felt another gust. She felt as though tiny fingers were grasping at her limbs, squishing them, before they'd tossed her aside like an unwanted toy. As she sensed that sensation again, although briefly, she swam away from it – imitating being in a body of water – and over the mountains.

She knew where she needed to go.

"Enough!" Isla demanded. "You've shown me enough. Let me go. Let me leave this place, and I'll find your Key. I'll go to Spellforge."

But the groping gust continued its pursuit. So, she diverted her course and dove down to Falls Creek.

She saw herself standing at the Searwood, her hand still placed on its current-filled bark. She reached for herself. Fingertips so close, her brain sizzled. Physically experiencing a fiery sensation spread through it, scorching and ruining.

Ignoring the warnings priorly given in presumed earnest, she pulled herself away from the bark.

Thrust aside by a force clasping itself around her neck, Isla was dragged by her chin through the sand and pebbles. Velyn took flight from behind Isla, undoubtedly, to avoid the riposte to her defiance that'd bruised her.

Coming to a halt with a jaw tightly clenched, Isla writhed as her muscles were so tense, she felt that they'd implode if she hadn't. Short of breath, she blinked into the darkness. Shapes materialised as her eyes adjusted. Tombstones rose from the flat soil, and a hole in the ground sat under Mother's.

Managing to lift her cramping fingers to her neck, she felt the laced choker relentlessly squeeze, felt the precious gem that had once hung from her mother's neck. The necklace from her portrait. The necklace she was buried with.

Clasping the azurite, Isla felt the power within surge through her from fingertips to heart, and back out again into various points of her rigid and pain-riddled body. A break allowed her to get to her knees – but the squeeze intensified once more, bringing her to all fours.

A tear fell as she gasped, wriggling its way down her cheek, ran beyond her heart-shaped lips, and dangled from her chin momentarily before dripping on the precious gemstone.

The necklace relented.

Panting, she peered down into the newly formed hole and glimpsed a skeletal hand. Her Mother's. Isla pulled away, but the stench of decay made her gag and retch; tears welled again, she needed to lean – to rest her aching neck.

Isla reached outward, blindly and without thought, and placed her hand on the Searwood once more. On realisation, she snapped towards it. A green leaf had sprouted between her ring finger and pinkie. Velyn circled above quicker.

She panicked. She blinked. She was transported.

The wind was strong, and it pushed against her from all directions, forcing her around like a buoy amid rogue waves. Yet her feet remained on the ground – stone, in fact. All remained black, as she kept her eyes closed. For that moment, she'd convinced herself to not think about anything, anyone, or anywhere. All was blank. And it was good.

Opening her eyes to see Velyn hovering ahead of her, thoughts returned like water through a floodgate, and she'd found herself atop a rough escarpment amid the mountaintops overlooking the town.

Miles away from the Searwood, Isla sighed.

Beholding the legendary tree's thick boughs, she couldn't fathom its capabilities – what it'd done to her. And she narrowly escaped it happening again. She came to terms with what'd happened. She evaded it – the out-of-body experience – and was instead teleported.

Teleported, Isla felt her mother's necklace and beheld a golden resplendence shimmer on the distant wavelets of Falls Creek's inlet, cutting through a secluded storm's nimbi brewing above the Searwood.

A skeletal hand flashed across her vision, Mother's, and Isla pulled at the azurite in a want to be rid of it. But it wouldn't budge. Why had it come to her? Why did it relent and not kill her? In moments like that, Isla wanted to believe that Leif had the answers. He usually would. And regardless of what Estrid thought about his career, Isla loved that he was all but a walking encyclopaedia.

He could've explained the Harbinger's role in greater detail.

"Did you hear?" she spoke to the faedragon in an uncontrollable quiver that'd ruined her pronunciation. "The Searwood called me the Harbinger, girl."

Velyn nodded her scaly head.

"Then you would've heard about the quest, too? Good. Remember Basem? Bet he'll be surprised to see us again, hey?

No, don't look at me like that. Like a varangian, I'll serve. I'll fulfil my duties."

When the bordello's edifice collapsed, Isla was drawn back to Falls Creek where she barely made out the night's candles being snuffed. Unharmed shutters were unbarred to roofless homes, and shrieking reverberated throughout the destroyed alleyways en route for her senses.

Summoning Velyn to her shoulder with a whistle, Isla searched her bag for the necessary supplies she'd kept for such troubling times. She knew what she needed to do.

Isla knew where to find the Key. Where he'd slithered away to that night. Spellforge.

A step towards the south, towards Hotham Heights and its mountain ranges, Isla felt the wind gust through the fissure in the rockface.

Isla had walked such a distance and through an abnormal humidity so acute that it made her despise her comfortable shoes, the only pair she'd enjoy wearing when not barefoot. Balancing herself on one leg, hopping as she struggled, and repeating the process, Isla threw both shoes and socks away. She didn't care which direction they went, or if she'd ever see them again, because feeling the soil between her toes invigorated her.

Inhaling the gorgeous scents of nightfall, accentuated by an aroma of unsullied lands, she carried on to Spellforge through uncharted passages to behold sights she'd only ever dreamt of seeing. Isla bypassed hillocks which possessed blue jacarandas and purple wisterias, dells of vibrant grass, and a crystal-clear lake at the base of an inselberg possessing a river ahigh whose water cascaded a transparent-cyan, all within the fissures of mountains.

Further, where a decrepit and broken bridge was situated at the foot of an old juniper tree that bore dangling planks of wood tied to its boughs, Isla came to a stop. To progress, she'd dipped down to an overgrown path eroded by time.

The passage was a land she'd recognised, but neither due to what she'd seen in person nor Leif's books bearing sketches. A memory deeply imbedded within her bones and soul; a memory belonging to thousands unknown to her before that time. Memories from those who briefly spoke to and through her. Of a time long lost. A time when Mystics were hailed as people and not monsters.

It was their voices she heard; their tales that they'd tried to project onto her. However, Isla doubted it a common occurrence for all Mystics that passed through the fissure.

She attested the voices to the Calling; that within the fissure of unrefined magic, it'd doubled – tripled – evolved into a collective to outshine her own thoughts and voice. But she didn't let it. Isla demanded unity or nothing, only it wouldn't relent so easily.

They ushered her to a place beside the new trackway: a cave of such height and reverence, bearing an entryway of intense proportion that'd initially terrify most passers-by, before they embedded their heels into the topsoil and declared it stone and not a monster.

It wanted her to enter it, as did the voices, and she saw stairs within. But she refused, lingering at the darkened entrance.

A wispy hand appeared to her and reached out to reveal a tome, although a transparent image and not the real deal. It'd then pointed at the mountaintops that towered over Isla. That's where she saw a winged beast fly, that's when she heard it screech.

The collective of voices drew her to the wisp again, and it welcomed her into the entryway. But Isla wouldn't budge.

"Do you show me the Codex?" she'd asked, and the wisp said nothing. "Surely, not."

Find the Key. Find the Codex. One can't be obtained without the other, Isla lingered, unsure. Curious. *Maybe it is.*

The transparent hand was eerily still. Isla inched forward. The creature above screeched again as it flew in and out of its home.

"If you lead me true, I thank you," she waved it away, "but I'll not be going in there with you."

VI

The Shattered Blade

On Deacon's twilight-lit rooftops, a filthy Leif over-watched Falls Creek's refugees collapse from exhaustion, burdenless of quarantine passes. He thought about his fiancée whom he'd left at the mercy of those lowlifes; he thought about her fate. All, however, was veiled by the monstrous obsidian chains that kept Deacon's floating, engirding islands at bay; just as his cowardice overshadowed him.

Following the barouche to Deacon and soon achieving vengeance for Mother, Leif hoped that what he'd planned to do would somehow make him feel less cowardly and more like his sister. He wanted to be better. Hoped that the broad man that wore the same black-obsidian vambrace as the Enchantress' men would help him sate these.

The man who'd sat beside the Comte on his ornate barouche. The commandant. That's what they called him. Nobody knew why.

Taking Seeker into his hands, he unsheathed it to admire Father's etching reflect the multi-coloured skyline. His silver-grey eyes were mirrored back at him, and he recalled *The Holy Writ...* special blood. Silver blood. He second guessed his lineage of northern nobodies. He second guessed everything.

It was time to move.

Leaping over the street below, as the river's breeze blew his coily hair out of his eyes and smelt of freshly-baked croissants, Leif caught a windowsill. Recalling a well-practiced routine, he prepared himself beside the neolyt sign that led upward to the rooftop balustrade. The sign itself was sturdy enough to withstand his weight, as it'd fizzed an image of a gentleman doffing his hat. He climbed.

Atop his vantagepoint, Leif adjusted his spectacles and gazed at the barouche and its familiar coachman. Alone, the commandant waved at all who caught his gaze. A man of the people, or so he portrayed himself. Leif knew the commandant's location. A striking one too, beneath a frieze depicting a nude woman whipping centaurs affixed to her carriage.

Comparable to the Enchantress and her pawns.

She'd called me the Conduit. Leif dabbed at his self-healed wounds on his forearm. *The commandant should know more. He'll help me understand. Before death, I'll make him. I won't be sacrificed.*

Pursuit in sunlight – no matter its scarcity – wasn't an option, however. So, crossing his legs, he'd waited. As he did, he'd admired the mosaic-like porphyry road, which led only towards that manor bearing uniformed snow-white brickwork that covered the building entirely to the spire atop the magnificent clocktower. Sleek and artsy.

Following the retreatment of the sun behind the various flue-gas stacks and Deacon's short walls, Leif took several steps backward before beginning a steady-paced jog that quickened into a magnificent sprint that'd led him to kick off from the balustrade.

Catching himself on a building by the river Argolia and above the city square, he was distracted from his goal and directed to an obscure and ghastly smell; to the obscenely loud flies that droned. Babbling brooks and a splendid shoreline weren't enough to make up for what he'd seen below. A grotesque and horrifying sight.

It was a slaughter. An arm had been trampled and detached from its owner's torso. Not the first extremity spotted. Palpitations narrowed his vision; the blood made him weak. Leif had momentarily lost sight of his destination and mission – baffled and feeling sick. He descended.

The first thing he'd happened on was a female's left foot. Blood, mud, and human excrement were bestrewn across the mosaics and carried upward and on the surrounding storefronts' baroque façades. Footprints too and belonging to a size ten boot.

Half the men in Gwynedd wear a size ten boot, Leif thought to himself, moving towards a hanged corpse whose urine continued to trickle down his leg. Removing the deceased's soiled shoe, Leif fingered the patterned and worn leather within and without before discovering the maker's mark and size.

As suspected, he tossed it aside. *Size ten.*

To stop himself from vomiting, Leif asked himself what the inspectors in his stories would do. And he'd envision all that was before him as an author's visualisation of a novel... at least, he tried to. The smell made it hard.

Against the fountain was a woman slumped forwardly, her arms and head submerged in the shallow waters. Within said shallows was a boy no older than eight, his chest cut open by a careless slash of a sabre. Parchment pinned on the pocket of his soiled waistcoat.

Submerging his hands within the red-coloured water, he extracted the child – whose irises and pupils were a hoary white – and placed him on a hedge that neighboured petunias. With his thumb, he cleared away the speckles of blood that defamed the boy's beauty.

What madness drives someone to kill a child? Leif straightened the boy's waistcoat and placed those little hands atop his motionless chest. He looked at the moist parchment, *Mystic Lover?*

Gurgling overwhelmed the sound of cicadas. From the square's south-east corner, closest to the river Argolia that divided the city, a man lay half-dead and bleeding; wanting to sit upright but lacking the appendages to help him do so.

Abandoning the child and kneeling beside the victim, Leif helped him upright; steadying the man's chin so to look him in the eye. It was the Comte. Leif recoiled briefly, choking back whatever tried coming out of him, before returning to the man and resting a hand on the stump where his arm once was.

Aiding Estrid in the past made the slaughter and deformations easier to bear, but even then, he found it hard to treat the wounded. Again, it was the smell.

More gurgling, and thereafter raspy breathing. The Comte's eyelids were heavy. However, something had been alleviated within him – a pain, perhaps – when Leif touched his wound. Unable to speak due to a missing tongue, he motioned his barely visible eyes in the direction of the child on the hedge.

Lips trembling, he sobbed.

The same parchment on his overcoat.

Mystic Lover, Leif shook his head.

"What're you doing here?" said a voice.

Leif unsheathed Seeker and flourished it amid an unpractised and sloppy turn on knee; the blade's tip finding the intruder's sternum rather than his throat.

He slapped away the blade as if it was nothing, and instead of retaliating, stepped into the light of night and wept. A deep purplish scar hacked over his right eye, contrasting against his ebony skin.

"Aivor?" Leif lowered his guard and rose.

They hugged, and Leif noticed that Aivor had salvaged his mandolin. A pretty, heart-shaped thing that mimicked the style of his favourite bard; it'd been scorched and burnt, and the masterfully painted decals on it had been reduced to black char.

Quickly pivoting, they saw that the Comte had passed.

"How'd you get here, Leif? And why are you so thoroughly filthy? Is Estrid with you?"

"I thought she'd be with you." His heart sank. "I'd arrived with the refugees, hidden away by the muck and soot. It'd concealed me from the vengeful eyes of old friends and neighbours. You?"

"I'd caught up on the road beside the old runestone." He pulled at his leather gloves. "Where's Isla?"

"I'd sent her away, told her to flee..." memories of Estrid overcame anything he recalled of his sister. "Where's Estrid?"

Aivor gestured towards the dismembered and dead, "They'd probably know more than I do. Barely remember a thing. I awoke beneath the remains of your cottage, feeble and bawling. Alone. F-first Estrid, then you and Isla... everyone had told me the worst. Everyone said that Isla was a Mystic. What's going on?"

Leif shrugged, noticing the visibility of his breath.

"You should know, Aivor, you're one yourself. Isla told me." As he went to speak, Leif cut him off. "These men and women were killed for being Mystic Lovers. Any idea what that means?"

Aivor cleared his throat, clearly uncomfortable with Leif knowing the truth about him, and knelt at the side the Comte. He then removed the parchment, studying both sides before looking back at Leif.

"Refugees who've lost everything, and they decide to murder the man who led them," he said. "What's not told in the mundane history books you study, is that Laics killed their own people following the Purge. Not only did Mystics needlessly die, but so did Laics that renounced the wrongful act. Those people were branded with parchment like this."

Aivor looked at his feet and cracked his knuckles.

"On the road I heard whispers..." Leif paced. "Ideas of finding and killing Isla – killing the one responsible for Falls Creek's destruction. I believed it was anger talking, and nothing more. Never imagined the people we grew up with were capable of... of this."

He feared for her safety, as he feared for Estrid's. But unlike what he'd felt for Estrid, that unique feeling in his heart led him to believe that his sister was okay, that she'd survived.

Looking about, Leif noted how regardless of their disregard for the dead and wounded, Deacon's sentries saw fit to block the eastern and western entrances to the square. They held back most curious people yet droves still bombarded the make-shift blockades for a chance to see something so to gossip with friends.

"Begone now, Aivor, we don't want to be seen here. I'll catch up to you later and we'll talk." Leif sheathed Seeker and climbed the closest tree, its firmest bough a walkway to a nearby balustrade.

"W-wait! Let me come with you," Aivor pleaded. "Whatever it is you plan on doing, I can help. You know how good I am in a fight."

"I do, but your no good on rooftops, and what I need to do is far beyond your capabilities."

"I can run on roofs, if need be!"

"Sure, but can you take a life?"

"Can you?" Aivor crossed his arms.

Leif attempted a retort, but hesitancy forbade him. Again, images of Estrid flashed before his eyes as he looked at her brother below. A liar, but a good friend. Leif feared putting him in danger – wished to repent for leaving him and Estrid behind.

He decided to go it alone.

Bypassing tall and short chimneys to arrive outside the uniformed snow-white manor, Leif watched the commandant dismount his barouche; having awaited nightfall to move.

If he was frazzled, Leif couldn't tell; if he was angry, he couldn't tell that, either. The commandant kept the same vacant expression on his face from when he'd first lay eyes on him.

Estrid, more flashes, *I hope you're okay.*

Unsheathing his weapon, Leif's arm froze – Seeker falling back within its scabbard as his vigilance centred on what was carried beneath the commandant's arm: an encumbered leather folder whose contents were protruding from every side and flapping in a brief and faint breeze.

The leather's tanned colour contrasted against his sallow skin, and the russet tones of his splendid boots paralleled what little Leif glimpsed of his irises.

Allowing the commandant to proceed onward and ahead for several paces before resuming his pursuit, Leif checked the moon's position. Midnight.

Curiosity outshone the want for revenge. He'd snoop.

From atop the clocktower, Leif overheard squeaky hinges below him and affixed himself to the sturdiest position before lowering himself down; arriving outside the commandant's window in time to see him poring over the folder's contents with a wide grin on his greasy face.

Content, and with a nod, he tossed the folder into a drawer with only a small black book remaining in hand. Then, and suddenly, he lurched in an unhealthy manner with an expression that was read as panicked – as if he'd forgotten something. Racing to the door, or as fast as he could manage, and without his folder or book, he fled.

Testing his hold on the building, Leif carefully equipped Seeker, inserted it between the window's white wood, and flicked upward. A click of the latch, a small nudge, and the window swung inward. Slowly removing his boots and setting them down by his entryway, Leif glimpsed the black book with a list of initials stapled to the inside sleeve.

One was separated from the rest with a checkmark beside it and a scribbled, cursive sentence: E.A., crucified and marked.

Within that book, Leif found entries amid sketches and notes which read like ramblings to a layman. Names and titles were noted: The Conduit, Daeva, Enchantress, and more scribbled down the page.

Stained by sweat, Leif found the most recent entry:

They turned on the Comte. My mission has failed. The Enchantress isn't pleased that we've lost another nobleman. She wishes to meet tonight after midnight.

Is that where he's going? Placing the diary into his pocket, Leif moved on to glimpse a grease-stained tumbler and crystal decanter.

A bump outside, a cough and sniffle. Peering towards the door where they resounded, a mesquite armoire caught Leif's eye. He tiptoed over.

In the middle drawer, he'd found the folder.

Beneath, it was a collection of letters, addressed to the commandant. The most recent correspondence read:

Commandant,

We grow impatient. Your Enchantress has promised us magic and immortality, and what little we've heard and seen hasn't helped ease our worries. During our last correspondence, you'd assured me that mana is magic – that it's proof Laics can wield magic. So, let us wield it.

I've heard whispers that the Enchantress has taught you and your lieutenants how to cast makutus. Why not us? Why not the loyal aristocracy that've come to serve her and her goals?

This has begun to worry our friends at the café-theatre. We want to become Mystics. We want to wield magic. We WANT immortality.

Mana is magic... It's as Isla said that night. Leif scowled; eyes surveying the rest of the letters to more aristocrats in a rushed manner. *But Laics becoming Mystics? There are few successful cases, and they were performed by Basem. The Enchantress is lying to these people, but why? Makutus aren't magic. They must be channelled through a willing Mystic... is mana the same?*

Pulling the diary back out in the hope to better understand it, Leif stopped randomly. He didn't know why, but that feeling in his heart had returned. And when it did, he'd wondered. The entry he looked at bore the same initials from before:

E.A. They've marked her body with the ancient runes, a language we can't understand. My lieutenants believe it points to a powerful weapon that'll aid in the re-surfacing of magic. But in the wrong hands, that could spell turmoil for the Enchantress. She doesn't tell us why, nor what her goal is with these new orders. I rather not wonder.

Ancient runes, he bit his thumb. *A powerful weapon?*

"Get away from there!" A sniffling sentry stood in the doorway.

Leif collected himself and stood as tall as he could, glimpsing the man's size and briefly feeling inadequate. Searching his way about his person, not breaking eye contact, Leif found his pocket and proceeded to place both the first-read letter and diary inside it.

"Put that back!" The sentry's hand reached for his sabre, and the mana-lamps flickered. "I'm warning you, vagrant."

Leif reached for the folder. The sentry attacked.

He thrust it upward and caught the sabre that cut through a third of it, destroying the contents. Leif pushed back but the sentry didn't budge; so, Leif revealed Seeker and stabbed for his head, yet that was perfectly parried and met with a riposte of strength and precision.

Astounded, Leif's stance faltered.

Forearms snatched, the grip on Seeker loosening, the sentry tossed Leif aside mightily and into the tumblers and decanter. The sabre followed suit in attack, destroying whatever glass remained in a swipe. As the sabre was lodged into the attacked furniture, Leif summersaulted aside and mislaid his weapon.

Seeing an opportunity, the weapon-less sentry advanced, grabbed the claymore at his feet, and in a single downward motion against his muscular knee, shattered Seeker into two. The ripples glistened weakly in the room's limited light before being snuffed entirely. Father's mighty work destroyed in an instant.

He then proceeded to undress. His grin enfeebling Leif.

Standing in nothing but his britches, the sentry extended his arms and slowly twirled. An opulent tattoo on his back shimmered into view like no tattoo before it – like treasure below the wavelets of some pyrate haven. It depicted two scythes crossing at their snaths and with a splendid diamond above them.

The sentry turned to face Leif again, reached for the small of his back with both hands, and revealed those very scythes. The mana-lamps practically dead.

"A sorcerer?" Leif blenched and eyed the windowsill.

The sentry chortled.

Lunging, the two scythes cut through the air and over one another, missing Leif by an inch as he vaulted over the desk. Making a run for the window, he was halted by a scythe cutting off his path and destroying the maple floorboards.

Falling backward, Leif re-routed his escape to the doorway. What he hadn't expected was for his foot to be caught by a snath. His spine popped and cracked in several places as he was slammed down to the floorboards. He rolled, avoiding a scythe, and again to dodge the other.

"I've you now, cur!" The sentry laughed and coughed.

A cough that'd persisted as he'd collapsed headfirst into the desk. A shard from Seeker protruding from the back of his skull.

The life in his eyes ebbed away as his pupils dilated. His nose mere inches from Leif's. On death, the mana-lamps' brightness returned to them in an instant.

"Please, tell me you're all right?" said the sentry's assailant.

"I'm all right, Aivor. I'm all right," Leif mumbled, beholding the ruined folder and its mangled contents.

Silence supervened, and it took the shrieking droves who'd broken through the barriers to bring back a semblance of reality. It'd shocked Aivor – evident by his flinching – into kneeling at the sentry's side to close his lifeless eyes.

"Did you find anything?" he asked.

"Diary entries and letters," said Leif, donning his boots and spectacles; the latter he'd lost in the fight. "They, at first, read like ramblings but I think they're much more than that. A look into whatever is going on. Why the Enchantress is doing what she's doing."

Aivor's eyebrows angled into a concerned frown. "You know about the Enchantress?"

Leif reached into his pocket and retrieved the letter; straightening out the corners, the folds, and the creases that'd formed across it to make it look like a washboard.

"Here." He held it loosely between his fingers and towards Aivor. "You can probably make more sense of this than I can. You're a *Mystic*, after all."

He stressed the word Mystic as he was still irritated by Aivor's secret keeping. Thus, he'd done the same and kept secrets of his own. There hadn't been a reason to share the truth about himself and Isla yet, and he was far too scared to mention the fact that he was the Conduit out loud.

The idea of sacrifice still haunting him.

Conscientiously accepting the letter, Aivor's eyes darted back and forth so quickly that he was done reading in a manner of seconds.

"Mana is magic, and magic is mana."

"Mm-hmm." Leif nodded, looking at the remains of Seeker and then out at the city. "Isla said the same thing. Is it true?"

Sighing, Aivor moved for the desk and leant against it heavily, his weight scraping it against the floorboards.

"Yes. Laics have been unknowingly using what they were raised to despise. Perhaps even ignored their similarities for convivence's sake."

"Can Laics wield it?"

Aivor shook his head. "They wish. Basem could explain it better to you, and in far greater detail, but from what I've gathered: they channel magic through a captured Mystic – a strong one – and use it to create mana."

"Like makutus," said Leif and Aivor nodded. "So, the Enchantress is lying to these men. She's lying to draw them to her side, but why? What's she planning? I thought she wanted to re-surface magic."

"She does," said Aivor. "But it's what she plans to do after magic is re-surfaced that should worry you. Should worry everyone. Whatever it is, it'll be our doom if we don't stop it."

Leif motioned outside where a disorderly commandant was jogging away at a quickened pace, shooting glances towards the opened window. He'd, most likely, heard or seen them.

"Barely scratches the surface of what I need answered. But thank you, Aivor."

"Don't thank me yet." He placed a hand on Leif's shoulder. "What do you plan to do now?"

Leif's mind swirled into loops and dead ends before recommencing to make light of things, and then hitting that same dead end. He wanted to feel fear, he wanted to cry. Leif felt as though every fibre of his being was so tense that he'd implode and bring the Dyadic Prophecy to an end.

And somehow, he didn't think that'd be so bad.

"Daeva's name was mentioned in the diary." He stroked a stubbled chin, "alongside mentioning of a weapon and ancient runes. Things we probably couldn't make sense of on our own. And we don't need to. So, we follow him," he pointed to the commandant's armoured back, "and we don't stop until we get the answers that we need."

VII

Kinship at the Crossroads

Beneath a rose-red sunset that cursed the low-hanging clouds with pink tones and lilac rain, Velyn flew above Isla as she entered a thin valley in the range's enduring fissures. Landing on a sweet pea branch, Velyn sat for a moment, twisted her head, and darted for Isla's shoulder before directing her snout towards the Heavens.

Following the faedragon's regard, Isla noted that she was beneath the rumoured location of Spellforge. Where she'd seen that winged beast fly in and out of whatever shelter it dwelt in; where the wisp showed a tome to be.

A tome she prayed to be the Codex, although remaining reserved. Isla refused to be elated without first laying eyes on it.

Scepticism prevailed over hope, and it'd done so again when she recalled the Searwood's words. The Key was still needed.

So, she approached the mountainside and ran an alabaster-white hand down it, seeing her reflection in the dark and metamorphic rock's dampness. The ashen had spread further.

While she did, a feeling struck her heart, and she knew it'd had to do with Leif. He was okay, but she felt a wave of depression wash over her. As if happening on something grotesque.

With that, she looked within herself with her mind's eye, searched her way towards that feeling... and snuffed it.

Whatever it was, if it was a bond shared with her brother, she didn't want to feel it. Not at that time. There was so much more at stake, and she believed in her heart of hearts that he'd be okay. That he'd survive to see her again.

For the greater good. For the Dyadic Prophecy. So, they can re-surface magic. Isla knew that Leif would understand.

Tearing away thin, frayed pieces of her tunic and fastening them around her hands, fingers, and feet, Isla prepared herself to climb. Velyn offered her spine to her as she'd usually search for, but Isla shook her head. Not this time.

Just like home, she told herself. *Just like home.*

Isla peered upward to be kissed by icy raindrops that'd made her frigid. Anxiety flushed away her ambition, cautioning her hand away from the rocky slopes. A couple steps backward and the valley shot downward into what seemed to be an endless fall. A thick smog lingering eerily.

Certain death if she'd misplaced a hand and fell. Something exacerbated by the deluge that'd chosen to moisten her route.

Wrinkling her nose, Isla kicked out a stone and planted her foot. Had she thought on it any longer, looked up at it for another second, she would've convinced herself not to climb.

Spotting a clearing through the rain, which pelted into her eyes, provided her with a sense of comfort; a chance to rest her bleeding and tender fingers. But on reaching the refuge, she was taken aback when sighting what chose to occupy it. An imposing beast that was both bird and lion... the spitting image of the mural above her parents' bedhead.

A mighty gryphon. Dormant, yet still a beast of great stature and greater strength than a harem of horses.

When she saw the winged beast fly – when she chose to seek it out – she didn't expect that. Not a gryphon.

Isla slowly approached and planned her route. The path she followed led alongside him, past his perked ears and sharp beak and further from the pelting rain. As she sneakily sidestepped to round his head, she glimpsed a tattered book's cover beneath a scuffed talon. The prize she'd sought within her reach.

Getting closer, she'd managed to read the title: *Initiate's Magic*. Its author's name all but destroyed through both abrasion and the weather.

I knew it wasn't the Codex. It's never that easy.

Disheartened, and knowing that she shouldn't touch it, that she should continue upward towards Spellforge without disturbing the creature, she'd, of course, done the opposite. How could she not? It was right there!

On all fours, Isla pussyfooted nearer to the imposing beast's talon and cautiously grabbed hold of the book's cover with bloodied fingers. The talon collapsed on the hay beneath, and the beast continued snoring as pleasantly and content as before.

Opening the book, Isla had a plan in mind – a stroke of genius that'd propel her journey en route for the Codex. She'd hoped to find a spell. Something to help her put a name to that island the Searwood had shown her. The Codex's location.

She'd assayed it on her own because she knew that she was capable. She was the Harbinger, after all.

Opening the book, she read over titles she's only ever known in Leif's literature. Things such as: cantrips and paramount spells, before continuing through and halting on a world map. Two pages were dedicated to each of the two Realms.

Above those pages was the same spell, or cantrip, as the book proclaimed it to be. A locator cantrip. Reading the necessary words written in Common, Isla attempted to verbally whisper it. But nothing happened. Thus, she tried again and again, but with no result.

Focus, she vanquished the air from her lungs entirely before taking a long and deep breath.

Uttering the words once more, her finger darted to the lower right-hand side of her Realm's map. To the southern Duchy of Rhegion; to Rimathea's Capital City, Coventry. As her breathing quickened and a light-headedness played on her, a name etched itself above her finger: Father's Smithy.

I said focus, she rebuked. *Find the Codex.*

Isla's vision strained beyond new ashen curls as she studied the map. She needed to get this right. So, she repeated the process again: carefully respire, and cast. It worked.

Her finger dragged upward on the right-hand page and headed back towards Gwynedd before it'd stopped on a sequestered and splendid island a small distance from Deacon. A familiar island.

Another name etched itself above her finger: the Codex.

Although the island had remained nameless, a sense of elation had overcome her. However, she hadn't time to celebrate for an unfamiliar rustling sounded from ahead.

Looking up, Isla saw the gryphon slowly broaden his wide and strong wings and release a screech which echoed the ranges when his observance fell on the book. She dropped to shield her ears from the blood-curdling noise.

The gryphon reared, relentlessly launching attacks at her, and not allowing her to stand upright. Talons clawed for her eyes, as his long lion tail whipped and struck her cheek.

Isla rolled away, avoiding another attack.

She swung her bag in a twist and struck the gryphon across his sharp beak, angering him and not repelling him.

Letting out another screech, he charged at her in a rumbling gallop.

Barely the size of his hind legs, Isla braced for impact. She held her breath, the book against her chest, and was launched backward over the ledge. Falling, Isla forsook the book and held out her hands – managing to grab on to the unstable, rocky mountainside.

She saw her honey-coloured faedragon come out after him, but Isla refused Velyn's aid with a curt shake of her head.

The gryphon swooped, yet instead of attacking, studied her person. A crash of thunder, a branch of lightning tore through the sky, and he dove rather than attack again.

Instinctively, Isla kept her head hidden within the crease of her arm as the gryphon proceeded downward.

Stupefied and relieved, Isla watched as he plummeted into the misty depths and convulsed with a sigh. He wasn't after her – he only wanted the book. The gryphon had attacked who he'd presumed her to be a thief.

A gust of wind soughed, it died, and the rain settled in.

All was quiet after that, and her attacker remained unseen.

Pelting against the mountainside and into the clearing she'd reached, the rain hadn't allowed Isla a clear line of sight until a screech echoed from the depths, and the blue-flame of lightning coruscated across the nighttime sky.

There, massy and intimidating in its ferociousness and dread, Isla saw the monster fly towards her.

Again, she braced; but when the beast neared, he'd opened his wings and slowed. He screeched as gently as he could manage and moved closer to the wrinkled-nosed Isla.

He didn't attack her. He didn't even look as fearsome as he had prior to his descent into the depths; his eyes, large and puppyish in lieu of the thin, focused slits they'd been.

There was a book in neither his beak nor about his awesome body, however. And for that Isla felt aggrieved.

As he gently nudged her arm, feathers drenched from the downpour, Isla said, "I'm sorry about the book." And she was. But she was also curious, lacking time, and had an idea. "Can you fly me to Spellforge?"

As Isla and the gryphon readied themselves amid the break of dawn, they admired the glorious view of the fissure's varied wilderness; smelt a coalescence of mixed berries on the brisk wind. It'd rejuvenated a sense of nostalgia and adventure once so profoundly sought when the Varangian Guard and knights was all she'd dreamt of.

The gryphon tilted his head left and right, rustled his feathers, and lowered his beak to the ground. Waiting.

Resting a hand beneath a wing, Isla proceeded to caress his elongated and muscular body, trailing along his neck, his head, and his beak. Her mind elsewhere, he'd remained as still as the dark rock. She then climbed atop his feathery back, both eager and nervous and without a clue as to how this'd worked.

Humans weren't meant for flying, and aeronauts dumbfounded her for that reason. Yet the idea invigorated that same nostalgia felt earlier, and she nodded.

The gryphon took off – the force almost sending Isla toppling over and into the depths.

They bypassed nests of giant peregrines and their hatchlings that equalled the size of a fully-grown kyojin, cascading waterfalls which ran the length of the mountainside, and biomes of pink and red mushrooms with spots. They corkscrewed within a circular and long tunnel, leading beyond an interior molten-fall with a fiery aura that kept the cave alit from one end to the other; and re-emerged as the air caught Isla's hair: rustling and whipping it about her face wildly.

The gryphon ascended! The wind against her face was so cold that she could barely feel her nose.

Her eyes were watering, and her fingers were cramping from how tightly she held on to the gryphon's massive feathers. Yet she'd loved it all the same; she felt alive!

Amid the clouds that smelt of rain and grass, Isla spotted the sweeping, mountainous vista below with pine trees flecking its snowy peaks as though green fleece on a black-skinned sheep from Enkhara. As gorgeous as an oil painting, yet as intimidating as a winter tempest.

They dove, the frigid zephyrs attacking her skin!

As her fingers dug themselves into him, the gryphon screeched and drifted upward alongside a looping, abandoned stairway of mossy granite. It led downward and into the fissure; it led into the same cave she'd turned away from.

Isla wanted to cry. But prior to tears, she glimpsed the prize.

Bewildering braziers in the shape of goblets contained multi-coloured flames and highlighted the pathway and entrance to Spellforge on both sides. Beside them, and placed between each, were seven humungous statues representing the magi that once dwelt within. They aligned the expansive mossy-granite, and at their backs were two clear streams with hints of magenta particles that cascaded over the edge.

Dismounting the gryphon, and patting him beneath the wing, Isla approached the magnificent mountaintop.

At the path's end, she came to be surrounded by purple, green, and sapphire flames which irradiated a single walkway that led towards a wall. There was nothing particular about the wall; it was a rocky surface moisture-ladened by dew and nothing else. In sooth, the room was no longer than one metre horizontally and three vertically if she'd to guess. Small enough to fit four more people, if they were anorexic.

A drip made the cramped space worse, and it'd drip every two seconds without fail. She'd counted.

Somewhere, beyond what she stood before, was the Key. Somewhere beyond the wet stones and colourful flames sat Basem Alpheniq, in the same inebriated state as he was in Falls Creek, she didn't doubt.

"So," Isla approached the wall, "is this it? Do I say something, or do I clap? Should I knock?"

She received no response but the echo of her voice.

Isla moved a little closer, placing her ear against the mountainside, and heard nothing but more dripping. She raised her hand to the blackness and knocked once. The rock bruised her knuckles. She stepped back. Nothing. The wall remained.

Clicking her tongue, she moved forward. She knocked once, twice, paused, looked behind at the gryphon outside, and knocked again.

The final knock was the loudest.

Nothing happened, until the ground rumbled, and the colourful flames were extinguished one-by-one. The wall didn't part, and the ground didn't move. In fact, the wall remained unscathed by the loud rumbling, and yet a single pebble had managed to wander onward through the wall and dissipate.

"Hello?" She touched the rock and sent ripples throughout it as though tossing a coin into a dark pond. "Bugger it."

Holding her breath and closing her eyes, she ran through.

Isla felt oddly moist as if her tunic was sticking to her chest like it would in humidity. Lightheaded also, as though she'd been spun around while looking at the sky – a game she played in childhood.

When looking at her pale hands, she could see twenty fingers wriggling like hungry worms instead of ten.

But as that subsided, she beheld a fountain ahead of her; the centre for where roads converged and formed a circle around it. A bit above its base were the same seven magi, each in a different pose yet each equally imposing.

Three of those roads led towards a collection of baroque buildings which she could hardly see above the first storefront on her left that'd stocked bolts of silk and cotton; some upright, others in piles from the floor up. Another led to a dried-out lake.

Looming over all in its imperious umbra, however, was a time-worn building. A ziggurat, in fact. Temples of prayer in most cases, but from what the barely-visible road signs dictated to her, it was once a school. Its intricate designs in its masonry visible even from the distance she stood.

Still, all was dark, and cobwebs grew on everything.

Mana was entirely absent. Huge, violet, crystal shards speared through points in the ground and walls of the enormous cavern instead. They glowed ominously with a throb and provided the slightest bit of illumination.

The buildings lacked any neolyt, yet a path ahead was sporadically alight with floating flames that aligned a single route through the city. It, Spellforge, had reminded Isla of simpler time – a time she never knew, but one missed by some. And it'd bore a familiar scent: burning timber freshly doused by drizzling rain with a hint of cinnamon.

With the Codex's location fresh in mind, and a lack of greeting from anyone or anything, Isla walked along the highlighted and tree-lined boulevard which led through the baroque and abandoned city. The path she took was constructed of pale-silver brickwork carefully arranged to create a symbol of a phoenix every third or fourth step.

On the fifth step, however, she'd almost cut her bare feet on the shattered glass that jutted out of a burgundy liquid.

A trail of it led to a narrow alleyway that bore signposts of debatable quality protruding outward, and sometimes downward, from the storefronts like unkempt vines. From there, she'd heard inexplicable noises that'd forced her hand back to Velyn's spine, but she stopped herself before stroking.

The faedragon was unbothered.

Pursuing that trail, Isla was led to what the sign above her head proclaimed to be a library, yet from the exterior was tantamount to a mausoleum that'd fallen into disrepair. Lingering at the threshold and bedevilled by a sense of intrigue, she peeked through one of the door's many holes while visualising the Codex's island.

And she kept that image suspended in her mind when she carefully opened the door to the bijou and dank library to see Basem admiring something with tear-filled eyes. A small, unframed portrait of a man with a young red-haired girl.

Isla noticed his diadem sat beside his scarred arm and a book, whose title she couldn't read but was marked by Basem, on the desk where he drowned his sorrows. She eyed the empty prong setting, her warm fingertips feeling their way upward and on the gem at her neck. Doing so, Isla felt it pulse through her fingertips – a gentle tug moving en route for the discarded jewellery on the desktop.

"Why'd you give my mother your gem?" She spoke up, garnering his drunken attention as he hugged the portrait to his breast.

Slightly and slowly, his head turned. Yet to reveal his ice-blue irises, he'd centred himself and sighed.

"I gave her my *gem*, so that she could read my secret messages," he freely admitted, and Isla doubted. "Readable only in the azurite's light."

"Don't lie to me! What power does this thing possess? Was my mother one of you – a Mystic?"

Thrusting a hand into his djellaba, Basem rose and revealed a gryphon origami that'd unfolded and refolded into his staff. Steadying himself, he snatched his diadem and recoiled into the sepulchral shadows that'd partially concealed him.

"She was, wasn't she? Was it Mother who gave you that parchment? A gift?" She approached. "It was, wasn't it? No, don't flee from me. You can't any more. Look at me! I do look like her after all, remember?"

"Indeed, same eyes." Basem fingered the many chains around his neck. His stubble had grown thicker. "But just because you look like your mother doesn't mean that I'll train you. You're not even supposed to remember me. How do you? Whatever! Look, I c-can't train you, all right? Leave me be. Return to Falls Creek and never look back!"

"Why did you give my mother your gem?" Isla's hands sparked with flame as her forefinger shook in a point.

Velyn dug her talons into Isla, yet she wasn't hostile towards the shaded Basem as Isla had expected her to be. Instead, the faedragon watched and listened.

Seeing that, and seeing Velyn, Isla noticed a change in Basem. The tenseness in his darkened silhouette had subsided, especially in his back, and he held himself upright. As upright as he could manage with the staff's assistance, anyway.

He approached them, neither of the pair flinching, but the stench of alcohol forced Isla to gag.

"A Familiar." His countenance twisted in apparent rejoice, narrowing his already thin moustache as he tossed away his diadem and allowed it to dent and bend. "I would've expected a cat. A rare piece of magic..."

Basem's eyes widened, stepping out into the light and in awe. He reached towards them, but Isla caught his bejewelled hand before he could touch either of them.

"My blood and what I am – a Harbinger..." she gulped. "Am I aenyr? Are we related? Did you love my mother?"

Basem hadn't responded, and only glared at Isla's red hair, at the point where the ashen colour had spread, before he'd felt for the portrait which he'd pocketed.

They lingered in that hold as the voices within her, the Calling, built. And as she investigated those ice-blue irises, they'd reached a crescendo... and then stopped. Unceremoniously, and without warning. The voices were silenced. Snuffed by an unforeseen blanket dousing the amber flames of some far-off wildfire.

As they were, Isla felt Basem's pulse through his wrist increase. And again, as she moved a little closer to him. Not once had he diverted from her – almost as if he was drinking her in entirely: her appearance, how she spoke, and even how she acted. But still, it didn't feel romantic. Loving, sure, but...

"Fine," Isla said, breaking the silence. "The way I see it? I am what I am, and that's all that matters. Live in the present, right?" She felt her eyelid twitch. "So, look, I know where the Codex is. The Searwood told me. It also told me that you're the Key."

His eyebrows quirkily spasmed.

"They Key to the Undercroft." She looked him up and down. "A man of six-foot-three. Now, will you help me and answer my questions, or will I go it alone? Somehow."

Raising his head and inflating his chest, he said, "Whether I help you or not remains to be seen. First, I must know that you're telling the truth. I must think. If you know what you are, then I've little more to tell you of your heritage. What matters now is the future. What matters is what we'll achieve together, if," he held a finger up, "and only if, you're telling me the truth."

VIII

Conduit, Curses, and Chains

On nightfall in Deacon, Leif and Aivor stalked the commandant. His stride was proud and unfaltering, even in its quickened pace. A need to be seen in a positive light outshone anything else, it was evident to Leif. When he'd stopped to nod at an aristocrat with a woman-of-the-night on his arm, it was all but confirmed.

At the pace they'd moved over broken rooftiles to keep up with the armour-clad schemer below, the night's icy winds found their way beneath Leif's loose-fitting tunic; especially when leaping from one roof to the other.

His skin was frozen, but his blood was hot and eager – pumping its secretions and motivating him onward. He hadn't even thought about being cold since he'd fled Isla's wildfire.

Leif wouldn't break the flow of free running – couldn't. When a roof ended, he leapt to a balcony; from the balcony to neolyt, and then to the drainpipe. Aivor lagged. His heaviness slowing him down and his unsure footing almost killing him.

Leif dove through open windows and into homes, slid beneath a table – or over – and leapt out the other side while his audiences within hadn't the chance to touch their dinners.

To keep up with the commandant, he needed to.

For all the armour he'd worn, the commandant was nimble. Alleyways were his best friend and the backroads his mistress. He came to a halt at a resplendent building named Jeu de Café and performed a patterned and paced knock on an ornate back door swathed in darkness.

The café-theatre, thought Leif, standing above the fizzing neolyt gentleman that'd doff his hat.

Eager to see more, Leif went to leap across the gap that'd separated him from the café-theatre and the commandant. Toes scraping against the ledge, judging the distance... he instead steadied himself against an old chimney, inhaled sharply, and pushed his spectacles against the bridge of his nose. It was too far. He couldn't jump it without serious injury, or death.

Leif focused entirely into the dark veil that enshrouded his quarry. Scratching his stubble, unused to the itchiness, he dreaded losing him. He couldn't. However, there was nothing within the void of stygian mass.

The commandant had disappeared.

Footfalls sounded from behind, and Leif looked back at Aivor who'd arrived breathless and tired. He bemoaned the aching feet and the bloodied fingertips – the callouses garnered from the mandolin strings torn off completely.

Leif was glad to see him alive.

Another glance into the blackness, another attempt to spot something, and Leif decided to wait beside his friend. As he had, clear skies allowed for the resplendent moonlight to reflect on ripples stirred by gondoliers performing heartfelt melodies. Yet that silver light refused to shine through the veil of nothingness.

I thought he was meeting the Enchantress, Leif brooded, watching the exact spot where the door was. *So, why would he come here for that? I need answers, and you'll give them to me, commandant. One way or another... you will.*

Aivor joined in on the melodies, strumming his mandolin lightly and singing of the good times – the better times. Of when his explorer father met his foreign mother; of their distant love being akin to his love for Isla. He sung of green moons and her emerald eyes, as she knew he would when he'd handed her the lyrics to that song.

With words of love and wonder flowing amid the scent of canola from the outskirt farmlands beneath the floating islands, Leif could no longer feel that supernatural phenomenon in his heart. Placing a hand on his chest, he searched himself for it. He inhaled the night air, the canola, for a chance to see within and allow it to be felt again.

Instead, he found that whatever it was, it'd been severed. No voices had told him, and nothing had convinced him of it. He just knew. And, somehow, he was okay with it.

Searching beyond himself and the rooftops, at the tail-end of the gondoliers' ripples and beneath the café-theatre, for a chance to understand what that feeling in his heart had once been, he instead spotted sludge and murky water that coalesced with the river Argolia. A sewer, and one Leif believed was built by the filth that'd occupied the establishment above.

Disgusted, he turned aside as something appeared in his peripheral vision. He'd glimpsed the front door swing open and rebound off one of the two ornate columns by the entry-way.

Halting Aivor's strumming, and lowly slinking, Leif peeked over the rooftop's edge and saw the commandant take off again. A new lantern was suspended before him as he continually checked his shoulders.

"Keep to the shadows." Leif nudged Aivor and pointed to the gutter; or, more specifically, the fragile pipe attached to it.

"That can't hold my weight," Aivor hissed through his teeth.

Rolling his eyes, Leif summersaulted over the edge, descending speedily into a swing to land on a balcony.

Aivor assayed to mimic Leif's movements, but the drainpipe bent, and his foot missed a brick. Freefalling, Aivor reached out ahead of him and threw himself forward – his hip colliding loudly with the rendered brick, ripping his pants and scuffing the grout.

A twang of broken strings echoed out, but the crashing of varnished wood outshone that in an instant.

The commandant swivelled, his lantern shaking amid his quivering. But he didn't redirect his attention from street-level. He regarded the sett road of rectangular and quarried stone with both scrutiny and malice and carried on.

Leif looked to his ebbing silhouette, to the light ahead of the commandant slowly becoming nothing more than an amber smudge in the background of an artist's painting, and then back at Aivor who'd writhed on the ground as he had in Falls Creek. Torn, Leif went to take off, but spotted the mandolin ruined at his feet. He couldn't leave him behind.

Not again.

"Sorry," he'd whispered, helping Aivor upright. "You did say... about the drainpipe, I mean."

Aivor disregarded the apology with a shrug but winced when Leif attended to his grazed hip with his healing hands; and cried when spotting his ruined instrument. Wordless, Leif caught Aivor's gaze as he looked towards the river Argolia and followed it to where the city square ought to be; where the commandant continued in the direction of, "Are you all right to run on it?" Leif nodded at the wound; its bleeding had ceased.

Arriving at a boutique bakery nigh the barricades, Leif pointed out that ahead of them, and between the tall build-

ings, were two neolyt advertisements that flickered with dimness. The mana within them waned, it struggled to keep the
street alight. Keen to move beneath those shadows, Leif ordered Aivor to await the longest flicker – five seconds, give
or take – before they moved to approach the barricades.

When it'd arrived, they crouched and shimmied along the
boutique's windowfront. Yet a nick in the wall halted Leif's
pussyfooting as he craned his neck towards the rooftop.

He scaled it, and Aivor clumsily followed suit.

Dashing forward, never tripping on the rooftiles, or
bounding heavily enough to break through somebody's ceiling, Leif came to a halt beside a collection of flu-gas stacks to
see that below, where bodies once lined the square, the commandant shook hands with a hooded stranger. The black-obsidian vambrace of consequence made apparent.

"The Enchantress," whispered Leif. "She came."

The hooded Mystic leant in, whispered something in the
commandant's ear, and retreated a couple of steps. With that
piece of basalt in her hand, she brought it to her ear and
licked it.

Without a staff, she remained tall; her stone skin doing
nothing to hinder her posture whatsoever.

"Thank you, Enchantress," said the commandant in a
shaky, yet relieved, tone of voice. "You've my assurance that I
won't fail you again. What happened with the Comte was out
of our hands, to be sure, but I've the café-theatre's aristocracy enthralled. I've assured them that all is going according
to plan."

"Users," she hissed, "the lot of them. They've no true loyalty to myself or Daeva. But you," she reached out an ugly hand and petted the commandant's cheek, "you and your lieutenants are different. As you once served Daeva, you serve me equally as loyal. You three will be the first to share in the immortality and magic my master and I've promised."

Was this why Daeva was mentioned in the diary? Leif pondered. *The Enchantress serves another... and one so foul?*

"We live to serve, Enchantress," he said, much cooler than before, adjusting his silver chainmail beneath golden-and-black armour. "How goes the search for the Conduit?"

Leif retched on hearing himself mentioned, his spectacles sliding down his nose. Notions of sacrifice spread wildly across his imagination alongside heritages, bloodlines, and again... sacrifice.

He stumbled, almost falling, but Aivor held him upright.

"Abysmal." The Enchantress advanced. "Once more, I still can't feel the bond between us. A bond Daeva promised would come. The slightest arrythmia in the heart keeps me hopeful, but then I recall the lack of ashen in my hair."

That feeling was a bond between me and someone else. He recalled the night of the fire. *Ashen hair... it can't be. Isla?*

"No point on your ears, either. Your faith is waning?" The commandant inflated his chest. "Are you not the Harbinger?"

Within the Enchantress, Leif saw something snap on hearing that question. Yet instead of acting on that snap, she buried whatever it was, because he didn't see any anger riddle anything he could spot of her. Her posture was still perfect, and her hands were steady.

"Leif Morrigan and I will re-surface magic. I'll make sure of it." She reached out and placed a hand atop the commandant's which held the lantern. "Now, tell me, how goes Ludwig's forging. I'm assuming completed, since you've arrived here unhindered by Imperial Troops?"

Cringing, Leif listened to the commandant's knuckles pop beneath the Enchantress' strength. As that happened, Aivor grabbed a hold of Leif's forearm – where a burn scar remained – and looked at him up and down. He'd felt the judgment and shock of secret keeping but brushed it off and took back his arm.

"No, Enchantress." He gritted his crooked teeth. "We've yet to receive the forged passes. Since I'd arrived with the refugees, I managed to avoid any suspicion. You?"

"Teleportation," she said, releasing her hold on him and admiring the moons – their position, Leif gauged. "Now, I've wasted enough time here, and I'm needed at the old cave. But know this: your task remains unchanged, as does your lieutenants'. Bring as many nobles to our side as you can. Lie if you must."

"And what of the girl my men killed? The runes?"

She turned, held the basalt to the sky, and said, "You needn't know what they say, just make sure your men carve them into the next victim. Make sure *he* knows the person, too."

And then she was gone.

A force dug into Leif's shoulders, and he was thrust against a flu-gas stack. Aivor's breath smelt horrible, and the scabbing scar over his eye was even more nauseating.

Peeking over his shoulder, and to the square, Leif saw that his quarry had disappeared.

All that effort and barely anything to show for it.

"You're a Mystic?" said Aivor. "Why didn't you tell me? Why didn't you tell me that you were the Conduit?" He grabbed Leif's hands, studied the palms, and then flipped them. "Your hands – healer's hands! The gift of Conduits. I should've known the moment you'd healed your first wound."

"Get off of me!" Leif shoved Aivor backward. "I didn't tell you for the same bloody reason you didn't tell Isla and I about what you were. Look, Aivor, I'm no Mystic. Whatever I am, there's no magic coursing through these veins – through these hands."

"Yeah, you keep telling yourself that."

Shouldering Aivor out of his way, Leif approached the roof's edge. He needed to process it – all of it – and for that, he'd needed to be alone with his thoughts.

If Isla was the Harbinger, if her ashen hair and pointy ears led to that... then so was Mother. That's why her killers took her ears; to sell them on the black market. The fact frightened him. The fact that throughout the years, he never once guessed that his mother – his best friend – was something so powerful.

Frightened that he never knew Isla was, either.

The bond the Enchantress sought could never be obtained, because Leif had already shared it with Isla. Although severed, he felt its exclusivity – more so after learning whom he shared it with. It was all then making sense, clicking into place like the pieces of a puzzle.

"Did you know what Isla was? Did you know that she was a Harbinger? The Dyadic Prophecy's Harbinger?"

"No," said Aivor.

"And my mother?"

To that, Aivor didn't respond.

"Forget about what they are, or were, and worry about yourself," he said. "Leif, to be the Conduit means—"

"—I need to sacrifice myself to re-surface magic, I know. Trust me... I know that all too well."

"Not only that..." his arms were akimbo. "Leif, once the sacrifice is official – once you willingly give yourself up... You'll be primed for possession."

"Possession?"

Daeva, he thought.

"Daeva!" he said. "The Enchantress wants to bring her back."

Diving into his pocket and grabbing hold of the commandant's diary, Leif produced it for Aivor. He searched the pages, bringing the mandolinist in closer so he could read. Fingertips damp with descending mildew, he drew to a halt on the passage marked with the old necromancer's name. It read:

The Enchantress has promised the return of our old master. And with Daeva's return, with the new era of magic, my master will sit the Imperial Throne. She'll rule a Realm united with magic and immortality with the aristocracy's backing.

It'll occur if there's strong enough magic to allow it, as I'd told Estrid. That's how she's going to return. Leif's upper lip sweated. *And somehow Daeva was already communicating with our world. How else would the Enchantress know her wishes?*

Closing the diary for Leif, Aivor wandered away on unsteady legs. Hands on his knees, taking a breather, he licked his lips. Aivor licked his lips. Licked.

Leif bit his thumb and thought on it – the word, the meaning, and its spelling. He wondered why anybody sane would carry around a piece of basalt and lick it.

The basalt, Leif adjusted his spectacles. *She licks it. Means of affection, perhaps? Either way, with that, the Enchantress receives her orders... orders she dictates to her men.*

Leif acknowledged the part he'd play in the future, but his task at hand wasn't to inhibit that. In fact, he needed magic re-surfaced more than ever if he'd wished to stop any of what he'd learnt from happening. With Mystics returned, they could thwart someone like the Enchantress.

They'd stand a better chance than Laics, anyhow.

But he didn't want to be possessed. He didn't want to die.

"Earlier you'd mentioned a weapon to me," said Aivor, cracking his knuckles. "Ancient runes too, right?"

He had, and he recalled what the Enchantress told the commandant about carving the runes into the next victim.

"Runes that point to a weapon that'll aid in the re-surfacing of magic." His thumb was aching from how hard he bit it. "A weapon that could be a hindrance to the Enchantress, according to the commandant's fears. Aivor, we need that weapon."

Hope became him. Hope that he'd be able to outrun the prophecy; that sacrifice was unneeded with the weapon in hand. He needed that hope. But first, they needed to translate the ancient runes. And to do that, they needed to find the body that contained them. And to do that... they needed the commandant who'd wondered off into the dead of night with no lamplight visible from their location.

Leif opened the diary again and read over the initials: E.A.

They were familiar to him, yet he didn't want to think about that. He couldn't afford to.

"We find the commandant again, and we make him talk," said Leif. "We find out about this victim – these runes – we acquire the final pieces to this bloody puzzle. And we kill him."

IX

A Noble Folly

Leif began by questioning the urchins. Hidden in plain sight, he couldn't imagine a better source of surveillance. He wasn't disappointed. Beneath disappearing moons and the first rays of sunlight, they told him all – and for little more than a ride on Aivor's hulking back and a silver coin. The last of Clan Alberg's dinero.

The bakery. As simple as that. The bakery they'd snuck by in the night was where they'd confront their quarry. However, standing in the middle of the street as the city awoke, Leif devised a plan. A relatively simple one, but a good one.

They'd pose as aristocrats; people that the commandant eagerly vied to impress, and then pounce at the opportune moment.

Returning to the snow-white manor to acquire the perfume and attire required to accomplish what they needed,

Leif retrieved the broken hilt of Seeker, hid it at his waist beneath his fashionable coat, and returned to the city square.

For vengeance. For answers.

At daybreak, seated alone and outside beneath an awning, Leif didn't take his eyes from the street. Modern apparel was a commodity among the characters of Deacon, so he didn't expect to be caught off guard by a man dressed entirely in golden armour. Nevertheless, and as his leg shook with anxiety, he restlessly watched.

The freshest croissant he'd ever seen was placed before him followed by tea and a complementary choux pastry. Both smelt terrific, as did the perfume he'd stolen. Still, he'd felt ridiculous. Especially when spotting Aivor lurking in the distance. Awaiting the signal. A signal neither of them had prepared.

Sat beside a parkland, it bore statuettes aside maple trees and knee-high shrubberies which produced splendid flowers all year round. Sparrows warbled, squirrels gnawed, and stray cats were welcomed by warm milk in saucers which the rotund baker would leave out.

The boutique bakery's fanciful interior was fabulous, and its aesthetic provided a sense of disconnect from the other ordinary bakeries in Rimathea. Rustic to Leif's eye. Barrels lined the baker's workshop – acting as stools – and the mezzanine was nothing but a storage area containing coffee beans and flour.

A favourite place of the commandant's, from what the urchins had said. They'd learnt his routine – his morning route.

Gesturing his hand above the steam to smell the delicate aroma of the warm pastry infusing with the rich hazelnut chocolate, Leif imagined himself opposite Estrid. Hoped that those initials were a coincidence – prayed to whatever divine would accept his botched invocation – and delved headfirst into a world of fancy. Remaining there as he'd pictured her incomparable temptation, Leif moved on to the tea.

In his peripheral vision, Aivor stirred; hidden behind the boutique's wall and awaiting his moment. A man that detested sweets and sugar, he'd priorly asked Leif to order only a black coffee to aid in his formulated arrival. But before he could do so, the heavy sound of armour startled Leif and a black-obsidian vambrace was before him.

It stunk of sweat, yet the commandant was well presented.

His hand was extended and suspended. It awaited Leif.

"Good morning," he said. "New to our fine city?"

Our fine city, is it? Leif half-smiled at him.

"Arrived the day before last, *actually*." Leif accentuated the latter word as he'd recalled his favourite fictional inspector doing the same. "A beautiful city, though death sullies its alure."

They met hands, and the commandant followed Leif's regard that was fixated on the city square. It was barely visible from around the corner, and still Leif envisioned it vividly.

"Merely a misunderstanding, as I've come to understand. May I?" The commandant motioned towards the seat opposite Leif. He nodded, and the commandant sat. "Sorry, I've not caught your name?"

"Don Alejandro."

"A Poirdelais?" He raised an inquisitive eyebrow that'd unnerved Leif. "Your accent is lost on me."

"That's because it doesn't exist. I was born in Poirdeaux, but my parents moved here when I was only an infant. Still remember the scents of fresh croissants, however. That's why I've chosen this place. Beautiful, isn't it?"

The commandant nodded, seemingly content with Leif's answer. Of course, it was all from the same fictional inspector novels. If it weren't for recalling the stories verbatim, Leif doubted that he could've managed the conversation. The archaic structure of his sentences making him sweat.

The commandant seemed to mimic the style. A want to be like the noblemen he recruited.

Ordering the same thing as Leif, the commandant leant back into his seat, revealed a new diary, and wrote something down. Briefly scrutinising the commandant when he'd finished and looked to the river, Leif feigned a smile and dabbed a handkerchief over his brow.

"Sir, may I ask what it is you're doing wearing full-plate armour?" He pushed his spectacles against the bridge of his nose. "In an evolving Realm such as ours, don't you fear being left behind? Will we not be fighting wars from afar soon enough?"

Inflating his cheeks before releasing the air contained within in a silent raspberry, the commandant leisurely diverted his attention away from the river. Sniffling, taking a sip of his tea, he proceeded to set aside his diary and pencil. Crossing a leg over the other and clasping his armoured knee with both hands, he returned Leif's smile.

Whether it was feigned or not was lost on him.

"Not really, no," he said. "It's for protection."

"Protection? With armour as thick as that, you'd think you were fending off dragons."

"Maybe." The commandant looked down at himself. "If the rumours of what lurks in The Horn are true, you should prepare armour of your own."

"And what lurks in The Horn, pray tell?" His croissant was still hot. "Mud, worms, and Settler bones?"

Expression lost from his deplorable countenance, the commandant leant over the table, "As you said, Don Alejandro: a dragon."

Leif recoiled at the notion and grabbed for his bag, stopping himself before he did. Daeva arising was one thing; sacrifice and possession was another... but a dragon?

"But they've not been seen since the Dragon Revolt." Isla's dream of a dragon came to mind. "You jest."

The commandant leant back, smiled, and shrugged. For how thick his armour had appeared to be, he moved with such fluidity that you'd imagine it parchment and not metal.

"The same was said about Basem Alpheniq, but he's apparently still around. Himself having survived both the Dragon

Revolt and the Purge. All manner of Mystics might've been killed, but you need something far deadlier than those to end an aenyr's suffering on this mortal plane. Dragons are similar. At least Coventry's dragon is."

Leif's palms sweated on his rich pants as he recalled the dragons of yore's promise to one day return and kill all humans. All of them except one... the first dragon. An experiment gone wrong; an experiment by the name of Ghulzar.

"That look on your face," said the commandant, "is fear. I knew it well. Knew. But now death worries me not, for I've seen the immortal plane. I've felt magic course through my veins."

Here we go, Leif banished the idea of dragons. *He's about to offer me – Don Alejandro – to join them.*

"What if I could promise you immortality?" He clapped Leif's knee with a gloved hand. "What if I could promise you magic? More power than the Empress herself – more than her imperium?"

"Well," Leif gulped. "Empress is just a fancy title to appease the monolid folks of the east. So, is that what you're offering me? A fancy title and false promises?"

The commandant broke off a piece of Leif's breakfast and carefully placed it into his mouth. "I offer you *true* power."

As a whistle came through the commandant's crooked teeth, and his leering smile persisted even when Leif turned away from him, a sense of pride and purpose emanated so fluidly and strongly from the armour-clad man that you'd imagine it was magic. What he'd lacked in looks, he'd compensated with suaveness and a beguiling countenance; but barely.

A predator, Leif understood his game. The commandant preyed on the weak who feared death – which was mostly all mortal beings. Nobody wanted to die, and nobody wanted to be normal. Another lost pebble on a beach of stones. And although portraying a character, Leif too feared death. He feared his impending sacrifice. And the commandant felt that.

"Good morning!" A failed accent encroached on their silence and received nothing from Leif or the commandant.

Aivor cleared his throat and tried again.

"Good morning."

"And to you," said the commandant, but didn't take his eyes off *Don Alejandro*. "I can see that you're not entirely convinced."

Lazily looking up, Leif took Aivor's hand into his own and shook firmly, thankful for the intrusion. Tapping twice on Aivor's knuckles, he gestured to the empty seat. As he'd sat down heavily, the commandant whiffed the air he stirred.

He'd caught Aivor's scent, his perfume.

He smiled again, "A friend of yours, Don Alejandro?" And extended his smelly vambrace to Aivor.

They shook hands.

"My brother-in-law, in fact. Don Martino."

Aivor gave a small, stiff nod to their quarry as his hand was still held. Then the commandant's flipped and he held tightly onto Aivor's; Leif watched it all from the corner of his eye and feigned ignorance. Even when the commandant sniffed at Aivor, leered, and brushed his modern vest with the back of his free hand.

When he'd seemed pleased, the commandant relented.

Clapping his hands and rubbing them together as if wringing out soaked socks, he rose; the muffled noise of gloves dulling the joy he'd thoroughly expressed through a suggestive countenance. He then inhaled the morning fragrances through clogged nostrils and broke away another piece of Leif's croissant before he'd sultrily placed it on his tongue.

Toying with the chocolate on his glove, he licked it.

"You don't see many noblemen with scars on their faces," said the commandant.

Leif got to his feet and grabbed at Aivor's arm for him to do the same. Aivor's squinty, pale-green eyes darted between Leif and the commandant as his wobbly chin appeared incapable of finding the right words. In that brief, silent window Leif felt his neck warm, his hands sweat again, and his heartrate increase.

The commandant wasn't wrong.

"We tried our hand at duelling," said Aivor. "Wasn't for us."

"No, evidently not." He chuckled and stared at Aivor's calloused palms. "My offer stands, Don Alejandro, and I'll be glad to extend it to your brother-in-law, too. With eyes like yours, I don't doubt that you've the blood of the first men coursing through your veins – strong blood. And for that alone, you should take up my offer. To sew your seed through your longevity will bring an extension to your forefathers' bloodlines."

Tossing two silver coins into Leif's tea, he nodded to the rotund baker, and walked away without saying anything more to the two of them. When he looked behind and brushed his sleek eyebrow with his thumb, they then followed.

They manoeuvred through unknown streets and alleyways, passing many aristocrats that bowed and smiled at the commandant, before arriving to familiar roads that their quarry had taken the night before. They'd appeared different from the rooftops, but in both regards were splendid.

"If you fear loneliness in immortality, don't," he said over his armoured shoulder. "Had I brought my folder, I could've shown you all those that're onboard – their fealty. So, instead, I'll take you to the men that signed them."

At that moment, his window, Leif lowered his nose to glower at the commandant's back. Aivor nodded at him and pointed towards a backroad away from civilians, and the commandant agreed. Hand on Seeker's broken hilt, Leif kept to their backs; he checked his shoulders thrice, and once more when they'd all but disappeared amid the antiquated road's tall and narrow buildings.

"Why bother with a contract?" Leif grabbed the commandant's pauldron and firmly drew him back with a force unknown to him; Aivor grabbed for their enemy's sword and unsheathed it for himself. "Personally, I prefer blood oaths."

"What's this? Who're you?"

"I'm asking the questions!" Leif pushed Seeker's broken blade against his neck, drawing blood.

The commandant spat on the claymore and chortled, "I should've known. A nobleman with calloused palms and scars. Duelling? Bullshit. Would've done better for yourself had your mate not joined us."

"Ah, but you fell for it all the same, didn't you?" said Aivor. "Where's my sister?"

"Aivor!" Leif hissed through clenched teeth.

"Sister? Who...?" The commandant's stiffness than eased a little, and Leif felt the laughter well within him through the armour. "Falls Creek. You're the ebony girl's brother, aren't you? Oh, you poor sod."

Leif kneed his back and pointed the shard's end into the commandant's throat. The laughter said it all. The initials from the diary were all but confirmed, and so he didn't want to hear it. But the armour-clad warrior said it all the same.

Crucified, mutilated... raped. Estrid was the one; the one who bore the ancient runes.

Aivor attempted to scowl, but the tears didn't allow him, nor the wobbling chin. He kicked at the road and paced back and forth, exclaimed at the sky, and waved a fist. Leif couldn't comprehend what was said as the shrieking that accompanied his words overwhelmed anything remotely comprehensible.

He charged – long, black dreadlocks flapping – but the commandant kicked at him, even in Leif's hold, and took out Aivor's knee. He fell to the ground, and instead of fighting, he wept. Sword in hand, he was of no use to Leif.

To forestall the same fate that'd bring him to ruin, Leif told himself over and over that it'll be okay and that he'll make it right. He had to. For Mother. For Estrid. For vengeance. And he'd repeat those encouraging notions over and over.

"You, with the broken sword," said the commandant. "Suppose I should've known that your silver-grey eyes meant more than a fancy bloodline. You're the Conduit, aren't you?"

"What do you know of it? My lineage? Speak!"

But he only shrugged, "What's there to tell? Powerful. Unique. Just what the prophecy needed. What else matters?"

"So, I'm the chosen one?"

"Chosen one?" He laughed again. "Harbingers and Conduits have been born throughout history to various bloodlines. Strong bloodlines, granted. You and the current Harbinger just happen to fit the bill for the Dyadic Prophecy, nothing more."

That's not what he'd wanted to hear.

"My mother," he continued, "you killed her?" The commandant nodded. "Because she was a Harbinger, too?"

"*Pfft*, no! What happened to your mother and father was unceremonious and personal. It had nothing to do with her powers. Powers she'd lost birthing your sister, according to the Enchantress."

Seeker lowered, appearing near the commandant's chest now, and then it was sheathed. Leif grabbed a hold of his quarry's arm, pulled him around to face him, clasped his shoulders, and glared intently within his eyes.

Aivor rose, his sword pointed at the commandant's back.

"We'll let you live," said Leif, "if you tell us about the weapon. The one mentioned in your diary. The one that the ancient runes apparently lead to. Is it the dragon you men-tioned in Coventry? Is it Ghulzar that'll help re-surface magic?"

"Maybe," said the commandant, straight-faced and cold. "Or maybe not. Kid, I couldn't tell you even if I knew. We don't know what the runes say. My men are following orders. They killed his sister because it's what the Enchantress wanted; they carved the runes into her because it's what the Enchantress wanted. We don't question it. We do."

"But you're curious, nonetheless."

"Sure." He shrugged in Leif's hold. "It's only natural."

"And where's Estrid's body now? The ebony girl. Where is she?"

The commandant didn't say anything, so Aivor pressed the sword against the nape of his neck.

"Hotham Heights. They'd expected you to travel that way."

"She wants me to read them, doesn't she?" said Leif. "She knows about what I do – or did. They're a message for me; for the Conduit. She's guiding me to this weapon so she and I can re-surface magic."

Aivor looked at him over the commandant's shoulder.

"Then we go to Hotham Heights," he said in a shaky tone. "We find my sister's body and translate those damnable runes. Leif, with that weapon, we'll go to Isla and re-surface magic together. We'll beat the Enchantress at her game before she even knows what's going on."

Appearing to be pulled from thin air, but was the speed he moved at, the commandant produced a dagger from his waist and parried the sword away from his neck. Leif moved in with Seeker but was bashed down with a hard backhander that spun his world and sent his spectacles flying. The commandant looked down at the broken claymore and kicked it.

"Isla, you said?" He stepped on Leif's forearm and pointed his dagger at a readied and keen Aivor. "Then the Enchantress isn't the Harbinger, as I'd feared. But no matter. The prophecy will still be fulfilled, regardless of what we now do. Things are set in motion that none of us can stop. Glorious, isn't it?"

He lifted his foot from Leif.

"Go," he lowered his guard, "to Hotham Heights. The both of you, go. I won't tell the Enchantress; you've my word. After all, I want what you want."

Voiceless, their gazes locked. Aivor attacked!

His footsteps were neither scattered in circles nor did they overlap, he'd stepped precisely where he needed to, a foot behind the other. As he had in Falls Creek.

The commandant smirked.

He feinted an attack at Aivor, swinging his dagger and missing the sword. Aivor didn't react. Not yet. Leif knew what he'd planned – performed so many times before. Prior to attacking, he'd shift his weight onto his toes before pouncing left.

The Danse Macabre.

Aivor shifted, but the commandant read him like a book. He lunged with the dagger and bashed away Aivor's parry. Moving to the right instead, Aivor jabbed the sword at his abdomen, but the commandant pirouetted and knocked the blade away with a bright spark.

The commandant attacked. Aivor parried down and pivoted, losing his footing as the commandant quickly slashed. Falling to his knees, Aivor caught the dagger against the sword before it zipped up along the blade and barely missed his head.

"Use your magic!" Leif shouted. "Cast at him!"

"I can't!" Aivor roared back, scurrying on the road as people gathered amid the tight buildings. "Leif, I was born magicless!"

Getting to his feet, Aivor retracted his arm, his fingers popping as he clenched them into a fist, and with all his might – and a cry – he threw it forward, staggering but managing to connect with the commandant's jaw.

They both lost their weapons.

Aivor punched again, this time clobbering his throat.

The commandant stumbled, cursing Aivor in a retching cough of phlegm and blood while struggling. But Aivor was merciless and swung widely, aiming for the ear or temple. With a dull clap, the commandant instinctively caught the punch with an open palm and countered with a jab followed by an uppercut that connected with Aivor's nose.

Aivor fell beside Leif. Knocked out cold.

Without him, Leif felt helpless. He wasn't a fighter.

Hells, he'd wanted to leave when the commandant had offered them the chance. But that chance was squandered. And with the armour-clad man standing over Aivor's unconscious body, Leif donned his spectacles and took up the broken Seeker.

For vengeance.

Rising, he'd jabbed at his quarry but missed when he'd ducked and weaved.

Leif swapped hands and pictured Estrid's crucified body – imagined the vile things they'd done to her – felt the rage welling within him. The commandant stood still and smiled. Leif drew back his left arm, giddy and incapable of regaining his balance, and lunged.

Pulling back, Seeker's hilt wasn't in his palm.

Instead, Leif glared at his hand that dripped a profuse amount of blood, knowing that it wasn't his. The hilt was stuck in the commandant's neck. He dropped to his knees and suspired a final breath, and still that smile persisted.

The surrounding people shrieked and swore as the commandant plummeted to the cold, hard ground. They called for the sentries and grieved for the death.

Leif shook Aivor awake, pulled him to his feet, and directed him towards the city's exit.

They fled amid alarm bells tolling, and more shrieking and yelling. They fled from Deacon to Hotham Heights.

X

The Thorns of Forgiveness

Isla loathly listened as Basem reviled her locator cantrip, adamant that it was unreliable and not *true* magic. Neither cantrip nor spell, he'd say over and over, although not explaining what the difference was. But Isla knew that she'd used magic in Falls Creek; she remembered the wildfire vividly. The heat, the smell, the sound of people dying...

Imagery refused to leave her. Haunting her waking eyes like the floating lines that cursed people's vision. And like those floaties, she'd learnt to ignore them. To an extent. When she was reminded of it, walking through the abandoned and cold Spellforge, Isla saw it all again.

It played on loop, forcing her to remember what she'd done.

Was it magic that did this to her? Did it want her to feel guilty? She didn't know. And truthfully, she didn't want to know. Isla carried the burden and would continue to do so. Yet she'd try refraining from acknowledging it until the time was right.

The time for penance.

Isla hugged herself and shivered. There was no warbling from birds, nor chirp of insects. Nothing but the thrum of the crystals that loomed above and the faint whistle of wind passing over the mountaintop above.

Basem hadn't told her where they were going, but she followed him because she needed him. All he'd say when she'd enquire about their destination was that he'd soon learn the truth of it; that he'd get to the bottom of her *hearsay* concerning the Key and the Codex.

Pausing outside the ziggurat, she felt anxious. Perhaps Basem was too, taking another swig from his flask; but she needed the Key, not a drunk. When feeling her eyes on him, he'd turned around and flared his nostrils before pocketing his vice.

From the entrance, routes were dictated by floating signs and hovering candlesticks. A sight to behold, yet archaic.

"My word should suffice." She rubbed the ball of her grimy, aching foot. "You knew my mother. Obviously, trusted her. So, why can't you trust me?"

"Trust is earned, not given out as inheritance."

Rubbing her other sole, caked in filth, Isla scoffed. She tapped the bottom of a candle, and it floated upward briefly before descending back to its original position.

"Archaic and an arsehole."

"The latter, perhaps, but we're not archaic by choice. Candles are used because magic and mana don't mix." He twisted his magical parchment in the manner of wringing out a towel. "The bordello?"

She crossed her arms, "But if mana is magic, and magic is mana... why don't they? Why'd I draw the mana into me that night when I've never done so before?"

"You drew it in because you'd acknowledged the Calling as magic within you for the first time." Basem hiccupped. "And the two don't *mix* because as Mystics we constantly draw on mana. Not on purpose, but because magic attracts magic. We could drain an entire city."

For how much he'd quaffed, Basem neither slurred his words nor walked crookedly. He appeared completely sober. At first the loose sole of his boot caught on a jutting stone in the road, and he'd stumble to his left or right, but within the blink of an eye he'd return to form and reach for his flask again.

"So, I'm trustworthy enough for this, but not for you to take my word on what a Searwood shared with me?"

"History isn't private, it's for one and all. What you claim is beyond common – it changes everything."

"Fine!" Isla grabbed his arm, not letting him indulge in the drug that turned good men evil. "An entire city, you said?"

"Sure. If you stand long enough and close enough to a collection before moving on to the next." He relented and pulled away from her hold. "A slow process if you're not casting. Over in a minute, if you cast a paramount spell. But secluded in a mana-less room, you should be fine."

Watching the back of his head – the glowing hieroglyphs – and how he'd half-turn when he spoke, Isla saw something in his eye that wasn't sadness.

From what she could see, he appeared scared. Or something close enough to mimicking scaredness, anyway.

"Pointless either way," he continued. "It does nothing for us aside from feel good and alert Laics to our presence."

Velyn soared above, shooting glances down at her master when Isla had looked at her. She remembered how quickly she'd circled her in Falls Creek. That Velyn had appeared a blur.

"How, though?" said Isla. "How can Laics use magic?"

"Use? They wish. What they've done is blasphemous and foul." He wagged a finger. "Those eastern scientists have secretly experimented on Mystics and magic for years, and now they channel it through a source. A husk that'd once been my chestnut-haired sister."

"I'm sorry."

"So am I." He nodded to a place beyond the ziggurat's schoolgrounds; to what the sign described as the Chamber of Wisdom. "Let's speak no more of it."

They entered the chamber to see seven seats spread-out on a wide dais which evolved into a thin stairway, broken and full of green fungi. Obscene and grotesque caricatures hung above them to create an opposite for each magus. Their likenesses comparable to night and day – hair colour and features inverted and morphed.

Only five of the seats were occupied by figures; four of them stone. Including Basem, there was only six.

Making his way towards the predominant seat decorated in a lemon-yellow banner bearing a phoenix crest, and situated between the rest, Isla watched as he bowed his head to the stone men. Mumbling something beneath his breath, he shivered and sat.

"Chairs? You brought me here to look at chairs, did you? Are they all-seeing and all-knowing? That one foretells truths once you sit long enough in it, right? Take another swig, maybe that'll help, too."

A figure semi-cloaked in shadow stirred at the corner of her eye, shapely and breathing. A blackened ring finger appeared next as the seat's occupant leant forward. The only other magus of Spellforge to remain conscious to the world since the rest were turned to stone by Basem at the tail-end of the Purge.

"Her name is Keziah Gaunt. Like you, she came to us when the Calling stirred." Basem toyed with his dangling hobgoblin earring. "As she grew to understand herself, and what she was, the Calling was sated. The same will happen to you. If, and only if, I find out that you're telling me the truth."

Keziah smiled at Isla, but she didn't return one. Instead, her eyelid twitched. She felt a twinge in her muscles, beckoning her fist to clench and unclench as she continued to glare at the aenyr.

"Despite what you think, I don't need your training. Give me a book and I can do so myself," said Isla. "What I need from you, *Key*, is to accompany me on my quest so I may see it fulfilled. Now, will you come to Deacon's coastline – to the island I was shown – or do I make you? We've already wasted enough time on your games."

Basem crossed his arms and chortled.

The shadowed Keziah fondled something stony within her pocket, adjusted a sheathed weapon at her waist, and rose. Dressed in velvets that hugged her tight, curvaceous figure, she sauntered in her approach. Her narrow and long face shadowed beneath locks of raven-black hair, as her lips, which were perhaps a bit too thick, contorted with a grin.

"First, he must read your mind," said Keziah. "As is the custom when we're brought information from an outsider. Can never be too careful with who you trust."

In a flash, her hazel eyes revealed shades of contempt while the wrinkles at her eyes darkened and appeared to deepen.

Isla flinched as something groped at her arm. Pulling away, but failing to make it to let go, she was brought to float. It was the same sensation she'd felt the night of the Emerald Eclipse. Basem had cast the same spell on her with a wave of his hand. Velyn, however, didn't react violently. Perched happily on Basem's seat, she only watched.

Keziah sauntered to Basem's side, brushing Isla's feet with her shoulder. Her blackened finger, which bore a ring that Isla surmised could either be a pretentiously expensive showing of love, or a promise ring, involuntarily shook regardless of what she did. An obsidian band with a masterfully cut pink gem in the shape of an inverted pentagram.

"Let me go!" Isla demanded, trying her best to flail her arms.

Keziah knelt by his side, "She's becoming far too restless, and soon the spell won't work. Shall I speak the first words?"

"No, it's my spell to cast." He shifted in the seat as the lemon-yellow banner became taut beneath him. "This may hurt, child."

He raised both hands, his palms pointing upward as if in prayer, and he closed his scared eyes. Isla then felt a strange sensation overwhelm her mind like thousands of tiny hands rubbing the wrinkles of her brain and searching them. It hadn't hurt at first, but when it did, she resisted it. She fought!

Isla felt her own hands burn as she pictured the wildfire in Falls Creek, only this time evoking the guilt to help free herself from whatever was about to happen. She channelled it all and focused it entirely into one point in her body. Her little finger.

Biting her lip so hard that she tasted the iron of blood, Isla managed to wag it and in doing so cast a stream of wildfire to pursue Basem.

Keziah didn't react, but Basem had. Clapping once, he evaporated the wildfire in an instant.

"Bastard!" Isla roared, before she fell to the cold ground. "Don't you dare try that again!"

Basem, his chin wobbling, reached into his djellaba – for the flask – and turned his back to Isla.

Keziah wanted him to continue, and to try again. His shoulders trembled, and he hunched.

Watching him reach for that drug she grew to despise, Isla spat at his old boots and crawled towards the empty seat. She felt defiled and grotesque. She wanted to bathe – to rid herself of the grossness she'd felt. That spell was the cause of it, and that's why he was scared. She knew it.

Heaving, Isla conjured enough phlegm and saliva to spit at him for a second time.

Basem's hand had frozen in place within his djellaba, and she watched as his scarred arm shivered. His face twisted as he turned, looked at the spit, and then at Isla. Sighing – deflating his puffed-up chest – he didn't retrieve the flask.

Keziah quickly went to touch Basem, but he pulled away in an instant. They fell into whispers, and Isla continued in her crawl away from them. All the fear in the world had amalgamated within. She wanted to cry, but she wouldn't.

Isla yearned for Velyn's spine, as the faedragon remained atop the seat – talons digging into the old stone. But her Familiar wouldn't budge, and she couldn't understand why.

You don't need to stroke her, she told herself. *That was the old you. You're strong enough on your own.*

Basem and Keziah's whispering was more like shouting in a forcefully hushed tone, and because of that she'd overheard them discuss all manner of things: her red hair, her green eyes, her mother. However, what'd torn them apart was the idea of Basem's inclination to believe Isla.

All it'd taken was for him to defile her with magic.

At the empty seat, and the furthest she could get from Basem and his schemes, Isla spotted a wilted rose. Curious, and wishing to think on anything other than what'd happened, she'd knelt and noticed the thick dust that'd settled on it; she'd noticed just how frail the wilted rose had become.

She reached for the stem, and as her forefinger neared it, it was stung by a thorn that drew a spheroid of blood.

It hadn't hurt her, however, but felt pleasant.

And as that singular spheroid fed into the wilted stem, its colour returned to it. What was once grey and dead had become green and red. A rose in its purest form.

Smiling at herself, forgetting where she was, Isla caught Basem's eye over Keziah's head. The smile was lost.

Those ice-blue irises containing a sparkle that she'd not seen before. Even from their distance apart, the sparkle was prominent and bright; tantamount to the dawn's rays glistening on the wavelets of Falls Creek's inlet.

Disgust waned and a fresh understanding descended on her as though she was carried away on a noiseless zephyr – carried to a point of knowing like the Searwood had done, but gentler.

Trust was fickle and vicious. In an instant it could be lost, never again to be mended.

In that sparkle, Isla saw that he wanted to trust her. That Basem feared irreparable certitude. The spell was cruel, and in their lingering stare they both knew that. She wanted to hate him but seeing him like that, she couldn't. What he'd done was wrong, but she understood the doubt.

Either way, she needed the Key.

Breaking away from their prolonged gaze, Basem paced and waved Keziah from his side. As he'd done so, the origami that'd appeared in his hand took the shape of an adult male and child holding hands. He shook his head, winced, and it'd transformed into the same wilted rose that'd morosely subsisted in anguish before Isla's touch.

"Isla." He waved her over without another squandered second. "I promise, I'll not cast at you."

Warily, and with the rose in hand, she obliged him for the good of the quest. Between the old magus and his stone friends, he'd continued to pace, but between footfalls he'd whisper. He'd appeared mad – holding entire conversations with himself – shooting glances at the rejuvenated rose and back to his origami. Isla readied herself in case she needed to cast again, or whatever it was she did with her little finger.

Keziah snarled and leered.

"I believe you," he admitted. "What you said about me being the Key, the Searwood, the locator cantrip... I believe you."

He gulped when saying the last part of his sentence.

"However, despite what you think, you're neither strong in nor capable of true magic – not yet." He twisted his nose ring. "What happened in Falls Creek, your outburst, was the magic within you looking for an escape. Your exasperation provided the route needed. Because of it, and because of my lack of... care... Falls Creek was destroyed.

"Thus," Velyn landed on his forefinger, "I'll accompany you to Deacon and beyond its coastline. We'll discover this nameless island; we'll discover the Codex."

"Basem, no!" Keziah touched his shoulder and Velyn roared at her. Quickly retreating, she said, "You've only returned. Why must you risk going out there again to find a rumoured tome? Let the girl do it. Let her prove herself by fulfilling this quest. I'm sure she misunderstood the importance of this... *Key*."

Basem glanced over his stone friends.

"No," he growled. "Once more the Realm needs me, Keziah. Once again it needs an aenyr – the Key. And I won't squander that opportunity. I won't abandon a quest given by a Searwood that my siblings and I had failed. Isla will have my aid until there's a time where I can no longer provide it."

Looking at the man in contrast to the grotesque caricature of him aloft his greasy head, and the person he was only minutes earlier, Isla beamed. If it took a personal goal of his to motivate him into action, to propel her quest onward and into accomplishment, so be it. She'd not argue.

"Forgive me?" He looked her in the eye. "Please."

Isla nodded, but she'd never forget.

"Please," Keziah whimpered, "don't act on impulse. Daeva did so with her blood magic and look what happened!"

"Impulse? Gaunt, this is far from that."

Taking Isla's hand, Basem led her out into the dark streets and pointed upward. Velyn took flight, and his magical parchment slithered peculiarly to form the shape of an origami wand. With it in hand, he roared unfamiliar words and the surrounding crystals brightened.

They throbbed attune to his heartbeat she'd felt through him.

Light overcame all and the city within the mountain appeared alive. Though empty, Isla caught a glimpse of how it could've looked before.

As his wand remained pointed, it trailed Velyn's flight-path. Isla called for her faedragon to return to her. She didn't. Isla whistled, clicked her tongue, jumped up and down, but Velyn continued to circle them, faster and faster until she became a blur.

"Speak these words," he said, and muttered something in an alien tongue.

Isla assayed to mimic him but failed. However, as she'd done with the locator cantrip amid her ascent, she'd done again.

Rose in hand, Isla controlled her breathing and spoke a command. Beneath the bright crystals, Velyn's speed increased tenfold, and she released a scorching trail of fire flecked with magenta particles.

Thus, as had happened before, all turned to black.

***

Velyn's squawking forced her eyes open when, in truth, well-hidden beneath ambition, she would've rather languished in the darkness of a welcomed repose. With that awakening, however, a familiarness played on Isla's recollections because she knew what teleportation felt like.

She knew what Velyn had done.

Admiring the honey-coloured faedragon, she understood perfectly. Velyn had teleported her away from the Searwood the morning she'd contacted the ancient and talking tree. Velyn had brought her to safety.

All she did was in service of Isla. Even when she'd appeared to simply watch from afar.

Hugging her scaly friend, Isla accepted Basem's offered hand as he'd outlined the monstrous, floating islands that cast augmented shadows across the plentiful landscape. Across Deacon's farmland.

Few could truthfully acclaim how large islands of terrain managed to keep afloat; though, Isla didn't doubt magic had a hand in it.

"Sorry about before," said Basem. "I've been hurt too many times trusting somebody's word." He took a long and deep breath, arms akimbo. "Anyway, see there? Atop that island I've an airship docked that I'd won in a game of four-pockets. That's where we must go. We'll fly directly out to sea, and from ahigh we'll spot the nameless island."

"But we're not aeronauts. Even if we were, couldn't we just teleport there?"

"No. Teleportation requires a placename and a memory of that place. We don't even know your mystery island's name. Come now, it's not that bad. You might even enjoy it."

Isla doubted that. Doubted how they'd ascend those massy chunks of floating land.

At the base of each chain an array of spiring obelisks surrounded a petite wooden door – what Basem had named a lichgate. Atop them was forestry that glowed as if thousands of fireflies kept the area alight, and the glow acted as lamps.

Giant lamps that illuminated the chains' wavering shadows as best they could.

Basem pointed onward, down the green dell and in the direction of the closest collection of obelisks.

Everything was briskly progressing, and yet it was exactly what Isla wanted. Had she wanted to experience a loitering adventure, she would've sought it. Thus, agreeing to where the aenyr pointed towards, she jogged ahead of him and raced him down that splendid dell that'd smelt of sodden veld.

Velyn flew beside her rather than above, and Basem failed to keep up as his laughter echoed in Isla's ears.

It was a lovely laugh, and one that felt homely. Homely enough to make her want to enquire deeper into how he knew Mother, but Isla refused to prod any further than she needed to. He'd agreed to accompany her, and that's what she wanted.

She'd acquired the Key and was one step closer to fulfilling her quest. Only a fool would complain or prematurely dig deeper.

As he'd said, her lineage mattered little. Where she came from didn't matter, nor who or what her parents were. What mattered, truly, was there and then. The quest to re-surface magic for the good of all Mystics. And if she'd to go on not knowing the truths behind what made her a Harbinger, or Basem's relation to Mother... sobeit.

The lichgate they'd approached was constructed of various types of wood – excluding rowan, the ostensible bane of Mystics everywhere – alongside nails which protruded outward and clawed at the handle. Without knocking, an iron panel flung back and a drop-tail garnok snorted his pierced nose through the hole.

"Who're you that reek of cinnamon?"

Basem revealed his origami as it took on a rooster's shape and blew on its tail, sending it towards the garnok's feline nose. Silently, the rooster pecked hard and sent the guard flying backward and against the cramped walls, dust swirling through the opened and iron hole.

Subsequent to the metallic clanking of locks and unfurled latches, the door was unhooked, and it swung, in an eery creak that'd numbed the spine, wide open. On the threshold, stood the origami rooster that'd proceeded to transform into a flat piece of parchment before evolving into a staff in Basem's hand.

Stepping over the unconscious garnok, they strode through a narrow, black hallway bedecked with peculiar veins of orchid-pink which shimmered beneath the distant light of torches suspended by hollowed horns. At the end of the hallway, a beaming light of a thousand colours travelled upward – invisible on the outside of wherever they were.

Isla took the first step towards it and held her hand out to Basem who'd felt for the worn and ugly flask in his pocket. A knotted stick sat next to it. It was the same hand which held the rose; its thorny stem intertwined with Isla's fingers.

Basem hesitated, tapping his hobgoblin earring, but accepted her hand when looking into her eyes.

Encircled by the beaming brilliance brighter than the fullest moons on the darkest night, they were propelled upward at lightning-fast speeds, and yet they could still discern the outside world. Specifically, the city of Deacon.

Through the dense and colourful smog that'd fringed their ascent to the island, the city looked to be torn straight from a disturbed illustrator's imagination. The hues were exaggerated, and the complexions were dulled, while the vibrancies of both water and greenery were saturated in vivid virtuosity.

There was no order to it, and yet that was the beauty of it.

XI

Desecration Beneath the Glow

Escaping Deacon's sentry defence of flintlocks by a hair's breadth, Leif and Aivor fled into the wildlands that separated the city from Hotham Heights. Their lead shots whizzed by in a flash, engulfed in the blue hue of ultimate heat and flame. They broke through soil, tree, and grass – scorching, splintering, and ruining.

They were pursued by that desolation until reaching a dyke and hid behind the manmade mound. There they'd remained until they were no longer fired upon, and they were allowed a moment's respite to compose themselves. It was then that Leif noticed the blood on his hands which'd caused them to tremble. And even though the clothes he'd stolen weren't his, he didn't want them touching the rich fabric of his coat. Detested the idea of sullying them.

At nightfall, they crossed a road bordered by sycamores, which thrived in Gwynedd but were overwhelmed by an unwavering fog. Rounding a trunk, tired and eager to be out of the open, they'd happened on lights brighter and warmer than any mana they'd known.

Glancing up at them, Leif beheld giant mushroom gills, rendered barely visible by the same fog which'd stalked them.

Shocked by the one, he was floored when spotting more. A closely clustered collection of tall, purple mushrooms, aglow beneath the gills and annuluses, that'd materialised on the road. Never had he read about a holt like it seen in or around Gwynedd's north-east, not even when magic was prevalent, and Mystics stalked the paths beneath them.

Aivor had no words, shrugging and holding his chest where his heart ought to be. Leif pitied him, and deep-down he wanted to grieve with him... but he couldn't. The commandant was dead, but he knew it wasn't the end of it. He'd received some answers, granted, but it wasn't enough. Estrid's whereabouts is what concerned him – her corpse and the runes.

They halted at a riverbank with magenta particles throughout it, colliding with pebbles beneath the current before being absorbed in the next. Leif washed the blood from his hands and splashed his face with the cool water.

It was then he'd felt the effects of exhaustion.

His world spun, and his knees became weak.

Bone-weary, on all fours, Leif glimpsed his reflection, and for the first time in a long time he didn't despise what he saw.

A short, scraggly beard had grown wildly and spread high on his cheeks. He touched the coarseness before rinsing it and his coily head of hair. The feeling of that cool, sparkling water on his head sending him into a state of bliss.

Collapsing to his back, he lay still in the soft reeds that swayed over him. The moons beaming down through gaps in the fungi-canopy with enough radiance to blind a naked eye, but Aivor was fascinated by the stars instead. He, seated beside Leif, watched the thousands of little lights twinkle as he cried.

"First Estrid, and soon Isla. I've lost them both."

"No." Leif rolled to face him. "Isla is fine. We've not lost her, and we won't."

At their feet, the frogs croaked, and around them floated blue, pink, and green phosphoresces that'd encircled red and white spotted stones at the bases of a rotund mushroom. They were the fae of the south, unparalleled to the books which described them as females in outlandish, sparkling raiment and tiny slippers. Leif got to his elbows, and then to his knees. Southern fae... in the north.

He bit his thumb. It was unnatural.

Come midnight, the fog had dissipated, and they happened on a gypsy caravan. Sellers had already laid out their wares for the night market that was in full swing. Stragglers that'd made their home beneath the glowing lights' warmth.

Rumours were born and died in the seconds Leif tuned in to the rare conversations in Common.

One pertained to a well-dressed hobgoblin peddling pocket dimensions from the comfort of his multi-dimensional, travelling home; another concerned an aurora borealis dancing amid the sunlight.

They passed a nude woman contorting her body, asking for a silver coin to continue the show; a pair of garnoks performing a balancing act on their scaly tails; and a devil-horned alsheytan who waved a hand through the air, producing coloured wisps of dust to create a misty rainbow. Leif didn't doubt the yellow-skinned alsheytan's magic, their hidden queendom was said to thrive on it, but Aivor chastised his deception and revealed his alchemical trickery with a slap.

"Bardic scum," the alsheytan snarled, packed up his phials and powders, mounted a donkey, and rode away into the foliage.

The other races and performers turned their noses up at them – their only human customers – before continuing their routines.

A disappointed Leif distanced himself from Aivor and sat by an abandoned campfire. Pricking himself on something that poked through the diary's cover, he flipped it open to the inside sleeve where the list of initials was stapled.

Seeing Estrid's wounded him deeply.

"Leif." Aivor cracked his knuckles. "May we talk?"

"Sure." Leif nodded, nudging a log into the fire with his foot. "What about, exactly? Wouldn't happen to concern this holt?"

"The holt? Nah, it's nothing out of the ordinary. Here because of magic. Known to happen often in the days of old, but rarely written about." Retrieving a stick from a drooping branch of an old sycamore, he methodically broke away pieces. "You killed the commandant, didn't you?"

Leif gestured away, closing the black book, "I did."

Tossing the branch-bits into the fire one-by-one, Aivor dusted off his hands. "It changed you, right?" Leif nodded. "For the better?"

"No." His lids became heavy; eyes stinging from the smoke. "Whatever I feel in me... it isn't for better or worse. I killed a man, Aivor, and that's not something I've ever wanted to do. I'm a writer. I write... things."

"You wanted vengeance though? You wanted this."

Leif glared at his tawny hands. He could still feel, smell, and see the blood on them – no matter how much he'd scrubbed.

"I thought I did, but now I'm not so sure."

Leif rose and parted briefly, but Aivor caught his arm. He hadn't attempted to budge and instead proceeded to regard the fire, stoke the flames, and sit by it once again – arm still caught.

"It's about Estrid."

"What about her?" Leif chewed the inside of his cheek.

"You can't put vengeance behind you because of one kill, that's what. I know it's hard, I get it, but think about what they've done to my sister – your fiancée!"

Snatching his arm back, Leif scoffed, "You think I've forgotten? You think I don't hurt? Rest assured; I haven't been waylaid."

"Why falter, then?"

Leif's mouth widened in shock as aphids swarmed to be swallowed, "I falter because I took a man's life, Aivor. To do so and not feel some sort of remorse is unnatural. It's... it's cruel."

With that declaration, although possibly unrelated, the holt's exit revealed itself ahead of their position by some otherworldly means. Trees parted, boughs were raised, and the roadsides were erected into short, masoned crinkle-crankle walls. It'd beckoned them as if a beautiful siren emerging from the ocean depths – luring, yet deadly.

Instead of rushing it, Leif glared at his hands that'd became frigid to the touch amid an icy breeze. They burned with frost, yet the fire took the chill off his fingers and the light from the mushrooms warmed his neck.

That same light, dazzling and uncanny, advanced towards Hotham Heights at the pace of dawn's radiance spreading across rousing vistas.

"I'm sorry," said Aivor.

"Don't be." He clapped the bard's knee. "There's something I wanted to ask you, though. Back there, when I told you to cast at the commandant." Aivor nodded and waited Leif to continue, but he didn't.

"When I told you that I'm magicless? Born that way, unfortunately. No cure." The mandolinist straightened himself, cleared his throat, and rose. "It's why I joined the Bard College as a child. Should've stayed there, too. I miss the days of lazing about, strumming my mandolin beneath the bay-side gazebo with other like-minded friends. Simpler times, I suppose."

Leif watched a mushroom's flesh pulsate; the organic lines gave off the appearance of an organ.

"Suppose that means you can't sense if dragons are still about." Neither the fire nor the purple glow could stop him from shivering when thinking about it. "Like, say, beneath The Horn in Coventry?"

Knitting his brows, Aivor walked away without looking back at the market or Leif and stepping sure-footedly and precise. He headed for the exit hurriedly. Leif followed.

"Dragons haven't been seen in years," said Aivor, "but there's been rumours. That they dwell in caves and sleep on caches of coin; that they'll only show their scaly faces again at world's end. But they're all rumours. All of them. Nobody knows where they disappeared to, and I don't think anybody really wants to know."

"Yeah, well, I *need* to know." Leif felt the coolness outside the holt hit him hard as they neared the exit. "Plus, if Ghulzar is the dragon beneath The Horn – the weapon – we'll be fine."

"Why, because he was once an aenyr?"

"That, and he never swore an oath to kill all humans like the others." He couldn't shake the fear. "What do you think?"

Stepping from the fungi-riddled pathway of pebbles and onto the dirt road that Hotham Heights bore, Aivor shrugged.

"I don't know what to think."

The holt's light irradiated an array of stone monuments and their intricacies. Monuments that were strewn throughout Hotham Heights: crumbled, darkened with lichen, and surrounded by shaggy cows. Their magi counterparts in Spellforge, who served as inspiration for the sculptures, ironically were also stone.

It was because of that light that Leif had smiled, thankful for seeing such splendidly preserved pieces of history... and it was because of that light that Leif beheld a horror. It was because of that light that Estrid's corpse ghoulishly glowed.

Leif floundered – breath caught in his throat, as he'd tried to breathe and failed. His feet were heavy – a burden. A pain in the chest, a hiccup, and the weight was alleviated; and his steps became strides. Estrid hung in a perpetual slaughter, a horrified rictus devastating her usually dignified countenance, and Leif neared.

Leif, weightless and numb, sprinted towards the crucified remains of his beloved whilst Aivor howled at his side – pleading for any of the merciful divines to return his sister to him.

Crows quarrelled over carrion, overcoming Aivor's pleads, as Leif breathed in the stench of rotting flesh. An odour that'd brought him to his knees, and then to all fours as he'd averted his eyes from the horror.

Crawling onward, nearing her ruined feet, a squelch forced him to recoil and squeal at the bloodied soil affixed to his palm. Minutes had passed before he'd mustered the courage to look, fearful of a death that'd haunt him forevermore.

But he needed to look – he needed to see those runes.

Leif raised his head and saw that Estrid's eyes were gouged out; and where there were once dark-brown irises, two black and everlasting holes burrowed deeply into her skull remained.

Leif wanted to hold her, to take her from the cross and hug her as he once had. To sit with her a final time.

He reached for her hand, yet decay had robbed her fingers of flesh. Pulling away at the last minute, Leif kicked at the bloodied topsoil and snatched at his coiling curls – trying to tear the clumps from his head in a single yank.

Head throbbing, he picked at his facial hair and tried to think, to aid Estrid from beyond the grave. He needed to see the runes.

This wouldn't have happened if you'd saved her in Falls Creek, he told himself – hated himself. *So, pucker up, and look again. Look at what happened because of you. Read those damned runes, Morrigan. You must! You MUST!*

He looked, and he cried.

Estrid was raped, her mouth bruised, and her chest mutilated with runes similar to Sandscript. In fact, he didn't doubt that the ancient runes referred to by the commandant were indeed Sandscript. The language only comprehended with the Archives' aid in Coventry.

Leif reached into his bag, bypassed *A Druid's Guide to Healing*, and retrieved his notebook and pencil. Unthinkingly, quaveringly, he spoke to Estrid's remains. And amid forgotten words, he'd managed to sketch the runes with cramping fingers. Sandscript, however, was as difficult to sketch as it was to translate or transliterate.

Its edges and corners were never exactly ninety-degrees, always slightly off; and if they'd a loop or circle, they'd be similar to a square spiral. Indeed, the runic alphabet was beautiful, and yet carved into his beloved's chest they appeared haunting and uncivilised. He told all of this to Estrid.

Leif assayed a touch of Estrid's decomposing foot but stopped himself short of the dripping blood that'd pooled beneath. Butterflies mud-puddled for nutrients.

If only his healing hands could resurrect.

"You *will* be avenged," Leif snarled, glaring at the runic mutilation. "No matter what, even if I've to walk through the Hells and back, I'll translate these. This I swear. I swear that magic will be re-surfaced; that Mystics will tear the stony flesh from the Enchantress' bones and boil the blood of her lieutenants that did this!"

Leif shoved the notebook in his traveling bag and spun to look at the multitude of rolling hills and knolls which made up the Hotham Heights namesake. Not knowing if he could take another life, the vow had been made and he couldn't go back on it. Wouldn't. A man kept his word, and he wouldn't devolve into the coward he once was. It was done.

He caught his breath and inhaled the fresh air of green pastures. Leif knew what needed to be done.

"Help me," a broken voice, which could only be Aivor's, said over Leif's shoulder. "Help me bury her."

And so, they buried her.

Digging with their fingers until their nails broke and bled, they slaved away for hours before reaching clay and going no further. It was shallow, but it was the best they could do.

Estrid Alberg was buried beneath the monument of Basem Alpheniq, the grandest of all in Hotham Heights, and where the moonlight shone the brightest. Marked by nothing but raised dirt, and a set of rocks in the shape of an E.

Through tears, Leif managed to say, "Will you continue on the road with me, Aivor? Will you help me see this through?"

Caressing the dirt over Estrid, Aivor struggled to get to his feet – using Basem's monument for aid – and made an affirmative, albeit lethargic, movement with his head.

"Coventry?"

"Coventry. But without a quarantine pass, it won't be easy."

They leant on each other, mud-caked arms wrapped around one another's neck, and glanced over the grave. In that moment, however, Leif didn't remember the good and the fun with his betrothed. Instead, he envisioned a translation.

He pictured the Archives.

"You boys look like you need a hand," said the devil-horned alsheytan. "Or a ride."

They spun and faced him entirely, frightened by the sudden company that'd initially made himself apparent in their peripherals before emerging completely.

Twisted around his right forearm were the reins to the weary donkey he'd rode off on earlier, and beneath his left was his trickster's kit. His sharp and black fingernails rapped on its oaken finish as he grinned. His teeth were sharper than any usual alsheytan, and his spearhead tail was almost as thick as a dragon-tail garnok's.

Drying his tears on his rich sleeves, Leif approached and asked what he'd wanted for the donkey. At first, he requested Aivor's mandolin, but when learning of its ruin, he refused anything materialistic. He instead requested that Aivor come over and see what he could perform with magic.

Leif obliged.

Together, they watched as the alsheytan placed his trickster's kit down, stood on it, and whispered something into the donkey's tall ear.

Stepping away with a bow, his different-coloured eyes flashed, and he sprouted furry wings that he'd wrapped around himself in the manner of a long, hefty cape.

Laughing level-headedly at first, it'd evolved into unhinged guffawing as the alsheytan winked and vanished in a spectacular cloud of dust and lights.

Aivor pulled away and grabbed Leif's collar, dragging him to his side and back beside Estrid's grave. Rubbing his neck,

Leif watched from afar as the dust never dissipated. Within it, sparks flew and then all ceased to be. It was only dust.

Ebbing, it revealed a tall, muscular, and proud destrier to them both. A knight's destrier in place of a donkey. They'd not walk to Coventry. They'd ride on horseback.

The road was long, their camps short, and their breaks were brief. Leif thought on the prophecy and his quest, as images of Estrid cursed him alongside the runes he'd vowed to translate.

He needed the Archives.

Conversations weren't forced and only grew when fertilised with need, like a well-grown vine. Riding sores ruined their legs, and an aching back befouled their posture, but Leif and Aivor carried on and on. For breakfast, they fed on berries, and for dinner they ate whatever they could. Rats, birds; even lizards that'd happened by at twilight.

Aivor hadn't sung a single verse to any of his songs memorised since childhood. He didn't hum, he didn't whistle. Sunken, malnourished cheeks; red eyes from crying; and greasy dreadlocks from how often he'd run his hand through his hair. He was a dishevelled wreck.

The routine was unchanging. Ride all morning, break at midday, ride all afternoon, camp at night, and carry on at the break of dawn. Without failure they did so, and they endured it without falter or argument.

Soon, after exiting the lowlands of a duchy, they'd reached the highlands of Rhegion and the hamlet of Rorkinstead through the forest on its outskirts: a quaint place outside of Coventry and its border town.

Ahead of them was a small run-down inn that sat on the outskirts. Leif examined the salvaged wood that kept it together: rickety and unstable, with windows stained in the colours of sepia and peach.

"Could do with a soft bed," said Aivor, stretching his back. "I'm sick of sleeping in holes and the dirt."

Dismounting, a shriek ran-out throughout the pitiful streets. It wound up the road and found the duo on the outskirts. It was the crier. His voice as irritating as a mosquito's droning.

Windows were opened, doors were flung wide, and the crowds gathered and whispered.

Stepping around them all, the crier readied his articles. Clearing his throat, he rang a handbell over his head.

"Oyez, oyez, oyez! The Empress' Birthday Tourney approaches! The final bonfire to be lit tomorrow!" The handbell rang twice. "A murder in the streets of Deacon! Murderers still at large!"

Leif quickly hid his face in his sleeve, in the fold of his elbow. Taking the destrier's reins, he and Aivor moved behind their mount until reaching the inn, and then peeked around it.

An individual placed a gold coin in the crier's palm, and without hiccup he'd changed direction and spoke at length about the forecasted weather. Yet the bribe isn't what fascinated Leif, it was the black-obsidian vambrace the individual wore.

"Aivor, look." He nodded to the vambrace. "The commandant wore one identical to it. One of his lieutenants, I don't doubt."

Aivor punched the inn's wall and dented the already weakened wood. Leif held him back, shushing him with a finger. There was a time and a place. Tired and sore from riding, they'd be killed in an instant.

Further down the barely visible cobblestone, and at Rorkinstead's border, Imperial Troops requested quarantine passes. They tossed aside the forgeries, arrested those without them, and turned away those without the required payment. One lieutenant had made it, no doubt with bribery, whilst the other one was held up.

Leif had ridden through the forest that separated Rorkinstead from the border town for that exact reason. He didn't think it'd work, and it wouldn't of, had the lieutenants not arrived with them. They were, in that instance, an aid to his quest.

"A rare coincidence that," said Aivor through gritting teeth. "I don't like it. Remember what the Enchantress said about their mission? They're here for a reason. They're here to kill again."

Leif agreed, she'd said so. Although he doubted it was only for that. Why'd they travel so far south just to kill again?

A feeling, like a tingle beneath his skin, began where Isla had burnt him and travelled up towards his heart. It wasn't the bond, that'd remained severed. Something else. A recollection on the verge of discovery: something overheard but placed at the back of his mind.

The Enchantress wanted another person close to me killed, Leif managed to recall. *But why travel so far to do it? I hold nobody dear in Rhegion.*

Pondering, his gaze strayed over the distant city walls. And on Rhegion's raised, pastoral land, he lionised the golden city's peaks, belfries, and steeples that towered into the clouds. The city which housed the Archives and The Horn.

Coventry.

Formerly the jewel of the south, adored for its historic architecture, it'd become a collective of old stonework bedecked in modern neolyt, hazily obscured by smoky plumes from civilian hearths.

"What do we do?" Aivor's feet shuffled as he cracked his knuckles.

"Let me think."

Imperial Troops, protectors beyond Coventry's walls, were stationed abreast of ballistae and catapults outside partially-opened hoardings on the two limestone mountains nigh the city and quayside.

A sight that hearkened back to a different era.

Their see extended beyond the bay and to land. From that height, they could see beyond the naked eye, and with their eastern spyglasses, even further again.

With such vigilance, Leif doubted that the lieutenants would kill in the open. They couldn't bribe those afar. Yet, with such vigilance, how were he and Aivor meant to get into Coventry? Furthermore, how would they convince the Empress to let them into her archives?

The second lieutenant had made it into the hamlet.

Leif felt the beads of sweat forming on his brow – the hair on the nape of his neck stand. Clouds were rolling in. The glint of the spyglasses obscured by the grey.

Someone was going to die, and he didn't want that. But... they could use it to their advantage. In the fracas, they could slip through the border town and into the city.

A bad plan – a cruel plan.

The only one he had.

Thus, they entered the inn – its corners covered in broken and new spiderwebs as the walls were overrun by the nearby forest's roots – and paid for a room with their rich coats they'd stolen from the commandant.

He'd get into that city one way or another.

XII

⁓⧜⁓

A Storm Comes

Aboard the cloud-faring airship, walled in by the perfumed lustre of rain, Isla and Basem were propelled onward by the complex technology keeping them afloat. A quasi-caravel that'd been bastardised into something alien. Basem tried to explain the mechanisms of it to her, but even then, it'd sounded like he'd made most of it up.

As the floating islands ebbed in the distance, and the disorganised city of Deacon became nothing but a small dot on the horizon, Isla produced a lengthy sigh and hugged her knees close to her chest. The compression against her breasts that'd limited her breathing somehow grounding her as doubts floated around the tumultuous murk of her head like several buoys struggling to keep afloat and roughly clashing amid a rogue swirl.

She grasped her azurite between fingers, its coolness easing her hot palm as a low hum trembled through her skin and tingled it. Almost akin to a mellow, gentle voice, the humming would ebb and flow, typical of a conversation.

Through that, Isla thought about the Searwood and what it'd shown her, and she kept that close to heart.

Images came to mind, both fresh and brutal. She blinked, drank in her surroundings to ground herself again, and they were gone. But as she released her knees and that compression against her chest evanesced, those images became her world. Surrounded by quagmires, a drunk's bloated corpse floated amid the dead of yore – their flesh turned into leather as they roasted beneath an aurora borealis in the daylight.

Basem's silhouette encroached, and she flinched away from the coolness of his shadow. The imagery having expired as quickly as wildfire spread. The sun behind him shone bright, like a painting of the first saint, almost akin to a halo.

Gently, he touched her shoulder where a single snowflake had landed. The glowing hieroglyphs on his finger were prominent as the origami wand remained in hand. Another flake joined its melting brother, and then two and more.

Whiteness descended on the airship amid the daylight and dissolved when reaching the ocean below.

They fell in pairs, drifting aside and along the airship's mahogany railings. As if they'd parted a sea, they cut through the snowfall. Its beauty suspended beside Isla's head as she'd touch one and sent it flowing towards another, melting when nearing her touch again.

It was beautiful, and unlike anything she'd experienced before. And the smell – burning timber freshly doused by drizzling rain with a hint of cinnamon – was something she'd grown accustomed to. The smell of magic.

As the culminating flakes of Basem's spell had dissolved on the waves below, or melted on their skin and clothes, he brought her to the airship's bow. Handing her a twenty-centimetre piece of knotted, twisted wood with a cushioned grip at the end, he outlined where he'd wanted her to stand. At a similar distance to when gentlemen of Poirdeaux practiced the latest craze of flintlock duelling.

Isla obliged, assumed her position, and pointed the wand.

The grip felt moulded to her hand specifically, as if the exact imprint of her palm was in mind when creating it. Well-balanced and with a peculiar sense of knowing within its grooves, too.

"Pay close attention," he said and planted his feet firmly on the deck. "This is a favourite of Keziah's."

Basem, a natural in his flare for the dramatic without even trying, manipulated a bronzed hand around the other and clicked his fingers. A duo of fiery rings was conjured and expanded before him, pentagrams occupying the space between the two rings. She smelt them burn, singe the fine hairs on his hand – watched as they flickered.

His djellaba still visible through the conjured element.

"Impressive. I've only ever heard how magic is gone." She lowered the wand. "So, how can we – how can I – cast anything?"

Basem enlarged the rings, "Magic was never *truly* gone. Akin to how our loved ones are forever with us, magic is, too. Some Mystics chose to cut themselves off, others dwindled due to defeat. However, and although it was lessened – pushed into the background of all Mystic and Laic minds – it was there. A slither or drop, it remained."

"So, weakened, but never gone?"

"Exactly." He nodded. "Now, I want you to cast *aqua pila* at me. Don't think on it too much, just cast it."

"*Aqua pila*," she repeated and nodded. "Must I say it aloud?"

"No. But doing so makes your magic more impactful. It packs a punch."

Feeling her wand and looking for Basem's, Isla focused all she could into that piece of rose-coloured wood. She glared at its tip, believed it an extension of her body – saw it as the only thing that mattered to her. An extension, and not an addition. That was the trick with swordplay, so why not with magic?

She breathed in, and out, and then spoke the words.

Aqua spheres propelled out from the knotted wood, but before reaching the fiery rings had evaporated into fine, wispy coils of smoke. A weak attempt.

Basem, extinguishing his spell, praised her all-the-same, or what she'd considered praise, with a simple nod.

"No, it was rubbish," she said in short. "Can't I cast your spell? I'm better with fire. Water isn't my element."

"Your element?" He glanced over the railing and to an approaching bluestone island she'd hoped was their destination.

It emerged from the ocean in the shape of a rotund, gliding bat.

"Isla, whether a magus or not, Mystics don't commit to using a single element alone. It limits them beyond the already existing limitations of spellcasting." His brow lowered, casting a shadow over his ice-blue irises. "Come on, cast at me again, but this time feel the words as you say them. Words are magical in their own right, and the closest thing Laics get to magic – closer than mana. Feel them, Isla. Know them."

Nodding, she closed her eyes and tried to feel for the words as instructed. Not knowing how to do that, she recited the Dyadic Prophecy that Leif had read to her. Inhaling as she recalled each syllable, Isla shuddered and felt a coolness run up and down her spine before expelling from her extremities.

Opening her eyes, she felt invigorated.

So that's what he means, Isla licked her lips. *Aqua pila.*

A torrent of water shot out from the wand's tip and sought Basem who'd promptly dodged the spell before catching it in an ethereal net that sparkled, and then tossed the captured water overboard to collide with the ocean in a splendid splash.

"Better!" He clapped and smiled a toothy grin.

It was. Isla felt it in her blood. But she couldn't see his origami – wand or otherwise – anywhere on his body when he casted. Basem revealed his parchment that remained in its wand-shape, and explained to her that if a Mystic hides a source in their sleeve, they're allowing it to touch their skin.

Drawing from it, they're able to use their hands when casting cantrips.

"So, we can't cast with our hands alone?"

"No, we can, but if we don't use a source, especially when casting anything other than cantrips, it's dangerous. Harbingers, like yourself, have the pleasure of not needing one. But to do so without training is dangerous to yourself and others. So, we'll begin with a wand."

"Why keep the tip touching your palm?"

"Because if we wish to draw steadily from the source, our hands are the best bet rather than, say, a thigh."

As Isla wrinkled her nose and shoved the wand down her sleeve, beside the rose's long stem, she struck a pose. The same pose she'd strike when engaging Aivor in the Danse Macabre. In that pose, she'd become irritated. A heat from that irritation beginning at the nape of her neck, before reaching its gossamer webs toward her pointy ears.

Why do I have to use a wand? She snarled at the deck, at Basem, and at the island – its flora now visible. Yellow, vivid grassweeds bedecked the darkened stone and the bright plains more than the muted and scarce greenswards.

Basem also struck a pose but thought better when he'd lost his balance. The magus then manipulated his hands, clicked his fingers, and the same rings were conjured. Their light spreading across the ship's deck, reaching Isla's toes, as the flickering would occasionally bring it up and on her shin.

Despising the wand since she didn't *need* it, Isla no longer envisioned it as an extension of her body. It was a thing. An irritating thing. She felt her eyelids become heavy, but neither due to the late night nor the flickering at her feet. Isla felt that gossamer web evolve into a ghastly cirrus around her earlobes.

Re-positioning herself in another pose, unlike what'd been done before, she proceeded to study Basem's person. The tips of her ears becoming warmer by the second.

Breathing in, sniggering, she lifted a leg and placed the sole of her foot against her inner thigh; her arms manoeuvring through the air like wisps of smoke caught in the wind.

Irked, she dropped the wand amid Basem's protests.

I can do it, Isla thought. *I'd done it in Falls Creek, and I can do it now. I'm different. I'm stronger.*

Conjured spheroids spat roguishly above her palms, appearing to want to seek and drown Basem as she thought on the spell. *Aqua pila.*

"Isla, stop it," Basem ordered. "I said stop – you're going to kill us! Listen to me, it's not a cantrip!"

As the magus attempted to touch her, a gentle hand on shoulder, his fingers were engulfed in a liquid that both froze and burnt them at once. Quailing, brows furrowing, Isla watched and heard the breath catch in Basem's throat. She tried to stop herself, but she couldn't. She was stuck in that pose, and the spheroids had vanished.

Straining through whatever trance held her in place, she glimpsed bubbling and brewing nimbi ahead of the airship that led a fierce storm above a whirlpool in the ocean below. The residue of conjured lightning sparking beneath her nails

– clouds about her waist. The rose was torn away from her, its thorns cutting into her fingers. Lost amid the storm, its redness soon disappeared into the distant ashen clouds.

Velyn flew in and breathed fire on Isla that didn't burn, but aid. The magenta particles remaining around Isla's hands before being absorbed into her skin.

Snapping out of her trance, she watched Basem spin the wheel to hopefully alter their course; his thick fingers gripping the wooden spokes tightly. Unable to discern their intended destination through the clouds and rain, Isla checked the direction the new wind battered their sails into and glimpsed where she'd needed to go to help – to correct her mistake.

The mast.

The rope was taut, sound enough, but the knotted and aged ladder would soon give out beneath her weight and the wind. Reaching upward, a rung unravelled and whipped her cheek. The rain pelted down, slashing at Isla's exposed skin whilst the aenyr struggled with the wheel.

Basem summoned his origami staff within his free hand and positioned himself in the direction of the eye of the storm as Isla briefly glimpsed him. Lightning tore a craggy and feral hole in the sky, accompanied by an outcry of thunder that'd made Isla quaver a whispered invocation. Basem stumbled, Isla screamed, and he'd lost his grip on the splintering spokes.

They plummeted quickly and suddenly, Velyn lost in the clouds ahigh and leaving Isla on her own. Basem too was waylaid; his limp parchment zipping by her head as she held on to the ladder for dear life.

This is all my fault! The howling wind in her ears sounded too similar to the haunting squeals that plagued her. *I need to fix this. I need to right my wrongs.*

Unsteady amid the bashing winds, Isla too had directed herself towards the eye. She held out a hand, closed her eyes, and inhaled deeply. But before she could cast anything, before she could even think of uttering the words of *aqua pila* – although she doubted its usefulness – waves crashed on deck!

The wood was splintered, the mast was destroyed, and Isla plummeted into the freezing-cold ocean's deep, dark depths.

XIII

◈

Blood in the Smithy

Leif uncomfortably rolled over as a misty rain fed through the inn's window. His damp skin sticking to the stained sheets and wrapping around his legs as he'd tossed and turned in the night. An act that'd carried on until the break of dawn. He hadn't slept a wink, or if he had it was scarcely for a minute or two. Unused to the humidity of Rhegion, Leif missed the cool nights and mornings of Gwynedd.

Rolling to the bed's edge, glaring at the sheets covering Aivor entirely, he'd glimpsed the finite rays of sunshine fight to cut through the hazy clouds. The golden glow akin to the amber flames of a dying hearth.

The crier should announce himself with his handbell soon. His heart skipped a beat as he held his chest and exhaled weakly; worried he'd hear the next victim's name called out.

Leif sat upright in the exceedingly short bed that felt like needles and pinecones and tore the sweaty sheets from his legs. Planting his bare feet on the wet timber, that'd conjured a tingling sensation in his soles, he hollered for Aivor to wake up. Aivor, however, remained unmoving without a stir or sound. Compressing his lower back with the butt of his thumb to ease the aching that'd conquered it, he called again, and still nothing.

Donning his spectacles and lifting his boots knee-high, Leif rose and slipped. The timber was wet. Not from the misty rain that'd found its way inside, no. It was a different kind of wet: slick and oily. Very sticky in certain areas, too.

Unable to see through the early-morning darkness that'd overwhelmed the scarce rays, Leif tread carefully across the moaning floorboards and to the mana-switch that'd lit up the room in a click with the buzzing lamp overhead. It flickered in dimness, but it was all he'd needed to see. To discern the hideous exhibition that'd sullied the already grim area.

Blood and viscera painted the narrow room's floorboards in a grisly shade of scarlet hues and cherry-red vignettes of a massacre. Aivor's bed, too.

Fighting to keep his cool, fingernails digging into his clammy flesh as he clenched his fists, Leif made his way, clumsily, across the carnage and tore the sheets off expecting the worse! Nobody but pillows remained.

Relief washed over him before realising that Aivor was still missing, and had that blood been his, then he was more than likely dead or dying somewhere other than that room.

Glancing at Aivor's clothes beside the bedhead, Leif's knees buckled, and he dry retched. He forgot how to breathe, focusing on the inbreaths and unable to exhale.

Get a grip! He warned himself. *Find him – anyone. Find Aivor, or somebody who's seen him. Get a grip! Get help!*

Dressing, he sprinted down the rickety staircase, bag in hand; the blood trail continued down.

At the bottom, he'd found the inn completely empty with nothing but a listless smog that'd permeated the air with a queer stench. The chairs were stacked against the sodden walls and, on the tables, rats scurried when hearing his footfalls.

"Hello?" he called, heart racing. "Aivor?"

He kicked-in the kitchen door and found only cobwebs covering the pots and pans, and a hefty amount of dust. There hadn't been a meal cooked in there for months, maybe years.

Seeing his rich coat hung by the entry and not Aivor's, he snatched it and ran out into the rain, rescinding his payment.

The trail of cherry-red viscera continued outside and into the streets where nobody was around to provide any context to the goings on. Alleycats meowed, a drunk puked, and the crier remained out of sight – but not out of mind.

The glint of spyglasses unseen.

Bribed again? Leif noticed that the trail led out of the hamlet and towards the border town. *The lieutenants!*

Looking back inside, hoping to glance somebody but seeing only more rats, Leif mounted his destrier and followed the trail.

"Aivor?" he called again and at the top of his lungs. "Please be all right. *Please,*" he whispered.

After passing through both the forest and border town, its name unknown to Leif, he arrived at Coventry's entryway beneath parting clouds; the expansive bridge over the border town moat that led to an ornate portcullis. Coventry's chief entryway. The cherry-red continued, although thinning.

A trooper was near the portcullis, head held high as he toyed with his rapier's hilt. An open chest of documents weighed down by a stone beside him.

Quarantine Passes, Leif moaned.

Retreating, he led his mount down a ditch that continued to a waterlogged walkway along the moat which reeked of seaweed. Eyes roving the massive walls for a break in the brickwork. A place he could sneak in. Instead, he found himself in a make-shift settlement aglow with neolyt and hooded vendors flashing unnatural and illegal wares at him.

In lieu of bellowing and shouting like hawkers, the vendors with twirled moustaches, turbans, and gold teeth whispered and leered. They invited Leif in with the mysticism of their eyes and foreign wares. Platinum lamps, exotic sabres with tassels as pommels, rugs and pillows, and books that glowed brighter than the surrounding neolyt.

Halting at the side of an eye-patched usāgi, the seller's race a familiarity that Leif clung to, he dismounted and looked about. He was in a dead-end alleyway beneath multicoloured neolyt – opposed to the Imperium's uniformed cyan and fuchsia. Leaning against the fluorescently-drenched brickwork, the usāgi caught his eye and a mischievous grin contorted his furry lips.

Raising a brow, he gestured for Leif to come over. He did. The seller then revealed a quarantine pass to him. The Imperium's seal of approval and all attached to it.

"Is this genuine? Who made this?"

"Names are for chumps, so we'll call them *the brothers three*." He emphasised the moniker. "Notorious for their forgeries. Now, give us your mare, pretty thing she is, and I'll give you the pass."

Petting the destrier's snout, Leif handed the usāgi the reins in exchange for the forgery – feeling dirty for doing so.

Nodding to ground-level, Leif asked, "Did you see what caused that blood trail?"

"Two armoured lads carrying a hunk of meat that I'd presumed was once a man. He'd donned a lordling's coat like yours, only tarnished with a sticky red." The seller licked his lips and ran his spindly paw along the destrier's backside. "Looked like he was breathing. Why? Your lover?"

Uncaring to answer, Leif sprinted towards the portcullis with the pass in hand. *Looked like he was breathing.* He clung to that notion.

Turning back briefly he saw the tall mare transform back into her original form. A donkey. Ascending from the settlement, out of the seller's sight, he heard him scream and cuss about magic before sobbing and squealing for "the boys".

Which boys they were, Leif didn't care to find out.

Handing the trooper his pass, and checking his shoulder thrice, Leif noticed the superlative bonfire the crier had mentioned. The final bonfire, and the largest, alit for the Empress' Birthday Tourney. Reminded of the occasion by the trooper, of how busy his day had been, he intently studied the pass; even smelling it where it was stained.

Clearly too busy to notice the blood at your feet, Leif thought, panting with his arms akimbo.

"Nobleman, are you?" He nodded to Leif's coat, placing the forgery in the pile next to him and beneath the rock. "Crest of Deacon is interwoven with that fine material. Foreign, is it?"

"Um..." The usāgi's ears popped up, a group of burly men behind him. "Yes, imported from Enkhara last week. So sorry, though, I must run. I've... I've a shipment waiting at the quay. Good day!"

Clapping the trooper's spaulder and evading the madness that'd ensued when the usāgi and his boys confronted the trooper, Leif fled through the portcullis to then be met by an extraordinary amount of people. Humans, chiefly, who each looked at him in disgust for panting so loudly. Intermixed with those revolted humans, however, were the usāgi caretakers and goblins. The latter working in the shade to avoid becoming sun-kissed, whilst the former stalked the streets humbly with their soft, fluffy paws.

Their modern garments were vibrant and far more colourful than anything Leif was accustomed to in Falls Creek. The humans also masqueraded in feline-shaped masks of burnt sienna and puffy shirtsleeves like characters from a children's novella.

Among those peculiar exhibitions, Leif noticed that the trooper had turned away his pursuers by unsheathing his rapier and flourishing it at their noses.

Taking a moment as he collapsed against a wine drum and breathed a drawn-out, stuttering sigh, whispers caught his ear: the Empress was attending the Tourney. A first. What'd concerned Leif, however, was that those who whispered also ignored the city proper's blood-flecked streets.

The city proper, the tension across his visage was relieved when he recalled where he was. *Coventry.*

Childish whim overcame his pursuit of blood; drinking in the sights like it was the first and greatest thing he'd ever seen. And then he spotted the waterfall mountain. The Horn. A dazzling centrepiece of the city that appeared buoyant; clear-blue streams gushing down on every side apart from the one which bore the chateau and old palace. Because of those streams, canals were created throughout the city.

The Horn, Leif shivered and jerked back. *A dragon. Aivor.*

Surveying the bespattered cobblestones in a vain attempt to glimpse the blood trail he'd lost beneath the multitude of shuffling feet, the City Watch patrolling along the crenulations, Leif knelt and dabbed a finger in what appeared to be black goo. Touching it to his tongue he spat it out.

"Metallic." He paused. "Blood blackened by people's boots."

Following the trail that'd devolved from its cherry-red, Leif came to face a drab brick wall with nothing perplexing or rather interesting about it. The droplets ceased to spread in any other direction and simply led there, and there were no footprints as the path he'd pursued bore no dirt whatsoever.

Stepping back, and taking in the building before him, he was subjected to an ugly smithy of no redeeming quality. It neither fashioned mauve taffeta drapes at the front nor did it withstand golden columns at the entrance in the same way that the other buildings had. Instead, it was dark-bricked and riddled with crevices, bugs, and hay; bearing a rickety and swinging old sign that was in dire need of oiling.

Father's smithy. The first time he'd seen it – not invited when Isla was. The last time he wanted to see it.

"Can I help you?" A man popped his head out from around the corner.

A short and scrawny man with three whiskers sprouting from his chin and five on his top lip which covered an old cold sore, he looked fragile enough to snap in half. Linen gloves spread beyond his elbows to a rich, Deacon-crest-embroidered coat; blood dirtying the white gloves.

"Did you kill him?" Leif's eyes widened, his knuckles popping as he readied his fists. "Are you in cahoots with those armoured monsters?"

"What? City Watch sent me here to assess the body, found this coat along the way. They're too busy with the hoards flocking to spot the Empress, see? I'm the coroner." He stepped back and pointed where Leif couldn't see. "Poor fellow. Killed only this morning, I believe."

Leif's stomach dropped. *Killed.* His knees were weak and barely let him walk around to affirm what was being pointed to. Dread befell him. If he saw, it'd confirm his fear. Leif would be responsible for another death. Another loved one slaughtered because of his stupidity.

The pungent aroma sickened him; an aroma that never ceased to permeate as a gust of wind swept beneath half-dead trees and unleashed a harrowing sough.

Knowing what awaited him, he'd cried.

Brushing past the coroner, recognising Aivor's burly yet dignified countenance, Leif felt his cold and decomposing cheeks, and cupped them gently between his warm hands. Tears of anguish flecked his reddened mien, and he puked.

"It's all my fault." He brushed his lips with the back of his hand. "Had I not waited in Rorkinstead..."

The lieutenants had mirrored what they'd done to Estrid.

Aivor's eyes were gouged, mouth bruised, and a carving on the chest. However, there weren't any runes, only the word "Murderer" highlighted by a makutu.

Icy beads perspired along Leif's increasingly furrowed brow, proceeding to trickle down and into his whiskers before dampening the ground below in pitter-patter. Leif bit his thumb, this time to terminate the idea of vomiting for a second time.

He diverted back and forth between Aivor and the coroner; his shoulders remaining tight, hunched, and shivering.

It only became worse when the coroner asked for Leif's thoughts.

"They've done this before." He pointed to Aivor's wounds that bled profusely; a crust of dried plasma covering his abdomen and legs.

A sharp pain in his heart brought Leif to crumple and fold in on himself. His eyesight strained, and flashes were made known to him in his peripherals. A headache.

Too many thoughts were rushing through his mind all at once, and it was ruining him.

Feeling responsible, Leif shifted his bag from his shoulder and delved deep. He needed to see this through; he needed to end this once and for all. Thus, he presented the coroner with his notebook. Tapping his forefinger against the Sandscript runes he'd sketched, he gauged the coroner's reaction and mouth forming the shape of an O.

"That's Sandscript." He blinked. "Never thought I'd see its like outside of textbooks. But there it is."

"You know it?" Leif gulped. "Do you know what they say?"

The coroner shook his head, "Only place anyone could hope to understand that language is in—"

"—the Archives. It was worth a shot."

He didn't want to look at Aivor any more; a friend reduced to a gruesome message – retaliation for the commandant's death, he'd deduced. However, how word had reached the lieutenants, and so quickly, baffled him. Maybe they followed them from Deacon, or maybe it was magic.

He took up the commandant's diary. Searching through the pages under a new breath he found the name he'd sought: Coventry. But regarding Aivor, there wasn't anything mentioning a premeditated murder, affirming his deduction, nor where they'd hide in such a large city. Unless it was both premeditated and retaliation. Two birds, one stone.

The Enchantress wanted another person close to me killed, Leif reiterated, remembering her conversation with the commandant in Deacon. *And that person worked out to be Aivor.*

Biting his lip, he drew blood and – still squeezing the diary between fingers – tore the black book in half.

"Do you know where the men who did this are?" He brushed the blood from his chin with the back of his hand.

"Mm-hmm." The coroner thumbed over his shoulder, to the smithy itself. Its front door barred by rotten planks of wood. "Told the City Watch, Imperial Troops – Hells, even a varangian who was receiving a nobleman for the Empress. All couldn't give a damn. More important things to worry about, see? Empress' Tourney is a big deal. As was the Imperator's before her. Rimathean tradition."

Leif punched the smithy's wall, bruising his knuckles and ripping up the skin, and stomped on the diary's tattered remains.

"Look, son, I see the look in your eye. I know it. No matter what I say, I can't stop you from going inside, right? Right. So, heed this warning: be careful. Folk have seen glowing glyphs in there. Few folk suggested magic, but we all know that's impossible. Magic and Mystics are extinct. Either way, be wary."

"Extinct? Did you miss the carvings aglow on my friend's chest?" Poking the coroner in the ribs, Leif spat. "That's a makutu. To cast one, you need to channel magic through a source. Through a Mystic."

The coroner shivered.

"Looks an awful lot like mana, doesn't it?"

The coroner caught Leif's eye before he'd looked away and to the neolyts attached to the surrounding buildings. Swinging his head back around, the coroner's mouth fell agape, and he'd gone cross-eyed. With a whimper, he fainted.

Slipping into Father's workplace by way of a shattered stained-glass window, Leif snuck across an oaken beam that ran the building's length. A single flame on a candelabrum beside the old furnace being the only commodity within the stygian expanse which emitted light. It lacked mana entirely inside.

Voices reverberated from deeper within, below Leif's location and the floor. *Must be them*, he snarled.

Descending a pillar covered in soot, Leif heard a loose padlock rapping against an iron handle; caught in a gust from the broken window. Reaching it, he opened the door slowly and peered inside. Hugging the wall when hearing the lieutenants again, he checked the darkness, took a deep breath, and moved down a flight of narrow stairs.

The stairs, which appeared to usher him into oblivion, led to an underground tunnel highlighted by spasmodic, phosphorescing glyphs which appeared numerical at first. On closer inspection, however, he saw that they were runes bunched together. They highlighted Father's old forging tools in a sheening magenta, like the neolyt of city streets.

They highlighted a crumbling pillar.

Leif knelt ahead of it, picking at the loose debris that came away at a touch. The base was almost entirely ruined, with pieces crumbling away after every breath taken.

Neighbouring that pillar was an archway, and he ventured a look inside. First, he smelt sweaty armour. A stench that suited Father's smithy, as he'd always stunk of it when returning home to the north.

There, with their crossbow-equipped backs turned, stood the lieutenants. Their individual black-obsidian vambrace reflecting the other glyphs they'd admired in the room.

"After we receive the passes, are we done here?" asked the left-hand one, removing his helmet to reveal blond hair.

"Did you pay the assassin for tonight?"

"Yep. In full, too." The blond knocked on the others helmet, who'd doffed it and flicked his grey curls.

"Suppose so, then. The Enchantress should be pleased. Perhaps she can finally show us something besides makutus. They're pretty," he ran a hand down one, "but they don't feel like *real* magic to me."

"Wouldn't count on it," said the blond. "She's weakened. You saw it that night in Falls Creek. It's that ring, I tell you."

"Oi!" The older lieutenant grabbed the other's gorget and pulled him close. "Keep your mouth shut, all right? We still don't know when the brothers three will be here."

The brothers three? Leif froze in place, his heart skipping a beat. *Forgeries.*

The lieutenants parted ways across the room, their countenances revealing exactly how they felt about one another. The older one's forehead wrinkles deepening the further he was from the glyphs; pupils dilated. Leif, weapon-less, planted his feet in the dirt.

The pillar was his best option if need be.

"Any bets on the weapon?" The blond kicked at rocks by his boot. "If we're right and the runes do lead to one, that is."

"Nah, not in the mood." He took the crossbow from his back and loaded it with two bolts, encouraging the blond to do the same. "Still miss him, you know? Won't be the same without the commandant."

They were then interrupted by ugly laughter reverberating throughout the narrow corridor. Searching the darkness, adjusting his spectacles for aid, Leif spotted a group stumbling along. A trio led by a tall, skinny man that the two at his side had called Ludwig. The same name Isla had mentioned in Falls Creek.

The leader of the brothers three.

Different to lieutenants in their golden-and-black armour, the brothers dressed in draping leather coats laced with animal fur and inconsistent lamellar armour. Their black-obsidian vambrace being the only thing in common with the lieutenants.

When they neared him, Leif pressed himself against the wall before they stormed through the archway. The last one's coattail barely missing him as he hugged the wall to hide his tawny skin; careful to not reflect any light.

At Ludwig's waist was a bagful of parchment.

"You're late," said the grey-haired lieutenant. "Leave the forgeries and be on your way."

Ludwig approached, unlaced gloves hung around his neck, doing so slowly and lethargically – a leg dragging after the other. Pulling a chair out from against the wall, he brought it between the lieutenants and straddled it. Lifting his hand, he looked at the longer nail on his right forefinger and tore it off with his yellow teeth, spitting it at the blond lieutenant's feet.

With a snarl, the blond aimed his crossbow at Ludwig as his two brothers readied knives at their waists.

"Our price has gone up," said Ludwig.

"You're dreaming." The blond screwed up his nose.

"Then it's a good dream." Ludwig tapped his feet in the dirt.

"Doubt it," said the grey-haired one. "Nightmares rarely are."

In a flash, he'd fired the two bolts, killing both of Ludwig's brothers without second thought. Their life hadn't ebbed from their eyes but was rectified within an instant. Their lifeless irises catching Leif's gaze as he hugged the wall tightly, again.

"Bastards!" Ludwig drew his dagger, cutting his bag and letting the forgeries scatter on the still air.

Several exited the room and landed at Leif's feet. Wanting to grab at one, or two, his clammy palms wouldn't budge from their hold on that wall. He felt ice in his veins as he was frozen in place. Forcing himself, pleading with his body to move, Leif managed to grab a handful.

Two were purposed for Coventry and two for Deacon.

One of the brothers twitched after death, and Leif's knees weakened and buckled. Falling, he rolled into the room and in full view of the lieutenants and a grief-stricken Ludwig who cried and pleaded for his dead brothers to return to him.

The blond, locking eyes with Leif, seized Ludwig, threw him to the dirt, planted his grimy boot on his cheek... and fired a bolt into his eye. Spitting in the fresh wound, he proceeded to cut a coin purse from Ludwig's belt and tie it on his own.

He'd admired it familiarly.

"Well, well." The grey-haired lieutenant leered, speaking in a monotone that maddened Leif. "The Conduit in the flesh, hey? Enjoyed our little display outside, did you?"

The blond lifted his crossbow and took aim. One bolt remained, and his finger was twitching on the hair-trigger. Upturning his lips, he chortled through his nose.

"Still lily-livered," he said. "Translated those runes yet?"

Silence diminished the leer that the grey-haired one kept on his face, and his dilated pupils had returned to their former shape.

Anxiously watching, his attention shifting between both men, Leif needed to think on his feet. His heart hurt – he needed to do something. Gnawing at his stomach, a feeling that persisted up his oesophagus, was the want to take their lives there and then. For Mother, for Estrid, and for Aivor.

But his fail-safe was out of reach. He needed to retreat.

"How'd you find us?" Leif shivered, stepping back to be adjacent with the crumbling pillar. "How'd you know about Deacon – about what happened?"

"A secret I'll not reveal, but it's also how I know you're not lily-livered. Not truly. Someone who is could never take a life, and yet you did," said the grey-haired one. "Just need a little goading, hey?"

The blond kept his crossbow trained on Leif, glaring deeply into his eyes as the grey-haired one slowly stepped over Ludwig.

"Lower your weapon. The Enchantress needs him alive, remember?"

Leif could see the blond one's finger still twitching, his gulping uncontrollable as his Adam's-apple went up and down.

"Why the runes?"

"Why?" The older lieutenant scoffed. "Because the Enchantress knew that marking your ebony friend's body with them would motivate you. Would bring you closer to what she wanted. Supposed to carve them on your mate outside too, but we relished the idea of a personal message."

"It's a weapon, right? That's what she wants to bring me closer to." Leif could see the debris he'd peeled away, but the lieutenants pursued his retreat. The blond one's crossbow still on him; bolt itching to be fired.

"Well, what my friend and I here presume to be a weapon." He shrugged. "We couldn't tell you even if we knew."

Eyeing the pillar, Leif licked his lips. *Just need a little goading,* he thought. *One sure kick and I'll bring it down.*

Vengeance at his fingertips, a rumble of laughter built within him, but was repressed. The pillar crumbled a little more, the blond lieutenant saw it – caught Leif's gaze, and fired his bolt!

Leif fell to his knees and turned, but the bolt was too quick. It scraped against his temple, shaved the hair from his brow, shattered a lens of his spectacles, and cut his aquiline nose.

It seared like fire. More painful than when the bolt struck his burn in Falls Creek.

Rage and fear than coalesced within him and Leif flailed madly, frightened that he'd never see again – that he'd never read another book if he didn't act. His foot found the pillar, and his blurry vision found the lieutenants. Through tears and screams, he focused all his might into a single action. Into a kick.

The room's roof caved-in, and the lieutenants were dead without a sound of protest. They didn't have time to, even if they wished it, before Father's smithy had collapsed on top of them.

The stairs were unobscured, but the ceiling overhead was falling. Leif reached for his wound, and with healing hands eased the pain as he jogged out from the underground.

He bumped into the door and the soot-covered pillar, blinked away the blood from his eye, and carried on.

Reaching the street, failing to catch his breath, and feeling the world spin, he'd collapsed to the blood-flecked ground beside the uneasy coroner and the crucified Aivor.

Three down, one to go. For vengeance.

A watchman was called as the darkness of sleep carried Leif away, and the coolness of Coventry's street delivered him to a state of bliss where thought ceased and only blackness existed.

XIV

A Sister's Regards

Awoken amid the repose of a shallower ocean, a shore-line, Isla stirred and beheld the airship's ruination. Its remains became driftwood in the same wavelets that'd damp-ened her feet. The storm had passed – the storm she conjured. And the night's breeze was warm, not cold, drifting in from the northern deserts of Enkhara.

Velyn sat at her side, perched on the rose-coloured wand's remains, and glaring at the island they'd arrived at.

They'd made it.

"Glad to see you, girl." Isla scratched her beneath the chin.

Basem, however, was nowhere to be seen.

She rose from the sand and seaweed, the latter's stench overpowering all, and looked about. *Where's that drunk?*

Neck killing her, she'd spotted a rusted sword close to grassland and a pathway. It bore a striking resemblance to a single-edged falchion, including the curve towards the blade's tip. However, an oddity relied on the fact that it lacked any form of quillon, single or double.

It was the work of famed hobgoblin crafters.

Equipping it, she measured its weight, and swung it around.

Isla smirked. She missed the feeling of steel; the weight and the control of something so deadly in the palm of her hand. However, as she toyed with its time-worn hilt, she glanced back at the destroyed wand, then to her hand. What was steel to magic?

What's a passata sotto compared to a fireball?

Moreover, and curiously, the Danse Macabre was better efficient in casting than with a sword.

Still, with an adoration for metallurgy, she buried the coveted weapon in a circular glen between the cyclopean ruins that were once a city. Velyn then took flight and glided over crucified skeletons that were little more than bone, sinew, and tattered, undiscernible robes.

"What happened here?" Isla called to Velyn, but she flew on.

She followed, avoiding the swinging feet of bones, and hiding her wrinkled nose in her damp tunic's collar. Destruction and death followed her as the night follows the day.

Further along the path were fresher decomposing cadavers that spread onward, each of them distinctively impaled through either their eyes, mouths, or sometimes rear-ends. And amid the horror, nothing but a simmered rustling of untamed grassland and a faint cacophony of gulls resounded.

What Isla had washed up on wasn't an island, but a tomb.

Distinguishing what she presumed to be remnants of a battle, she passed giant memorials of fallen legends and imperators, a small medina quarter, and a smaller casbah. The latter's roof had collapsed, destroying the murals that'd decorated the walls.

Velyn called from above, and Isla followed. She didn't know where to exactly but taking her on faith she continued – hoping that, somehow, she knew where the Codex was. Something Familiars could feel that Mystics couldn't, perhaps?

It was a beautiful and diverse island. But being so diverse presented many places to hide a tome. The Codex was there, but where? Arms akimbo, Isla took a moment's respite and considered the quagmire to her right. To bury it beneath water was the best idea she could think of. Dive beneath – draw it entirely – but you'll need to dig after, too. Dig deep.

Yet the quagmire produced nothing of note aside from bony fingers sprouting out of them like a small henge of stones.

Guided on the idea that her Familiar was capable, Isla soon felt certainty in where she stepped. And with each step she prayed to spot Basem or the Codex; both if she was lucky.

He was the Key to the Undercroft, and without the old drunkard, she feared not finding the Codex at all.

Passing over thin gullies and climbing knolls, Isla found herself at a dead-end within a bluestone henge atop the mountain island's tallest peak. Looking up, Velyn circled. It was there that she heard a desperate man's haunting wails, wallowing in self-pity and despair. She recognised the tone of voice and diction, although the latter was hindered by slurring and self-defamation.

There, against the bluestone henge, Basem writhed in the bedewed topsoil, covering his amaranth djellaba in muck before suckling on the flask he'd carried. Yet to spot Isla, she used that to her advantage by rounding the henge and getting closer.

"Another dead b-because of me," Basem muttered to the moonlit beaches. "I've failed. Magic re-surfaced? A stupid d-dream and want to make amends." He hiccupped.

Isla shimmied closer, careful not to make any noise.

"Yet still I found the Undercroft for her." Basem took a swig and drained what remained in the flask – judging from the fruitless slurping. "And I did it for you, my daughter."

Isla peered around to see him fawning at the same picture he'd covet. The picture of himself and a red-haired girl. A child that Isla finally saw in detail. She was tall for her age – what appeared to be around seven or eight.

And as axe splinters shield, a truth had struck her hard and true. Basem had lost his daughter, as he'd said so in the bordello; he'd lost his daughter as Isla had lost her mother. A tall red-haired girl with green eyes. A tall ashen-haired woman with green eyes.

Seven seats, and only one was vacant. The rose.

Isla looked to her finger where the thorn had pricked her.

Her heartbeat pounded sternly against her chest. Aggressive and painful. It'd skipped a beat – Isla lost her breath – and then it'd resumed in an arrythmia. She stumbled but caught herself coarsely against the bluestone. She whimpered.

"Your daughter," said Isla and revealed herself in the moonlight, "was my mother."

Basem swivelled, clicked his fingers, and forced the soaked parchment to transform into a phoenix – aflame and primed. Suspended in that state, the phoenix danced above his forefinger, itching to swoop onward and attack its prey; to attack Isla. And she'd believed it would've, that Basem would've allowed it... had something within him not softened after he'd looked into Isla's eyes.

"Grandfather?" she said, as a tear slithered down her cheek.

Reaching for her, he winced and brushed down his stubble. Basem rose, took a step towards Isla, looked at his flask and threw it far across the mountain. So far that they'd lost sight of it before it'd fallen. They heard the bashing of metal against stone.

"You haven't failed," Isla held out a hand to him, "and you've shown your worth."

His bottom lip trembled as he watched her hand. Gently slapping it down, he held out his arms and before Isla could react, he'd wrapped them around her head tightly.

Isla returned the hug.

***

Sobering quicker than a mortal ever could, Basem pointed at a stone that'd contributed to the henge. Yet from what Isla could make out, there was nothing mysterious about that stone, only that it was slightly less crumbled than its counterparts. Though, what Basem pointed to was the spread-winged phoenix that represented his kin; small and hidden away from the naked eye.

As if drawn to the phoenix, her alabaster-white hands started to become red and hot – they sparked. Fingertips brushing the bluestone, the phoenix flapped its wings.

At once, the ground wickedly shook and it'd moaned as the henge descended below them anticlockwise and in succession, creating a stairway into a new hole. One that'd made itself apparent with a loud and hefty thud.

"Very well done, Isla," he'd complimented.

"But... you're the Key? How'd I unlock the Undercroft?"

"A key can be much more than the counterpart to a lock, my dear." Basem winked at her.

Pretending to know what that meant, Isla led the way forward as Velyn, settled atop her shoulder, offered her spine. She received a scratch beneath the chin instead. Her warm belly, like Isla's fiery hands, which'd sparked again when stroking the faedragon, acted as torchlight but brighter.

Stopping on the last step and ahead of a dangling pendulum of iridium and silver that'd swung without a breeze or reason, Isla allowed Basem to pass her. He donned his hood, equipped his origami staff, dashed it twice against the step, and whispered into his hand. A blinding light radiated from it and spread across the underground; exceeding lands Isla never imagined to be beneath her feet.

From what she'd envisaged, wasn't what she'd lay eyes on. It looked to be dug recently without a fleeting thought to construct walls of clay, or something that'd keep the contents inside safe. It was muddy and uninviting. Yet, and ahead, the Undercroft expanded greatly with every step taken until becoming as wide as Falls Creek.

Naturally formed, perfect cubes of pyrite jutted out from the walls and ground. They reflected a blueness ahead.

A lake became clearer on approach, and it emanated a cool-blue glow that highlighted the cave following Basem's pulse. Beside it sat a melting castle and a rickety dock that bore a single pier which'd stretched out to the lake's centre. Isla couldn't tell if they too were blue, or if the cool glow had saturated them in its colour. As for the castle itself, regardless of its age-given imperfections, it was marvellous and made of ice.

Basem's lips curled.

"You know this place, don't you?" Isla admired the ice-blue columns and archways that dripped their carefully carved friezes into the lake.

"Only in stories." Basem rubbed his gurgling stomach. "Amid the First Imperator's time, a group of soldiers broke off to find their own kingdom rather than fight the Settlers. Unable to establish anything on the terrains of Rimathea, and not wishing to leave the vibrant country, they decided to build beneath the terrain and on the Realm's verglas-line. Hence the ice."

Basem lurched forward to hold his mouth and shivered after swallowing whatever tried to come out.

"Rumours had proclaimed that when magic re-surfaced the Kingdom of Pelmora will once again thrive and cease to defrost." He motioned for Isla to take the lead, and she did. "That only someone gifted in blood magic, someone strong enough to summon an Emerald Eclipse, will do it."

They continued up a short flight of wide steps that led towards a thawing pathway connected to the ice castle.

"Still, and even though rumour is just that and nothing more, whoever summoned the Emerald Eclipse was certainly strong in blood magic." He petted Velyn as they walked. "A great deal of flesh would've been sacrificed – they'd be disfigured for life. And the source to channel that much magic... it'd be a weapon befit for my race."

Cloaked apparitions floated by them, some halting to study them whilst others lingered and stared – if they'd eyes to stare with. Isla searched her mind for answers as the ice castle neared.

"Daeva once used blood magic, right? Keziah said so."

"Right." Basem brushed away an apparition that got too close, "But I know for a fact that she was banished for good. I'd done so myself many a year ago."

When Isla's muddied sole touched the impressive castle's threshold, the most imposing apparition amid the flocks of black cloaks and ghastly moans, appeared before the two. Its dead eyes surveyed them, and its breathless moan demanded something; something entirely lost on Isla.

Basem, however, revealed his pinkie to the apparition that viewed the finger as if it'd give it life once again. Extending a rusted dagger towards Basem with a hand that appeared sinewy and decaying, the apparition waited. Its moaning had abated, its movements non-existent.

Accepting his task, Basem's forearm was caught as Isla locked eyes with him. But with all possible haste, he shook loose of her hold as the apparition drifted closer, seemingly intent on something dire.

It desisted mid-flight when Basem held the dagger between Isla and it, paused, and resumed its menacing float to await the sacrifice.

"I do this willingly, Isla," he said, "as is my task as Key. Your sacrifice would never work here."

The apparition moaned as horrifying eyes spoke what little words he wished to say or curse. In response, Basem bowed towards the black figure and readied the rusty dagger. With an inbreath, he lopped off his pinkie without so much as a squeal.

Aenyr appendages regenerate, she told herself, fidgeting for reassurance. *Cursed to never die, they can't be so horribly maimed... surely? Surely, I'm right?*

Allowing for the blood to soak his attire, Basem presented the finger to the apparition.

Permitted to pass, Basem magically cauterised his wound, and they entered the castle. They found their way to the throne room where a single, small, and sad throne was occupied by a decomposing and moist corpse. A brass and poorly smelted crown sat crookedly on his brow as strands of hair dangled over his vacant and dead stare.

Beyond his throne was a statue dedicated to a divine long since lost on the world. It was built to convey authority; depicting an aged, angular skull and eyes that would've glowed bright had they not been stone. Its bony chest bore no heart beneath its ribcage, but a dagger, and at its feet was a runic alphabet that'd instead looked like chicken scrawling; an alphabet lost on Isla.

Quivering beneath its gaze, Isla gestured Velyn's glowing belly towards the decomposing king and distinguished something in his hands. A dusty and aged tome.

As they drew nearer, she was able to discern the cover: a Searwood and a Phoenix entwined ahead of a lunar eclipse.

Isla's leathery soles had felt an amalgamation of terrains and surfaces after leaving Falls Creek, but none were as queerly pleasant as the soft, yet damp, carpet they'd plodded on. An old carpet that led to the Codex.

At the feet of the king, Isla looked to Basem. He winked, and she smiled. She stepped upward and onto the decomposing king's dais, eager to achieve her goal. She made her move.

Taking the large tome into her hands, which possessed more locks and clasps than the lichgate, Isla felt a rush course through her fingertips, her flesh, and into her veins.

The decaying king lost his impeccable and upright position and collapsed from his throne at the feet of Isla Morrigan.

Brass crown rocking, a king on his bloated belly, and the Codex in hand. *I've done it*, she thought.

A rumble re-routed her concentration to the surface; another caused Basem to rush outside the castle as Isla barely kept up – his origami staff in his bloodied hand. They passed emptied cloaks and skeletal remains, until reaching the stairs and ascending into the crisp outdoors.

On the fifth step, a rush of fresh air was caught in Isla's hair. And on that air, a zephyr, was an agitation that'd seized her.

"What is it?" Isla gulped.

Basem sniffed about like a keen hound dog before he'd held an ear out to the sea, "A foul voice is on the air. A voice I prayed lost to space and time. Daeva!" He spat. "She's reciting a necromantic spell!"

Swords were drawn from below the mountain in a unified hissing more likened to a nest of serpents, and Basem forced her behind him. She'd wrestled against his insistence to no avail.

Isla brandished the Codex at Basem's back, hopeful that he'd accept her insistence that it'd solve all their issues – truly believing it would. She wanted to lead the charge; she believed it was her duty. This was what the Searwood wanted.

Magic will re-surface!

But Basem refused her. In a flurry of red and blue, and before she could argue the fact, he'd managed to whisk them below. A step forward and they found themselves within the quagmire and surrounded by the white columns and cyclopean ruins.

In the distance, she saw the fresher cadavers being devoured – their limbs gnawed.

Undead burgeoned from the ground and fell from the crucifixes which lined the causeway. Their legs still caught in another's mouth.

"Revenants!" Basem roared. "Isla, your attacks stand no chance. Let Velyn teleport you away from here. Please! No, don't take a step closer. Unlike a lich, a revenant will tear you apart without thought. Brainless and cruel, they've no notion of their own that isn't death!"

Isla leapt from the sodden reeds towards her grandfather, yet before she'd reached the bank, more skeletal hands rose from the water and in her path. She turned, the mire sucking at her feet, only to find another revenant clasping her toes and scratching its malformed fingers across her pliant skin.

Isla bashed the Codex's latches down, but the metal bounced off her target. He was right. No chance.

Basem's right hand irradiated scarlet-red while in his pinkie-less left the origami transformed into a sword, and he cut down a corpse that reached for his forearm. They rose from beneath! Another snatched his ankle.

Commanding the skies to aid in his endeavour to repel the undead, he'd summoned a surge of lightning, caught it within his origami sword, and directed it to the quagmire.

Isla launched herself from the waters onto a collapsed column, escaping the hold on her toes as Velyn circled above.

"Daeva's spell is weak." His sword sparked. "She can only localise it, and for a few minutes. I'll keep them here. Go, now!"

The sword's sparking reached a crescendo and exploded with thunder and lightning! The quagmire was alive with magic. At the centre of it all, Basem caught an additional revenant and levitated it metres from the ground, plunged the whetted parchment-blade within another, and brought the levitating undead zipping towards him to skewer them both.

Seeing a break in the electrical currents, Isla ran at Basem amid the rising revenants, their hands sprouting from the loam like poppies in an open field. Their moans overpowered the din of gulls, and Basem's booming voice drowned them both out. Metres from him she noted that he was overrun.

"Run, Isla!" he demanded.

"No! I'll not leave you here!"

Slicing through more undead, his ice-blue eyes softened as Isla watched his shoulders ease. The revenants continued en route for him, but he did nothing to stop their advancement, smiling again as they tore at his djellaba, destroying it and leaving shreds at their decaying feet. He'd allowed them to do so.

No! Isla refused to be still but slipped and landed face-first into the murky, shallow waters. Gripping the Codex, she'd turned her body and shouldered raised turf to cease her sliding and to protect the tome, glimpsing Basem's irradiating scars glow and grow – spreading and digging.

Codex in hand, Isla reached for him in a breathless and wordless scream. Building from her chest to her bicep, her forearm, and piercing through her fingertips, Isla sent out a force of magic stronger than a mountaintop's winds! Both water and undead were thrown across the quagmire and into dells and ruins.

Stillness befell the battlefield, and Basem panted on his knees. However, the battle was far from won. Isla felt it on the air: a coolness in the brisk wind that brought with it the same foul whispers that Basem had heard.

In a flash, dark robes appeared ahead of him; a hood draped over the stranger's face. Isla tried to move in and protect her grandfather from this encroaching menace, but the Codex's weight kept her in place. It vibrated with magic. Its cover imprinting on her skin as it weighed down.

What revenants remained whole and standing parted for the hooded woman – the Enchantress – as she held up a piece of basalt ahead of her forehead that bore an aura. The foul voice, Daeva's voice, spoke through it. The spell concluding and silence befalling them as the Enchantress stood triumphantly before a beaten and deformed Basem.

A stiletto was then produced and thrusted with the hand that bore the blackened finger. Driven into Basem's chest, she pulled away and left it to twitch in the rhythm of his heart-beat.

"Enjoy your dreams," said the Enchantress. "Your beloved sister sends her most *heartfelt* regards."

Isla froze as Basem's smile persisted; his regard fixated on her and not anything else as the colour drained from his face and irises. The origami unfolded, and the parchment was lost in the waters below alongside the portrait.

Surely, an aenyr can't die?

The Enchantress turned her head, stone skin revealing it-self alongside a snigger from a cursed mouth. Isla recognised those hazel irises in a heartbeat. Not wanting to believe it, she shook her head – rising and clasping the Codex, whose weight had relented, tightly against her breasts.

Keziah approached her, her ring glowing as her stone skin persisted. Leaving the stiletto embedded in Basem's heart, she allowed him to fall into the quagmire.

Lifeless, from Isla's perspective.

"Give me that book, girl!" she demanded. "The spells are lost on you, anyway. You can't read it!"

"I can try!" said Isla through sobs.

"Fool! The best can rarely ever translate or read Sand-script, and you think you're any different? You think your special for being here? You were a puppet – my puppet. We'd left you alive that night in the forest for this exact purpose. You were a pawn in a game that's soon to conclude. Now, if you wish to see how it ends, bring me the Codex. Deliver it at my feet, pawn!"

Isla felt her world constrict and close in on her. Guilt for the deaths she'd brought on exasperated by those words spoken, haunting her already daunted mind like a furious poltergeist. Although a light shone through, tantamount to the blessed kiss of dawn: *Translate... Leif. The Conduit. We're the Dyad.*

"Address me as Harbinger, or not at all." Isla closed her eyes and took a deep breath. "Either way, you'll learn your place."

You can do this; Isla shook. *You can do this.*

Taken aback, the rage in Keziah's visage said it all. But when she reached for her hair – ring sparking violently as her form returned to human – she searched for something amid the raven-blackness.

"You've the ashen hair," Isla heard whispered. "How do you...? No! I'm the Harbinger, not you, pawn!" Keziah conjured the same rings that Basem had aboard the airship. Her favourite spell. "It's you who'll be learning her place. At my feet, you'll beg to worship. Once magic is re-surfaced and my plans are fulfilled, you'll see."

Then you'll die before you see it done.

Isla prepared her pose as the revenants became corpses again and collapsed into the quagmire's waters. Keziah continued conjuring her spell. Isla investigated her body from afar, curious about her source.

The basalt.

Keziah manipulated her hands around each other and clicked her fingers. Fiery rings were conjured, expanding to proportions unmet by Basem. Pink, inverted pentagrams, akin to her ring, occupied the space between.

Isla smelt them burn her, reaching into her skin and scorching it, but Keziah was unflinching.

In her pose, the same struck on the airship, the same struck when practicing the Danse Macabre with Aivor, Isla was scared. Seeing Basem's limp body hurt her, and she wanted nothing more than to let her emotions run ramped. She wanted to explode. However, before Keziah – the architect of her pain – she could only think about how scared she was.

She closed her eyes and tried to feel for words. Recalling the syllables of *aqua pila* and acknowledging them as part of her spirit, her mind, and her body. Isla shuddered. A coolness running up her spine, but not down. Fleetingly, she felt that same coolness expel itself from her extremities; however, even with the Codex in hand, it felt weak.

Opening her eyes, she felt feeble.

Spherical water shot from her hands and seemingly attacked the fiery rings but had instead turned into wispy nothingness. Worse than her first attempt against Basem.

Keziah retaliated; the quagmires aglow with the fire that spat from the pentagrammic rings.

Isla quickly held up the Codex as a last-minute shield, and the cover absorbed the magic.

Keziah spat, cast again, and roared for Isla's head.

Looking for Velyn, who still circled above, Isla knew she needed to get out of there. Chastised herself for not fleeing when she'd the chance. She needed to grant Velyn an opportunity to transport them – teleport them. But where?

As the spell attacked her and the Codex, Isla wrinkled her nose. She needed someplace safe – she needed a place where she's been before and whose name she knew.

Preferably where Leif would be, too.

Leif, she thought, and opened the connection between them again.

A tidal wave of emotions overwhelmed her. Pain. Loss. Anger. Purpose. And through those, she knew where she needed to go. Coventry. Through those, she knew what she needed to do. She'd fight; create a window.

Unleashing a squeal, Isla cast down the Codex and held forth her hands. Harnessing what she felt through their bond; harnessing her feelings for Falls Creek's ruination and Basem's death, Isla outfluxed a torrent of wildfire so bright and scorching that the water at her feet boiled and bubbled.

She'd let go.

Isla glimpsed the fear in Keziah's eyes before she dove for cover. She relished it.

Guffawing at the power she wielded, a pause in her perceived invulnerability made her lurch. The torrent ceased, but the wildfire sought and destroyed without her guidance.

A pain brought her to knee, and quickly she grabbed for the Codex again, but it was too late. Beginning from her fingertips and etching up slowly, like vines on an ancient frieze, the same hieroglyphs she'd seen on Basem carved themselves into her skin. A hieroglyphic alphabet unseen in any of Leif's works. An alphabet alien to her world.

The pain was unbearable, and seeing that, Keziah seized her opportunity. She cast spell after spell, cantrips too, and sought Isla who continued using the Codex for a shield as what felt to be a searing dagger carved an alien tongue into her skin.

"Exerted yourself, sweety?" Keziah laughed.

As the vines ceased their etching and crawling, so did the pain. Her entire right hand was tattooed in scarring. A cantrip ricocheted from the Codex, forcing it to bash against her head.

Through tear-filled eyes, she understood Basem's warnings aboard the airship. Although a Harbinger, she still had limits like every Mystic – limits unexplored without training. She'd exceeded those limits twice, and both times proved she wasn't ready. Though, she would be.

Closing her brief connection with Leif once more – before he'd felt what she was experiencing – Isla vowed to Basem, beyond the zapping spells that highlighted the battlefield in all the colours of the rainbow, that she'd learn. For him, she would.

But first, she'd fulfil the Dyadic Prophecy.

Calling to Velyn and holding the Codex above her head, Isla ignored the casting, Keziah's cackling, and her own remorse. The hot and cold of spells, some that smelt like sulphur, zipping past her vulnerable body.

Isla thought about Coventry – of the times she'd visited with Father – saw Velyn turn into a blurry circle in the sky, and then everything faded to black.

XV

Hero's Scars, Healer's Hands

Like winter snow, the promised bonfire's ash coated the razed smithy and Coventry in a hoary sheet. A reminder to all, without seeing the flames, that the Empress' Tourney had commenced. The only person that could grant Leif access to the Archives had revealed herself to the public when he'd needed her. An omen of good fortune, he'd hoped.

And although in pain, that headache evolving into a brain-splitting migraine, Leif envisaged what was next. The river of vengeance flowed without hinderance, and to close the floodgates amid the rushing current would've proved detrimental.

For Mother. For Estrid. For Aivor. I will re-surface magic.

So, he said to the watchman, "The Imperium is in danger. Get me to the Tourney. Bring me to the Empress."

Beholding the razed smithy, Leif's fresh scar, forged quarantine passes, and Aivor's crucified body, the watchman relented at Leif's insistence and led him wearily through the city. They left the coroner, who'd yet to recover his senses after what'd been told to him about mana, en route for The Horn.

Leif's wound hadn't bled since it was healed by his touch, and it hadn't hurt, but judging from the watchman's reaction, it wasn't pretty to look at, regardless.

After a ride on a bespoke gondola, Leif had arrived at an island separated from the city proper by two branching canals. The Horn's nobility segregating themselves from the other classes in more ways than one. However, for its magnificence, Leif feared it; feared what was to come by showing himself at the Tourney.

He feared the rumours of a dragon within The Horn.

The watchman, to mar the silence, pointed out that unlike a castle, the chateau they'd approached bore neither sturdy fortifications nor turrets. That it was a home, first and foremost. Thus, Leif believed it no better than a manor with a fancier title. How could that, for all its beauty, withstand an attack from an invading force let alone a dragon's wildfire.

It sat above the old palace – the Settlers' initial residency – high atop The Horn. Undoubtedly, its beauty was unrivalled by most other modern architectures that'd obscured the beauty that'd once been Coventry, and yet Leif couldn't help but consider its vulnerabilities. Couldn't help but compare it to that old palace that'd retained both fortifications and turrets.

Reaching the top of the wide, winding stairs that'd connected everything upon The Horn, they'd arrived at a landing where olive trees grew wildly alongside grapevines that'd intertwined with painted gazebos.

Beneath their shade sat dignitaries, picking at those rotund grapes, and plopping them into their mouths to then wash them down with a cooled challis of imported wine. Because, and as the watchman stressed, their grapes were okay for eating but tasted like vinegar when aged into alcohol.

Only, it wasn't their eating and drinking habits that'd sickened Leif. It was the fact that his friend had been murdered in the city below, not too far from The Horn itself, and yet atop their fanciful mountain – a place likened to the Heavens – the nobility ate, quaffed, and giggled like nothing was amiss.

As if his fiancée wasn't crucified, and the Massacre at Deacon was nothing but a footnote in the annals of Cymeria.

Passing more noblemen beneath an arch created by crossed swords, hiding his scar and missing lens, they approached a broad, tall, and hemispherical structure. The First Imperator, a balding man with a long and wizened beard, looming above. A tome in one hand while the other was authoritatively pointing.

The entrance alone was taller than the bordello in Falls Creek; doors painted golden and mauve.

At the watchman's say-so, the massy and ornate entryway swung open, and Leif was greeted to an exalted foyer. An antechamber to the renowned interior. Staircases of mahogany were adorned with mauve carpets, the coffered ceiling bore the largest chandelier he'd ever seen, and various colourful paintings hung tightly abreast of one another above foreign-motific vases.

Entering the hallways deep into the chateau, however, they were both dark and disheartening; only lit by a single brazier every five columns or so. Leif thus briskly followed the watchman, bypassing statues, cats, and armour, before they stopped in the middle of a wide corridor. There was a uniformity about the place, and it was mana-less.

The fact that it was had been the biggest surprise to Leif, given how advanced the rest of Coventry had been and the fact that the Empress was from the east. That alone, he'd imagined, warranted a profound adoration for what her peoples had created. For mana and all its *greatness*.

On his right, a stairwell led upward to the place he needed, feeling drawn to it as he read a sign: the Archives.

The watchman introduced himself and Leif to a varangian standing guard. In response, he lifted his helmet above his mouth, spat at the watchman's feet, and inspected Leif menacingly with downturned lips. When Leif heard whispered "silver-grey" in a gasp, the varangian stepped back and opened the doors for him, dismissing the watchman with an obscene gesture of hands.

Rather than move through it, however, Leif remained beside the dismissed watchman and glimpsed a sparkle to his left. A sparkle that'd borne a lustre attested to the painted jewels illustrated in the rarest tomes. He saw the Empress' throne.

The varangian's sabaton tapped on the flagstones as he curtly shook his head, which Leif ignored.

Carved of a sharp, massy, and black granite that protruded from The Horn, the throne was naturally enamelled with uncut gems of varying rarity. Overtime, and through the reign of previous rulers, extra features were added to the throne and its surroundings. Such as the elaborate dais, the gold filigrees, platinum-coated religious icons, and the chateau itself.

It was as he'd pictured when reading about it – when admiring those illustrations of fantastical jewels and treasures.

The varangian stepped closer, warning Leif to move away, but he'd peered deeper into the throne room, awed by the splendid bas-reliefs that covered the walls depicting known historical events. The stained-glass windows – that all reached up to the vaulted ceiling – also serving a similar purpose, although of different tales like the Searwoods' recreation of nature.

The stained-glass windows reflected their stories on the ground and throne, slightly touching an ironwood trapdoor beside it before a blueish glow – attuned to inbreathing – disproportioned the images and caused them to vanish alongside a quake that'd rumbled the sturdy walls.

In that moment of awe, accentuated by the parchment lanterns, he wanted to stay there. Pain, vengeance, and purpose hid themselves deep within him – again, only briefly – but it was a briefness that stirred a feeling of childish bliss to overwhelm him and make his skin tingle. Leif inhaled the air, as it'd even smelt royal: like jasmine and chocolate.

Drawn out of that phase by the watchman's sepulchral tone, however, he was then bid good luck and left in the chateau's dark hallways. Leif, composing himself, touched the dented frame of his spectacles, where the lens had broken away from, and cringed. He remembered why he was there.

Tut-tutting, the varangian went for his sword hilt and motioned his head onward. Leif couldn't see his eyes beyond his onyx helmet, but he knew that he was serious.

Thus, withdrawing from the room and away from the Archives too, Leif went where the varangian gestured towards. He went to the Empress and her tourney.

Notable clan heraldry flapped and cracked in the wind as bleachers spread throughout the open-roofed hall where the Tourney was taking place.

Leif was sat by a spindly man, eldest of the Varangian Guard, who hid his eyes with the dark lenses of half-moon spectacles and bore a large beard with tints of silver streaked throughout the blackness as though someone had painted the hairs individually. Black, bushy eyebrows came together as Leif informed him of all he knew and encountered.

On Leif's other side, pampered with the finest makeup and perfumes, was the Empress. She wore long wine-coloured robes, which hung above her feet; the layers of velvet and silk draping over her skinny arms as long fingers protruded from their warmth. At her waist was a scabbard-less sword, its hilt and pommel hidden by the wine-coloured material. A sleek black blade meant it was a rapier.

What stood-out to him, however, wasn't the rapier nor her eastern features and monolid eyes. It was the fact that she'd half-hid her face with a gold-filigree mask. A fluid weeping from beneath it that one of her several handmaidens would dab away with a silk handkerchief. They too journeyed from the east with the Empress, as had a small portion of her courtiers whose seats surrounded hers.

Their fashion and features striking in contrast to Rimatheans.

The Empress, though, had yet to welcome or speak to Leif, as she was far too busy focusing on all the clans in attendance that'd brought knights of their own to fight for their honour and name. Alongside the swords, standards, and heraldries the combatants emerged, and the Empress yawned.

When realising she'd not converse with him anytime soon, Leif also directed his attention to the spectacle below. Although they were so high up, he could scarcely make out anything without straining his eyes and focusing.

Some competitors, to Leif's surprise, still utilised full plate armour whilst others chose gauntlets, gorgets, pauldrons or spaulders, sabatons, or variations and combinations of those, while wearing doublets. The latter also chose the utilisation of dirks, stilettos, and rapiers to follow the Poirdelais in their semi-armour-less elegance in lieu of the archaic Varangian Guard.

Even the troopers and watchmen had done the same. Something pointed out to Leif, in heartfelt disgust, by the eldest varangian before he rose and announced the notable knights and esteemed guests to everyone in attendance with a booming voice.

With that addressing, all eyes fell upon the announcer, the Empress, and the stranger that'd sat between them.

With so many eyes on him, Leif had abandoned his endeavour to hide his wound, but when becoming aware of his shirt sticking to his chest, he'd felt embarrassed. Especially beside the Empress.

The sultry climate of Rhegion's coastline was far from anything he'd ever tolerated, and he preferred the prospect of inland Enkhara's arid steppes over it. A dry heat was manageable, or so he'd read and come to agree with, unlike the stickiness of humidity.

The eldest varangian threw wide his arms and the crowds cheered. Leif didn't know what he said – he didn't hear it, either. Alongside his considerations of heat and its various forms, he'd come to realise where he was and how he'd got there. In fact, that notion alone had floored him and caused that stickiness to evolve into a slickness that he'd tasted when it'd pooled on his lip.

When peeling away his shirt from his chest and noticing his rich clothes, he knew why he'd been admitted into the Tourney and beside the Empress. Or, at the least, he assayed a guess. Had he looked as he once had in Falls Creek, they never would've allowed him entrance to the chateau, no matter his claims.

Then again, he paused and assessed the rich, thick sleeves of his coat and recalled what the varangian had earlier whispered. *They're certainly not silver-grey.*

A single boo sounded from the crowd, followed by many, when a semi-armour-less trooper revealed himself. Goading them by at first flailing his arms, he pulled his eyelids to the side to mock the Empress' monolid eyes and laughed at their collective gasps that'd soon mellowed into a deafening silence.

A tall man with a wide nose and straight, thick eyebrows then emerged, his helmet beneath his arm. A varangian that'd donned black-and-onyx armour; a grey surcoat over it with an indigo and upright cross on the front and back. The sapphire Imperial Crest affixed to his breastplate remaining visible due to a circular opening in the surcoat, which was pinned around it.

"So, you want access to the Archives." The Empress didn't look at Leif. A lock of her long, straight, black hair sat in her mouth. "Mm, yes, I heard everything you've said to my varangian. So, speak up." Her head bobbed and weaved, following every move made by the prospective combatants.

"Speak up, I said. I don't want to be here any longer than I need to be, boy. Appearances must be upheld, see?"

The below varangian donned his plumed helmet and ran a gloved thumb across his neckline. The trooper stabbed at him but the varangian performed a parry, pirouetted, and glided his blade through the air as silk across a lady's soft skin.

For how thick the armour was, he moved flexibly.

The trooper struck downward and towards the ground, to the left, parried, and receded.

Leif explained all that he could to the Empress without having a moment to think, but still she kept her attention on the battlefield. Chewing her hair and crunching her fists; evidently more invested after the trooper's mocking display. She didn't blink when he'd mentioned the crucifixion of Estrid and Aivor; not even when he'd relayed the Massacre at Deacon.

"If I can translate these runes," Leif pulled his bag into his lap and revealed his notebook beside *A Druid's Guide*, "then I can stop the Enchantress, Your Majesty. Your throne will be secured, and all will be right in the Realm. Or, somewhat, at the least. I believe I can translate Sandscript. I'm ready."

When he said so, she'd looked at him. Her crow's feet wrinkles harshened as she squinted, although not uglily. He then watched her mouth the words she'd wanted to say to him, but instead faltered and produced a mere whimper.

The Empress stared at Leif's eyes, then at her helmeted Varangian Guard, and back to Leif.

"The colour... how do you...?" The Empress cleared her throat and diverted her attention back to the fighting. "Mm, following sufficient training as an acolyte, you'll have access."

Sloppily lunging with feet scurrying behind to catch the weight of his blade, the trooper attempted another attack. The varangian pivoted and disregarded it with a parry before he'd knocked the trooper off balance with a bash of his hilt against the nape of his neck.

Cheering reverberated throughout the grounds followed by the chanting of the varangian's name.

"An acolyte?" His migraine pounded his skull. "Your Majesty, I'm not looking to become varangian. I'm not even—"

"Highborn?" She smirked. "Mm, think I didn't know that when first seeing you approach? Takes more than clothes to hide that fact. You walk like a blacksmith with blood fever."

Hearing that hurt him. A blacksmith is the last thing he wanted to look like. Like Father.

"Yet you granted me an audience all the same?" Leif watched her chew that lock of hair – irritated at her consistent moan. "Look, Your Majesty, I'm grateful that you'd even consider me as an acolyte. But... but I can't go through that training. Years of it, to fulfil this quest. The need is far too dire. Can you not see the danger?"

"Mm, only the Varangian Guard and myself are allowed access to my archives. So, make your decision, and quick. My bonsai misses me."

Looking at the Empress' horny crown, Leif felt his throat tighten as he found it hard to swallow. He needed the Archives effective immediately. *Want* was no longer at the forefront of his mind, replaced with *need* when he discovered Estrid's body on the road. Training to become a varangian was Isla's old dream.

He didn't want it.

Below, an exhausted trooper kicked loose topsoil at his opponent who, in a flash, cut through the trooper's calf and shin – reaching the bone. Collapsing to his knees, he refused to concede and revealed a concealed flintlock. Firing a shot at the varangian's breastplate, the bullet tore through the surcoat but barely made a dent in the armour. In response, the varangian brought his sword over his head and awaited the crowd.

Thus, they cheered for him as the trooper's decapitated head wetly thudded and reverberated throughout the hall. Murmuring and the passing of dinero followed, tailed by the upset of some and the joy of others – those who betted and won, and those who lost.

As the varangian presented the trooper's head to the Empress, she brought her challis to her lips and drank.

Emptying it. She smiled.

"Make me an honorary varangian and then strip me of the title when I'm done, please."

"Impossible. With no heroic deeds witnessed or spoken of by great bards, how do you expect my knights to accept such an appointment, honorary or otherwise?" The Empress rose, her handmaidens and courtiers doing the same. "Think on my offer. Mm, think on the benefits. You'll have quarters in the chateau and fresh clothes until a decision is reached."

She looked at his eyes again, studied them.

"My party is at the old palace tonight. Come, if you'd like to pursue this path, return to Gwynedd if you want otherwise."

Everyone bowed as the Empress strutted by, ignoring them as they whispered at her back. Leif cringed at the pain in his head and again when looking into his lap and seeing the cover of *A Druid's Guide to Healing*. Estrid's last gift to him. He'd lost too much – was far too close to achieving vengeance.

Leif couldn't let this stop him. Not now.

The eldest varangian continued to clap and chortle at the display below; his brother-in-arms still parading the trooper's head around like it was nothing but a child's plaything.

Antiquated fools, he thought, loosening his shirt from his sweatiness again. *They host these tourneys to hold on to a dying era, hoping to retain the days of knights and princesses in towers. A bygone era. A lost era. But I'll play along, for now.*

Come nightfall and the notable absence of twinkling stars in the nighttime sky, he'd arrived at the party amid revellers and drunks. At a time when most partygoers were too drunk to make conversation, and those that weren't were too boring to consider mingling with. For Leif, however, who'd preferred the quietude of a library to a mazurka, saw it as nothing short of fortuitous.

Alone, he'd investigated his environment.

The old palace sat prominently and proudly on The Horn. It's architecture astounding Leif; unscathed and unsullied by the ever-present neolyt advertisements that befouled the city proper. The bespoke limestones were perfect and painted golden, the stained-glass windows patently purple, and flags flew high and proud above the celebration to mark a long and prospering alliance among all companies and clans.

You'd never think there was a crucifixion this morning. Leif took a sip of pinot noir that'd helped ease his migraine, shifting to look out over the serpentine walls that twisted into alleys which intersected yards; bell towers pushed up against the mountain at either side; and ribbons of smoke drifting from tall chimneys. *Not being up here with the aristocracy and bourgeoisie. Not when you've made it to the Heavens and lived.*

Then, over the heads of clamorous merrymakers, a well-dressed Leif discerned the most magnificent hairdo – greater than anything the palace had offered and grander than the chateau's clocktower. Gorgeously oiled, it possessed violet petals accompanying the braiding that complemented the Empress' fair skin and resplendent lilac gown.

With the rapier still at her waist, Leif glimpsed a blue gemstone on its pommel radiate a bright glow amid the moonlit grounds. A familiar blue he'd seen before, in book, painting, and in person. It was azurite, and that sword at her waist was the black-bladed rapier he'd seen in *The Holy Writ.*

A rare relic which he didn't imagine she could so easily wield. A Mystic's weapon, she flaunted it as if it was her right to do so, and the people sneered at it.

Regardless, Leif admired how the Empress held herself: chin high and an ever-raised brow that suggested she knew more than anyone. Certainly, more than the guests that'd toast one another with pinot noir, and, in a hushed manner, curse her name.

The Varangian Guard at her side led her into the palace, and Leif followed. The two knights never easing their straight backs or lowering their towering kite shields.

Enlisted soldiers from various countries with no loyalties but to the person they served, they neither spoke nor acted unless instructed to do so, or necessity arose.

Leif could have never pictured Isla doing that. She was too free spirited. He smiled at the thought of her. He missed her.

Waving the two from her side, the Empress halted upon the dancefloor in the east wing's largest room, amid everyone else that'd waltzed in circles. And then she pointed to Leif while chewing a strand of her straight, oiled hair.

He didn't budge, not a muscle, so her knights grabbed his arms and brought him to her.

Dictating where Leif's hand should sit on her hip, the Empress placed hers atop his shoulder; their free hands abducting from their sides and pointing straighter than a sword.

The Empress instructed Leif to mimic her every move and to not lift his head until he understood the footwork. The band then began to play at a larghetto before evolving into andantino and then allegretto, or so she noted in whisper to herself; and as their tempo morphed, so did the dancers' footsteps.

Leif struggled to keep up, but he'd lasted.

When the music ebbed and the crowds cheered and clapped, the Empress' hand dropped to Leif's waist and the small of his back: feeling the rectangular outline that he'd hoped to be hidden well. She smiled at him, and he returned a half-smile before he'd revealed his notebook to her.

"Mm, the runes." She raised a brow and groaned. "That's why you brought this."

Watching her tilt her head to the side, comparable to a feline's inquisitiveness, she shook it. As she turned her back to him, her rapier's black blade touched his leg – cutting through his pants – and he swore that it'd burnt.

Like Isla's wildfire, it'd burnt him.

Moving on through the crowd, she took his hand and parted the dancers with a mere look. She didn't comment on the burn, nor did Leif mention it. Instead, he smelt her exquisite perfume.

"Majesty, please," he ventured. "What I've told you is hard to believe, but you *must* trust me."

"Must I?" The Empress motioned her head, and a handmaiden dabbed the fluid that ran from beneath her mask. "Don't get cocky, boy. Mm, I danced with you because I like the colour of your eyes, nothing more."

"Not the fact that I'm the Conduit, then?" Leif assayed.

Her breath caught and the Empress paused, smiling at whoever's eye she'd caught, but resumed a cruel countenance when regarding Leif.

"Just because you say you're the Conduit, doesn't mean that I believe you. Besides, don't you think that someone with healer's hands would've remedied their wounds without delay? Mm, say, a cut from a sword, for example."

She nodded to his leg where the material was singed.

Leif's breath then caught, as though they'd taken it in turns to rob each other of air.

"Why would I lie? I've told you the truth. I've told you that I need the Archives to save you – to save the Realm and your throne. What more do you want?"

As Leif's voice raised over the music and the Empress' eye widened in a despotic leer that'd prefaced a lecture, he was thrust back by a firm hand on his chest.

Breathless, he collapsed to the ground between jaunty prancing, and flowy gowns that were both long and wide. Kneed, stepped on, and waylaid, Leif had lost sight of the Empress. The Varangian Guard nowhere to be seen.

Raised voices boomed across the heads of many and found Leif amid their legs, and the scraping of steel against flagstones.

Those people, whose legs he'd come to know, had then departed long enough for him to rise and watch them gather so densely that he'd scarcely managed to get back to his feet before they'd brought him into that compacted mass. Glass shattered, water plashed, and a collective gasp ensued.

Over the heads of some, over a waiter's filigree tray precariously shaking in a dainty hand, and between the shoulders of others, Leif managed to glimpse the Empress at knifepoint.

The curious onlookers didn't move a muscle to protect their Majesty; in fact, they looked relaxed.

Far more relaxed than the assassin whose nostrils flared, as he'd shot worrisome glances towards the spilt water. His boots shuffled away from the puddle, he rounded the Empress, and then turned his back to the gathered crowds but not the Varangian Guard who'd arrived too late – them, he kept in his line of sight.

The music had been deadened and murmurs were here and there, but barely the volume of ants feasting.

The look in the assassin's eyes was deadly. Leif feared it, yet the Empress barely reacted to it. Her attention focused on the blade pointed at her throat, nothing more. The assassin, though, continued to ponder the water. The still liquid which he'd feared more than the swords that'd come to surround him, wielded by the scarce easterners, loyal to their leader, and Varangian Guard.

Stillness overcame all and the simultaneous holding of breaths made the room appear dead – a tomb for the living. A footfall forced Leif to flinch. His migraine had returned in force, heartbeat pounding behind his eyes, creating an illusion ahead of him; rings that encircled the assassin – that encircled his quarry.

A squat, stout man.

The rings aided him; helped him think of something other than what he was about to do. Something stupid, but something that'd further his goal. He needed access to the Archives. Needed. Not wanted. The Empress needed to live.

She did, after all, want a heroic deed.

Again, the assassin looked at the water.

He sweated and feared that, too. His mad eyes deepening with hatred and purpose.

Aquaphobia, Leif stroked his hairy chin. *He's scared of water. Even that which he creates himself.*

Leif grabbed at the dainty-handed waiter's tray of golden filigree and took hold of a jug, presuming the condensation on the exterior would be enough even if whatever was inside wasn't water. And then he ran, as quickly as he could manage – shouldering one and all to cut through the crowds.

The assassin closed the gap between himself and the Empress, "The Enchantress has promised me immortality for this!" he said, punching her chest so firmly that she'd staggered and collapsed.

Leif was too far away, and the crowds stirred to become thicker. The Rimathean aristocracy still doing nothing. He could no longer physically step in-between feet, nor did his battering-ram technique work. The jug sat heavily in his palms.

He assessed it. He inhaled.

With a terrific thrust, Leif managed to throw the jug over the heads of many and drench them all in both condensation and chilled water, and his quarry received the most of it.

The assassin writhed on the flagstones, saturated in water. Tears flowed freely as he clawed at his face to create rivulets of blood. The people gathered watched on in a morbid curiosity that'd kept them and Leif in an unwavering standstill. Soon, however, the spectacle was quelled when a varangian approached and stabbed the assassin through the neck.

The Empress, however, had yet to be at ease as she too writhed on the flagstones, clawing at her chest instead of her face. She cried and kicked her feet, slippers flying from her small, perfectly formed foot as she struggled for air.

Something in Leif then clicked. He'd read about this, not too long ago. *A Druid's Guide to Healing.*

"The Empress is s-suffering from a myocardial contusion!" he declared, finger wagging overhead. "Her heart is compressed between spine and sternum. Listen to me, her right ventricle is possibly injured, or the aorta is ruptured. I... I can try to treat it, but I require a stiletto. Now, please!"

The eldest varangian revealed a small dirk and offered that instead, and Leif accepted it quickly and asked the other Varangian Guard to restrain the Empress. Agreeing, they gently held her down. The eldest, though, grabbed a hold of Leif's scarred forearm, tightly enough that it'd hurt him, and intently inspected him before the Empress was even touched.

It was a stern look that said, "If you try anything dodgy, you're dead."

Opening the Empress' robes and revealing her ample breasts where the bruising was, Leif gulped.

"You may feel a sharp prick, Your Majesty."

Leif held his breath and awaited the blood, and sure enough it came. Quickly, he threw aside the dirk and placed his hands against the wound that'd proceeded to heal at his touch but not so rapidly that people would question his mundanity.

Opening her eyes as her breathing returned to normal and her writhing ceased, the Empress glanced up at Leif and said, "Healer's hands."

Clapped on the back and hoisted atop shoulders, he felt hands grope him in places he'd never wanted touched, accidently or otherwise, to be paraded around and lauded. The eastern courtiers cheered and thanked him for saving the Empress' life, while the Rimatheans politely clapped and feigned smiles.

All, however, called him a hero.

XVI

The Varangian Gambit

Met by the mana-drenched city streets of Coventry, Isla collapsed to her knees and ran a shivering finger down the burgundy-coloured vines that scarred her hand. She roared at the night sky – at the moons overhead – without care for whoever was about; wholeheartedly believing it the only way to express how she'd felt. To know family, only to lose it again.

After the scarring, she'd felt physically drained. As though the power she'd coveted had ebbed into the deepest recesses of her soul. Isla feared exertion. Feared how the Calling still stirred within her, experiencing the same feelings she'd hoped lost when finding Basem; yet thankful that at least the voices hadn't returned. That much, at least, she could be thankful for.

Punching at the stoney street, forcing the small bugs at her fingertips to slither or crawl away from her outburst, Isla restrained her tears. She felt like she was going backwards. Biting her lip so hard she'd felt it bruise, she kneed the Codex closer to her fingertips and groped it. Urchins got to their feet and scattered, and Velyn landed at her hands.

Taking a breath, Isla remembered where she was and how far she'd come. She remembered where she'd asked her Familiar to take her. But where Isla had expected to see Father's smithy, she beheld a ruin. All that'd remained were the sign in shambles and the tools of metallurgy unscathed by the building's ruination.

Wanting to enter its remains, Isla felt the azurite at her neck tremble like it had on the airship, heard it hum deeper. Isla heard a male's voice. Cool and calm and wizened by years. It came through the azurite in search of a niece returned from the dead.

"Niece?" it repeated. "*I feel the presence of your azurite. Have you returned to us? Somehow, have you returned to the mortal plane?*"

Isla held the azurite to her lips and looked towards The Horn, but before she spoke into the gemstone, a glint from a blade caught her attention. A watchman overhead vying to see through the bitter darkness where neolyt didn't reach.

Her gaze returned to the razed smithy, and she did long for it. She missed her father, but his memory and teachings had done enough. This was her quest, and she'd no longer rely on a memory to empower her. Thus, Isla fled against the crinkle-crankle walls of Coventry to get her bearings. To recentre.

Avoiding the fuchsia and cyan neolyt, her hieroglyphic scars glowed whenever she neared them. Glowed like Basem's.

Slinking into the squalid quayside, Isla crouched low on the narrow spine of a fisherman's roof looking over a collection of square crates, some riggings, and coiling, weathered ropes. Nose wrinkling at the awful stench of cesspits, which'd overcame the salty air, Isla relished the sepulchral darkness.

A darker part of the city with little neolyt, Isla relied on the moons' brief light, when the clouds hadn't obscured them, to guide her way forth when that gloom which she'd delighted in for the moment had dwindled.

She reserved the use of magic until the time was right, especially after hearing whispers of wildfire in Falls Creek by two stocky fishermen who'd one beer too many before returning home to their fishwives. The scarring that goldenly glowed from her paleness returned to its burgundy.

Codex in hand, she assessed murky wavelets and tried concocting a plan that'd open it. She knew no magic that could do so. Stone skin had then flashed across her eyes – a stiletto, a death! Isla clenched her jaw and gritted teeth, fingering the Codex's cover.

Where are you, Leif?

Startled by the incessant knelling of an enormous bell, which'd descended on the city like a hoary gloom from the smog of industry, Velyn breathed fire. Translucent, crimson smoke rising from the faedragon's nose and into the city's real and grimy smog.

Perhaps the voice will know where he is, she toyed with her azurite. *But can I trust whoever speaks to me?*

An aggregated caw from a murder of crows, and Isla ran her tattooed hand down the Codex. From what'd happened on the island, she surmised that the terrific treasure was invulnerable to magic, or the scarce magic she knew of.

Rapping a fingernail against it and producing bone-white dust from the depiction of the Searwood and Phoenix, Isla grabbed at the latches and pulled hard. Achieving only sore fingertips, the alien dust twirled and swirled amid the scarce moonlight. Velyn, crawling onto the Codex's cover, breathed fire again. Magenta glimmering, she'd flapped her wings.

Velyn breathed fire, Isla gawked. *Magical fire!*

Collecting the Codex and suspending it between herself and her Familiar, Isla indicated where to breathe.

Velyn's breath curled around the latches and locks: the intense heat was unburning. The wispy, coiling fire instead slithered around the unopened clasps in the manner of water serpents: seeking, unlatching, and unlocking the Codex's restraints one-by-one. Ceasing, the electrum clasps rocked in the faint breeze which'd rustled Isla's ashen curls.

Born from her own magic, Isla felt a tinge of pride for the honey-coloured faedragon and for herself.

Opening on its own accord, the Codex's ancient parchment possessed an uncanny chill which radiated outward and touched her skin. However, when glimpsing the first runic passage written by a divine thousands of years ago, Isla understood none of it. Velyn squawked, and Isla tried her best to comprehend any of it, but she wasn't her brother. Thus, as she did as a child, she'd resorted to looking at pictures – at the flamboyant illustrations.

Must be it! She found a glimmering image of an Emerald Eclipse with a broken staff in the foreground. *It must be the spell to re-surface magic. One line – one spell. It must be!*

Glancing about, spotting not a single piece of neolyt that could be drained by casting in the lower-levels, Isla got to her knees and recalled the gryphon's tome. All she needed to do was find Leif, and she'd just the cantrip to do so.

A locator cantrip.

Repeating the process, but with no map to point to, her finger instead darted through the air as if an arrow and pointed to The Horn's obscured peaks beyond the smog. To the chateau. Even from the lower levels, even with that impenetrable barrier discharged from the rectangular and tall edifices and their sister factories, the denizens could see the Heavens, or what the aristocracy prized as being such. The Horn.

Having been there before with Father, Isla felt for her azurite. And recalled what she could about it, although minimal.

"Hey." She scratched Velyn beneath the chin, the little creature yawning. "Think you can do me one last favour tonight? I promise you, it's not much."

Her reptilian head followed Isla's regard, a forked tongue flicked, and she nodded – stipulating agreement. However, the faedragon's scales no longer reflected the light so splendidly as they once had. In fact, her leathery wings appeared wooden. As Isla had felt, so had her Familiar. The pair were exhausted.

Lifting her little friend into her hands, they locked eyes. Through that gaze, a truth was made known to Isla.

"I'm so sorry." She cupped her mouth to muffle her own blubbering. "Velyn, I never knew. If... if I had, I would've never asked you to exert yourself. Like mana, you channel my own magic, don't you? An extension of my body. My Familiar." She hugged her to her chin. "Opening the Codex ruined you, didn't it? You need rest. So do I, girl. But..." she glimpsed Leif's location, "... one last spell, and that's it. I promise."

Velyn nuzzled into Isla's thumb before taking flight, her wings flapping stiffly and almost mechanically. She circled Isla, eager to help in any way possible. Always.

As she did, the azurite's trembling and humming had intensified, and in that instant a feeling of intense and raw magic had seeped into Isla. More so when she looked back at The Horn. It'd begun through her pores before spreading into her skin and reaching her veins. There it'd dwelt and heated her blood. It gave her a message.

The powerful presence was neither her own nor whatever the Codex emanated. It came from The Horn. Closing her eyes, she grasped the azurite firmly and felt Velyn's teleportation spell build. She glimpsed a large, winged beast in her mind's eye.

A dragon, she shuddered, and everything became black.

***

Through the chateau Isla wandered, following the route she'd recalled when visiting with Father. The first time she'd seen the Varangian Guard, and the last time. A memory she'd clung to that'd evolved into an aspiration. Honour in duty; she fulfilled it in another way – to Mystics rather than the Imperium.

The lack of mana helped her sneak through the wide and dark corridors, and the armour let her hide when a dignitary or knight strode by with their hand at the ready on a sword.

Even the cats meowed, never hissing at her or Velyn, before they slinked away into shadow once more.

Her azurite trembled, and the voice within spoke to his niece. Isla felt its presence again, only this time beneath her feet. He'd mentioned a Searwood that continued to blossom in places hidden – ramblings of lunacy to Isla's ear. The mellow voice then trembled through not only her gemstone, but the ground itself and up through the chateau. The vibrations tickled her soles, and she sprinted to evade them.

Whispering into her hand, holding the Codex close to her chest, Isla cast another locator cantrip and her finger darted to another corridor. It'd evolved to become narrow, with mauve carpet. Up a flight of stairs that felt to last an era, she'd reached the heights of a tower.

And that's where her cantrip ebbed.

Leif must be nearby. She'd thought, twirled a lock of hair, and spotted a door. *Closer than I thought, perhaps?*

Her finger lowered to her side as Velyn landed woodenly on her shoulder. Isla felt the door between fingers, the wood-grain ancient and worn, and she knocked. Tightening her abdomen as she held her breath, she readied herself for whatever was beyond.

"It's open," she heard, and twisted the handle.

Isla's knees felt weak when she saw him, slumped over at a desk. A groomed beard and a scar too, Leif was dressed in a knight's gambeson. Something she never pictured him donning, even for a joke. He'd evolved into a man she didn't know, and yet when he looked up from his old notebook, those silver-grey eyes sparked a fire within her.

Seeker wasn't spotted, neither the sword nor its scabbard. And searching her brother's crinkled brow, she knew it'd been lost. Steel for flesh; Seeker for Leif.

She approached him, wrinkling her nose and feeling for Velyn's spine. But she stopped herself, and timidly waved to her brother. A queer stirring had then briefly overcome the Calling's, replacing it with what felt to be butterflies in her stomach.

"Isla?" Leif straightened in his seat and gulped. "I... I see you've almost come into a Harbinger's ashen hair."

"And I see you've grown a beard." She smiled and picked at her fingernails. "Gained a warrior's scar too, huh?"

Lips downturned and wobbly, Leif ran to her and fell to his knees at her feet, hugging her waist tightly. He wept into her dirtied tunic, and pawed at her back as though doing so somehow brought him closer to her. In that hold, their emotions ran free, and they'd wept for the Albergs as Isla petted Leif's coily hair.

Leif then insisted that she eat.

So, he fed her, had a bath drawn, and requested fresh clothes be brought to his chamber. Unable to recall the last time she tasted food so good, Isla devoured all she could: bread, apples, and portions of salted pork. All while, they endlessly chatted, and when Isla felt up to it, she mentioned their adventures. Centring them back into the present and their reality. That's when she revealed to him the Codex and explained all that she could.

Leif also provided what he'd learnt including the reason behind their bond that remained closed off, before revealing why he'd dressed in a gambeson in the dead of night. He was preparing for his induction into the Varangian Guard for services to the Empress and Imperium; namely, saving her life. At first, Isla hated the idea of someone so inept with a sword taking her dream from her, before she'd recalled what truly mattered.

Isla recalled what he'd said about a weapon.

"And you don't believe the weapon you speak of is this?" Seated together at his desk, she tapped the Codex's cover. "You believe it's the dragon in The Horn? The dragon I feel beneath our feet even now?"

"I still can't believe there's really a dragon beneath us." He glared at the flagstones. "But it must be, right? The Codex, although powerful, can't be what she meant. It can't be."

He bit his thumb, as she remembered him doing.

"Or it is, and you don't want to believe that's the case." She lay a hand on his forearm that she'd once burnt. "Leif,

Keziah never once mentioned a dragon to me, nor can a dragon do anything to re-surface magic. If they could, don't you think they would've by now? This tome is what she'd sought. She wanted me to find this, for me to deliver it to her so you and her can re-surface magic."

"Then... she never wanted me to find a weapon, and her lieutenants were wrong. She anticipated you to find the Codex, since that's what we need to re-surface magic. That's why she left you alive in the forest," said Leif. "She killed Estrid only to goad me into finding her, and Aivor was the next planned message. How am I so stupid?" He punched his legs. "Should've never have assumed – I don't know what I was thinking!"

"Leif, it's all right. We're going to make this right."

"We can't, Isla!" he exclaimed, pulling at his coily hair in a panic; feet tapping on the flagstones. "Don't you see? My sacrifice is assured now. I... I need to die. The Codex isn't a weapon, it houses the spell we need to fulfil the Dyadic Prophecy."

Coldness surpassed any heat which the fireplace dis-charged, and the touch of Isla's clammy fingers caused Leif to flinch.

"We're not going to let that happen," she whispered as tenderly as she could. "I won't let that happen. I promise. Leif, we've the blood of Basem Alpheniq coursing through our veins. You think we'll die so easily?"

He shrugged, "It's as the prophecy says, Isla. We can't change that if we want to re-surface magic. I was a fool to think otherwise." Beads of sweat popped out from his tawny skin. "I'll die, and my body will be primed for possession."

Lifting his depressed chin with her finger, Isla searched his silver-grey eyes and then looked towards the armour that awaited him. A tinge of envy struck her, as she'd envisioned herself in the Varangian Guard's black-and-onyx uniform.

"You still haven't translated the runes you found on Estrid, right?" She guided him to his feet and brought him to the armour, helping him don the tightly linked chainmail. "Then you still don't know the message. What're your goals, Leif?"

She shepherded his hands to the black-and-onyx breast-plate and together they'd traced the metal's design.

"To translate the runes that'd marked Estrid's body... to understand the message left for me." He looked at Isla, adjusting his dented spectacles. "To transliterate the spell that'll re-surface magic. To find and kill Keziah."

Taking the breastplate off from the mannequin, Isla fitted it to his chest sturdily and reached for another piece.

"Good. But we must kill Keziah first. If we don't beforehand, her plans with Daeva will come into fruition."

Leif nodded with a thousand-yard stare before cringing like he'd tasted sour fruit.

"It's what she plans to do after magic is re-surfaced that should worry us, right? Should worry everyone. Whatever it is, it'll be our doom if we don't stop it," he said. "Aivor told me that in Deacon."

"Well, he was right." She shuddered. Hearing his name hurt. "With those quarantine passes you've folded in your notebook, I'm sure we'll have no trouble in deciphering their location. Deacon or Coventry you said, right?" He nodded and she continued, "We've got this."

Able to discern more than her own reflection in the onyx, it mirrored all else. Isla observed not only her countenance, rounded and disproportioned, but another... Aivor's. Rather than cry, however, she bit her cheek and held her breath. It wasn't the time. She needed to remain focused. An inbreath helped her, followed by a steady and levelled exhale. A coolness travelled from neck to lower-back, and she sighed.

Leif, fully dressed, stood beside Isla as they beheld the resplendent armour. The centred crest glittered blue.

"I'm glad you came." He reached for her scarred hand and caressed it with a gloved thumb. "Perfect timing, too. We're meant to have somebody hand us over to the Empress."

She wrinkled her nose, worried that Velyn's scales were still woody. "A walk down the aisle, then it's silver blood down the hatch."

"Sure, but... Isla." Leif waved a hand between her and Velyn. "What about the dragon?"

She'd clasped her azurite, ordered Velyn to hide in her travelling bag, and felt for something through her soles. Still, the dragon spoke to his supposed niece. Isla had no idea whether he mistook her or her mother for his scaly relative.

"What do you think about it?" She brushed her knuckles against his groomed beard. "He's been trapped for so many years."

Leif, storing his notebook beneath his breastplate and leaving behind his old bag and its contents, stepped between Isla and the door. He shook his head.

"You said it speaks through Mother's azurite, right? You said he tries to speak to his niece who he'd presumed dead. What if..." he scratched at his beard, "... what if it *is* Ghulzar? What if it's Basem's brother? I'd a feeling earlier, but... Isla, it must be! We can ally with him."

Basem's brother, Isla's shoulders eased.

"He also mentioned a Searwood. One that still blossoms."

Leif excitably clapped, "The Searwood of Coventry. The first Searwood to plant its roots to restore nature! A Searwood the aenyr commissioned the dragons to protect before their revolt. Isla, don't you see? Wherever this Searwood is, that's where Ghulzar resides."

Isla stopped Leif from biting his thumb again. From her experience with a Searwood, they weren't all too friendly.

"One step at a time, Leif. First, let's get through the ceremony."

XVII

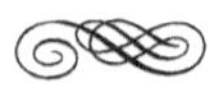

Silver Blood, Black Blade

The two strode side-by-side before reaching an archway bedecked in friezes comparable to what'd decorate a cathedral, which led to the throne room. Through it, Isla smelt jasmine and chocolate. The scent of royalty.

There, Leif apologised to Isla alongside a wish that it'd been her in his place – that it was her who'd be receiving what she'd always considered an honour. He'd apologised, sincerely, but not with words... instead, with tearful eyes and a lingering stare.

Adjusting the helmet he'd borne beneath his arm, Isla rustled his coily hair and nodded through the prodigious doors where horns were sounded, and censers were swung by priests; the frankincense and myrrh blend cutting through the chocolate and jasmine. Although pleasant, she'd preferred what was.

It was a moment Isla dreamt of, and it'd pained her to see it taken from her, but when Leif had reached out to hold her scarred hand and half-smile, she remembered why they were there: their goal. Rejuvenated, she felt strong again, but the Calling still stirred. Unlike in Falls Creek, however, it'd hurt.

"Mm, who comes before the Imperium?"

"Leif, of the Clan Morrigan," Isla responded.

"Who bears him?"

"His sister, Isla Morrigan. Who receives him?"

Silence befell the ceremony, and hushed whispers carried themselves through the room towards the entryway. A single courtier then ran out, and when spotting Isla gasped and prayed to her divine.

"Mm, the Empress," she said loudly, drowning out the whispers before clearing her throat. "Approach."

Passing through the narthex at the entrance, the throne room was shaped into a more modern cathedral compared to a ziggurat, and it bore writing over the doorway – in Common and not runes. Although an older dialect, it was a language she understood. Most people were raised to.

It read: *ROBUR. POTENTIA. UNITAS.*

Three aisles were ahead of them, but they took the central one – the nave – and came to a halt at the crossing and transepts. There, at the open choir, surrounded by the ambulatory and ahead of the apse, sat the spectacular throne that awed, an ironwood trapdoor, and the Empress beside a stoup.

Seeing the Empress sparked a memory of being at the chateau in youth. A memory of an eastern woman with a mask that covered half of her face; a memory she repressed or was made to. Still surrounded by parchment lanterns, seeing her again broke whatever repression lingered.

Nearing her, Isla saw that the Empress' wrinkles provided a matured look that framed her mien perfectly; more akin to a fine, temperate wine than a woman. She was unchanged from when Father had spoken to her, aside from a limp that forced her to favour her right leg.

Why had Father met with the Empress, she twirled a lock of her ashen hair again and snarled at a courtier that gasped.

Isla then beheld the rapier.

It was an ornate sword with a black blade that trembled and hummed. The twisting quillons were etched with bijou runes, and the grip was covered in an uncommon scaly sha-green. Wincing at the light reflected from the rapier's pommel its shine painting her in a blue beam, she couldn't help but note the double-edged and straight blade's intricacies.

But it was the azurite that'd ensnared her more than the amazing blade of a material unbeknown to her. Azurite was the gemstone of aenyr, and it didn't belong to the Empress. It shouldn't belong to her.

A Mystic's weapon, Isla pondered how a Laic could wield it; how the wayfaring Basem hadn't reclaimed it.

She looked again to the mask that'd concealed half of her face from the world; that'd concealed a disfigurement. To the sword, and then to the azurite.

There, on that blueness, Isla lingered as she'd toyed with her own, feeling the smoothness of its cut.

A weapon befitting Basem's own race. The Empress caught her eye, and a smirk lifted that mask slightly where fluid leaked and was dabbed away by a head-scarfed handmaiden. *Is the Empress responsible for what'd kickstarted this whole thing?*

Leif had arrived ahead of the elegant majesty and her Varangian Guard that all stood in a semi-circle and on a dais.

The Empress reached into a rose-gold stoup with a human skull, worn and cracked with teeth yellower than urine. A stoup bearing the silver blood of the first men. Crooked like a twig and thinner than a blade of grass, the Empress' forefinger stirred it. Dissimilar to how the books depicted it, the brief silver shimmer within the crimson blood is what'd given it its name. Not the fact that it was entirely silver.

"Kneel." Isla heard the Empress hiss at Leif, a lock of damp hair dangling from her lips.

The eldest varangian removed Leif's gloves and added a drop of his blood to the skull's contents with an unyielding press on a fresh and small wound. Leif's too bore silver particles.

It's as The Holy Writ said, she'd thought, feeling a scowl wring her prideful countenance. *The Dyad's blood is special. But I've never noticed it until now. Not until looking for it.*

Looking around, all the Varangian Guard had their helmets tucked beneath their arms. Each one had silver-grey eyes; an apparent side-effect of drinking the silver blood. When she'd learnt about them in her youth, however, silver-grey eyes weren't mentioned. It was meant to be hereditary.

Velyn stirred in Isla's travelling bag beside the Codex.

Ingesting the blood was meant to extend their life in service of the Empress, as the first men lived longer. It changed their genealogy, sure, but Isla hadn't known to what extent. She doubted many did.

The courtiers allowed into the room being sworn to secrecy.

The Empress, donning a glower of her own, extended the skull towards Leif as his mouth twisted queerly in disgust. Isla's nose wrinkled, worried about what'll happen to her brother since he already bore the remarkable gene. She stepped forward, anxiously massaging her fingers.

He brought the skull to his lips and tasted the old bone. With a clench of his jaw, and a twitch of his cheek, Leif flung back his head and quaffed the skull's contents. Falling and groaning, he pressed a hand against his mouth. Dropping the skull, he needed both hands. Isla wanted to go to his aid, but the eldest varangian shook his head when seeing her attempt to move.

The crowd edged, whispering.

The Morrigans looked at one other; then, grabbing at his M-shaped hairline, Leif yanked his coily hair and forced the final mouthful down. Quivering limbs brought him to all fours, and it pained Isla to watch him struggle; his palms slipping on the marble mosaic.

Getting to his feet, however, the eastern portion of courtiers ardently cheered and hoorayed as the others docilely applauded and smiled at the tips of their teeth – a trait of the weak-chinned nobility. The Varangian Guard themselves not moving a muscle. That was until Leif looked to them and they'd recoiled, gasped, and reached for their swords.

Where once beautiful silver-grey eyes were... they'd been replaced by glowing irises that'd reminded Isla of mana itself.

The knights donned their helmets, drew their weapons at the eldest's say-so, and encircled their empress. But she merely waved them away with her handkerchief and descended the dais with an earnest smirk.

"A descendant of the first men." The Empress reached for Leif's spectacles and gently removed them from his face. "With such precious blood coursing through your veins, and with the blessing of our divine mixing with that of your ancestors, your sight is made anew."

Isla ran to Leif's side, pulling him around to look at her. The Empress halting the eldest varangian before he'd grabbed at Isla.

His irises blazingly smouldered that it'd hurt to look at. Yet he'd seemed, overall, unchanged.

Sir Leif donned his helmet and gloves, and the Empress asked him to face the crowd. Cheering ensured, encouraged by the Empress, but love was unfound amid the majority. Isla felt it.

Reaching for her azurite, anticipating the voice to hum, she'd instead heard a warning from the dragon. A warning that'd told his niece to flee from the chateau, if truly she was there. To abandon her folly and seek solitude away from the world of men.

The cheering grew louder by the second. The Calling cramping her stomach rather than merely stirring – unsated, it was dangerous. Through the pain, her fingers sweated on the azurite, and it'd warned her to flee again – to take up arms, if she needed to. Anxiety loomed over Isla, as did the tall Empress.

Leif caught her as she folded in on herself, panting for air.

"*Flee*," said the dragon. "*Flee or fight.*"

Clattering of armour resounded from down the hall and raised voices to boot. They were coming.

Leif, catching her frantic eye, cocked his head to the side and squinted at her. Had she known any better, she'd think he was curious, though not panicked. That trait she'd the honour of bearing alone, as it was Isla who'd been warned.

Rounding her brother in a moment of supreme hysteria, Isla took the black-bladed sword from the Empress who hadn't moved a muscle and felt the azurite pommel resist her – aggressive like her mother's azurite once was.

The eldest varangian swung his claymore in a mighty war cry, but Isla caught it on the black blade that'd sent forth a force which then toppled everyone but herself and Leif. The clash of metals convulsed her scarred hand and ached it as she'd grimaced and bore the shockwave that'd advanced through her.

Rapier in hand and Codex at her back, Isla felt a surge of acute power pursue that aching blast and snuff it. The pommel's azurite glinted and the one at her neck warmed; the two sparking, wanting to touch.

Isla grabbed Leif and bolted from the dais.

Bowling through the Imperial Troops and the frightened courtier from earlier, Leif asked what was going on, and he was answered by a trooper that'd assayed to slice off Isla's hand. Seeing that, Leif threw himself forward and head-butted the helmetless trooper so hard that he'd broken his nose before Isla could attempt a parry or riposte.

"What're you doing, you mad bastard? She's a bloody Mystic!" said the broken-nosed trooper. "Burnt down Falls Creek with her wildfire!"

Closing both doors on the throne room's occupants, including a smirking Empress, Isla summoned Velyn to breathe fire on the handles and melt them together to create a makeshift and somewhat malleable lock. A temporary barrier against their unanticipated enemies. As the flames ceased, however, a shock shot through Isla from head to toe.

Something was off. The bulky doors rattled as fists and undiscerned instruments pounded against them.

"Word has already reached Coventry," Leif panted, his neck a deep shade of red. "The induction was for nothing."

"No." She grabbed his pauldrons and forced him to face her as the shock ran through her again and she'd felt the heat of his fear. "You drank the blood; you wear the armour. The Archives will sense that. Your induction was everything."

Nodding, his glowing eyes so bright even beneath his helmet, Leif said, "To the Archives."

A step forward, and they were halted by Velyn landing stiffly on Isla's palm. She hadn't even made a noise. Her scales had devolved, and her wings were as straight as a nail. Shaking her head, Isla tried to stop what was happening, but the final and strongest shock travelled through her.

As the pain relented, a wooden toy sat hotly in her palm.

The desperate rapping on the doors across the corridor became louder, as grunting and a cacophony of orders to destroy the ancient entrance resounded. The malleable look solidifying into something stronger. A rage welled within her, and what'd devolved into honey-coloured wood had become sawdust.

"Come." Leif motioned towards the Archives as the sawdust sifted through Isla's skinny fingers. "Don't let her sacrifice be in vain. Let's finish this. Let's finish the fight. For Mother, for the Albergs, and for Velyn. Isla, we must go now!"

Isla's cheek twitched and eyes largened. The Calling tore apart her insides, and Velyn's loss struck her heart.

She wanted to let loose, to allow wildfire to consume the chateau and seek out Keziah wherever she hid – to end it all in a fiery blaze, as it'd began. Poetic justice to bookend their story; something Aivor would've appreciated in song.

Scarring be damned, Isla seethed, and moved to strike a pose. Leif's protesting didn't bother her, and the rapping of fist and instrument against the barred entryway only lent to her fury. She readied herself – wanted it!

No, she weakly exhaled. *I'm better than that.*

XVIII

The Searwood's Embrace

At the winding staircase that'd led to the Archives, Leif felt sick to the stomach. Yet, and after drinking the blood, a sensation washed over him that'd made him stronger – as though nail, tooth, and bone were hardened. When the first men's blood mixed with what'd already flowed through his veins, boiling and bubbling, he was changed.

Deep-down, however, was dread. The dread of responsibility. That's what sickened him. Too many people relied on them, and he didn't know if he could live up to their expectations. He didn't know if he could surrender his life for the Dyadic Prophecy to be fulfilled.

Skipping two steps at a time, they ascended as Isla glared at her hand where remnants of sawdust remained in the creases of her palm. Leif let her pass. She then skipped three at a time.

Reaching the top, Isla rapped her knuckles against a mahogany door until an affixed eye, centred where a knocker should be, opened; eyelids peeling back slowly. Hiding his sister behind his back, Leif stood as still as a mouse and allowed the eye to assess him. The veins riddling the whites grew thicker the longer it unblinkingly stared.

It'd squelched, the pupil dilated, and then the eyelids drew wetly to a thin slit before closing. A click followed, like a clock's hand, and the door swung ajar; the ruckus from the throne room almost drowning out the creaky hinges.

Cringing, they entered on tiptoes.

A smell, like what'd be expected when entering an elderly couple's home who drape their furnishings with musty coverings and off-white doilies, filled Leif's nose and congested his sinuses. Although unlike that, the Archives were blanketed in a thick sheet of dust which covered everything but the area where somebody had been working.

Leif assayed a meagre holler and received nothing in return. Not wanting to risk their exposure, however, he tiptoed among the bookshelves looking for a varangian behind every corner, potentially flailing a sword around wildly, but instead spotted a keyhole in the floor to a thin and sleek key without teeth.

"Nobody's here," he exhaled, removed his helmet, and looked up.

Awed, he'd staggered backward when gazing at the high shelves – almost floored by the number of books that'd lined them. Some were chained at their oldened spines, and others were so brittle that he imagined a single touch of oily flesh would disintegrate them.

Leif was where he'd always wanted to be, and he loved every second of it. The smell alone, almost enough to alleviate all the weight of responsibility – of dread. But Isla's tutting brought him back into reality.

Walking amid books numbered in the hundreds of thousands, Leif rounded numerous varnished corners and cobwebs, until he'd spotted a desk with a bonsai tree.

On it, he glimpsed scattered pages – notes – on the eastern advancements in the west. More parchment was half-revealed from within a slimline drawer of a florid composition. Particularly, the sketching of an eclipse and something written in Sandscript beneath it in a red ink; a viscous ink.

Brushing them aside, he reached for a tome that bore no heading or name. There was no design as captivating as what'd bedecked the Codex, and yet there was folded parchment jutting out of it like he'd done when translating in Falls Creek.

A marker to remind you of certain words.

Heartrate quickening, he opened it, studied it, revealed what he'd sketched in Hotham Heights, and then placed it on the plain tome's pages to compare them with what was recorded. Closing the book with a short inbreath, pressing the sketch between the pages, he smiled.

"This is it," he said and looked at Isla. "This is it."

"Are you sure? You're one hundred per cent?"

"Ninety-nine, I'd say." He opened it again. "Whoever's desk this is," he took the red-inked page and handed it to Isla, "they were translating Sandscript, too."

"A varangian?"

"Couldn't say for sure, but possibly." Leif pulled out a seat and removed his gloves. He hunched over the tome. "Estrid's first, and then the Codex."

Hours passed them by as he'd got to work, and the pinkish-purple shades of sunrise, complemented by the sporadically golden clouds, overtook the silver glow of moonlight.

Isla remained, not saying a word, and glaring at the red-inked page. Leif worried about her; about the scarring; about if she could do what they were meant to.

He wondered if she felt the same dread.

Nobody had rushed them yet, and no varangian had entered the Archives. Seemed that nobody, but one, had done so in recent years. So, he continued, struggling to translate the runic alphabet. Sandscript had been the most difficult language he'd worked on. But in that moment, with his sister at his side, Leif knew that he could do it; that he was capable. He wholly believed it so.

The runes' edges and corners that were never exactly ninety-degrees, always slightly off, made sense to him. The loops and circles, that were similar to a square spiral, becoming nothing more than another letter. Punctuation was the most difficult, as it was absent entirely, yet when making sense of sentence structures and syntaxes, he was confident enough to add his own where he'd felt necessary.

Sat within a spruce chair with a low back, unable to slouch and rest his aching neck, Leif pored over Estrid's runes and cross-checked them back and forth. Amid it, the Archives' stale air made him sweat. Leif likened his work to sport of the mind.

Dabbing his brow, he stretched and wiggled his cramping fingers. Wrists aching in their stiff position. Yet the oddest of all that he couldn't shake or wiggle away, was the feeling that the knowledge before him was somehow ascending from the page and intermixing with the light of his eyes.

Physically, he felt it feed into his pupils.

In the thick of that peculiarity, the Archives' tapering, grandiose windows allowed the eventide light to spread itself richly along the cold, stone walls and highlight Leif's work in a reddish hue. Almost a day had passed, and still they were undiscovered. Yet at the tail-end of the day, lips dry and with exhausted eyes, Leif had accomplished his task.

He'd translated the runes.

Bringing his notebook close to his face – so used to doing so when he wore spectacles – he smiled a full gap-toothed smile.

"You've done it?" Isla yawned and stretched, coming up from her nap on the hardwood floor.

Leif pointed to the sentence and said, "'Conduit, your other half awaits you beneath thespians and coffee.'"

"Thespians and coffee?" Isla knitted her brows.

"Yup!" Leif beamed in a boyish glow. "Although..." he felt his cheeks twitch, and his shoulders ease. "Doesn't make much sense, does it?"

Receding into his mind, Leif bit his thumb. Pondering, he deflated and fell back into the low-back seat.

"Well, hold on, what do the quarantine passes say?"

Quarantine passes? That's it! Leif shimmied forward and flicked through the notebook until reaching the title page. There, where he'd written his name years ago, were the four passes he'd taken. Two were for Coventry and two for Deacon. *Thespians and coffee,* he thought again, glaring at the remarkably forged seals.

Coventry, and then Deacon; Coventry, Deacon, and then back to his translation. Thespians and coffee. A theatre. A café-theatre. Leif leapt from his seat and grabbed for Isla's hands.

"The café-theatre in Deacon! She's beneath the café-theatre! Jeu de Café, Isla! Jeu de Café!"

After sharing a hug, Isla handed Leif the Codex and pointed to the spell they needed. Kissing her on the cheek, he got stuck back into it. It didn't take him long to transliterate the spell, however. Not after he'd become accustomed to the language.

Again, feeling the words and language feed into his pupils in a queer, sludgy manner.

"We're all set." Tearing the page from his notebook, Leif handed Isla the transliterated spell. "Now, we need to go to Deacon. Once we find and kill Keziah, we'll be free to re-surface magic without worry of aiding her plans. Two birds, one stone. Maybe then I can avoid possession."

"Sure, but how can you know that she's there now, or that she'll be there when we get there?"

"Think about it." He donned his helmet and gloves. "She's nowhere else to run. Her own lieutenants said she was weak. That ring is eating away at her day-by-day, or even quicker. She's on the ropes. Plus, I reckon that she'd always return there. Proud as she is, Keziah will want to make sure that her plan worked. That I translated the runes she'd instructed to be left for me. She wants me there."

Isla clapped Leif's pauldron with an open hand, "For Mother and the Albergs... for Velyn."

"For vengeance!" He hugged her again. "Isla, she's taken everything from us... and for that, she'll pay. Though the journey between Deacon and Coventry is long, and I'd rather get there sooner than later in case she's anything else up her sleeve."

"True." For the umpteenth time, Isla looked at the creases of her palms. "I'd teleport us, if I still had a Familiar."

Separating, Isla wrinkled her nose as he remembered her doing, and Leif bit his thumb. Dragging his feet, he found himself at those grandiose windows. Coventry's cityscape was distorted by the stained-glass imagery that bedecked them almost entirely, and again by the consistent smog and hearth-made smoke that'd lingered. If he didn't know any better, he'd think fire spread throughout the mana-lit streets of a modern society.

Seeing that, seeing the smoke plume into coiling clouds, he pondered; physically feeling an idea brewing.

Packing the Codex, his notebook, and the tome into Isla's travelling bag, the idea bashed through all other notions and presented itself. "Fire." He clicked his fingers. "Your Familiar... a faedragon. A dragon. Isla, Ghulzar! Find the Searwood and we find a *flying* dragon. Deacon here we come."

At the door, Leif held out his hand for Isla. Pocketing the red-inked page, she took it. Turning the handle, a clap from behind halted him from stepping over the threshold and making his exit. Another made him release the handle before the final one forced them both to turn around.

Isla drew the black-bladed rapier and pointed it.

The two stood a distance apart from a woman in shadow; Leif and Isla at the entryway kicking at a creaking floorboard, whilst the stranger leant against one of the many tall bookshelves and dusted it with her long fingers. It was a casual lean, although her tallness made it awkward.

It was her hair, however, that'd given her away. As strands of it – a shadow to Leif – were dangling from her mouth.

"Your Majesty?" He assayed and squinted to see through the darkness.

"To be amid these old, dusty books soothes me; helps me escape this world," she responded. "When I'd arrived here, bringing with me the technological advancements from the east, I was coveted as a beacon of advancement. Mm, but as the Rimatheans I soon ruled saw beyond the gifts I'd brought along with the changes to their Imperium – a change of title from imperator to empress, they saw the real me. The colour of my skin, and the shape of my eyes... they'd changed."

The Empress inspected the dust particles on her fingers.

"Contemporary edifices erected in a heartbeat, mana spreading like wildfire, and the people celebrated. They lauded it. But not me. Mm, never the Empress."

"That so?" said Isla, lowering the blade and holding up the red-inked page; obscuring Leif's view. "Is that why you studied Sandscript, sacrificed your flesh, and stole an aenyr weapon? Is that why you summoned the Emerald Eclipse? You wanted magic re-surfaced so you could rule with it." Isla looked at the page, "*Seud alqamir alkadhari. Amjad waeadu basahr.* Did I get that right?"

"What?" Leif's heart fluttered.

The Empress scoffed, hobbled forward – a disability following the assassination attempt – and revealed herself in the scarlet light. It glinted off her filigree mask and painted her in the colours of her homeland. The dragon design on her robes accentuating her heritage.

"Mm, magic can never rule, only serve." She shook her head and sighed. "And no, that's not why I summoned the Emerald Eclipse. Although I'm quite proud of you both. The Dyad together. Mm, finally. After using blood magic and sacrificing..." her hand trembled and floated ahead of her mask. "As for the rapier, Basem's sister entrusted it to me when I'd briefly returned home."

"To liberate her? Great job, *Your Majesty*, she's still a bloody captive!" She turned around, Leif seeing her ears turn redder by the second. "Her people have our great-aunt. They're—"

"—channelling her magic to generate mana." Leif nodded, rounded Isla, and doffed his helmet. "Why'd you do it?"

The Empress shrugged, "To see the scientists answer to the injustices performed on helpless Mystics; to live among like-minded magic folk that don't look at me as if I'm different." She looked over Leif's shoulder to Isla, "Mm, it was your father that'd told me of the prophecy that day he'd brought you to my chateau, Isla. Do you *remember*?"

She took a book from the shelf, ran her hand down its cover, opened it to the title page, and slotted it back into place. The Empress then tapped her slipper on the keyhole Leif had spotted earlier. A mechanism clicked beneath their feet, and the thin keyhole deepened.

"He'd told me that there'll be a day when his silver-eyed son would return with his daughter of ashen hair – not red as I knew it. Mm, that's why I let you stay in my chateau; that's why that blade," she pointed to what Isla wielded, "*accidently* cut your leg at my party. I needed to know for certain that you were the silver-eyed Conduit. That you've the healing hands. Mm, wasn't expecting an assassin to show up."

Leif didn't know what to feel. Everything up until that point had appeared preordained. Known ahead of time. What'd happened then felt like a long-winding play of fools. As though he was merely a piece on a chessboard to accomplish another's goal. The Empress' want, and not his own. Remnants of the conversation between the lieutenants then came to mind. They'd hired an assassin before killing the brothers three.

Was that also preordained? Leif twisted a coarse moustache hair between his fingers. *What isn't?*

"Look, you two, your mother and father knew what you both were. Mm, they prepared for it."

"And you believed him?" Leif flailed his arms in disbelief. "A random blacksmith, and you took his word for it?"

"Mm, he'd provided enough proof." She straightened her back and appeared as tall as the bookshelves. "Asked me to cast a spell on Isla, knowing what I really was, to help her forget what she'd heard. To live a normal life until the day prophecy claimed her. Mm, claimed you both."

Leif, so overwhelmed by feelings that his skin itched at his neckline and his gorget warmed, shuddered. Yet as he'd attempted to ask her another question that might rid him of the bottled and confused emotions, the Empress held up her slender, bejewelled hand.

She curtly shook her head.

The way she'd carried herself was beyond graceful, regardless of her awkward lean. There was a certain air about the Empress; an elegance unseen if you only read her on the surface – judged her physiognomy. If you only saw her disfigurements and deformity. An air of nobility flecked her every move, which she was powerless to escape. Not arrogance, although it was present in her mien, but something else.

Through that, Leif adhered to her want for brief silence.

"Open it." She broke what she'd sought and pointed down to the keyhole. "With the blade you stole from me," she looked solely at Isla, "place it here, and open the floor."

Leif glimpsed the black-bladed rapier appear at his right, and Isla followed. Holding her stomach, clenching at her clothes, she moved towards the Empress without question.

Watching the sword vibrate the closer it got to the keyhole in the floor, Leif shook his head.

Slapping it down, he disarmed Isla with the flourish he'd seen Aivor perform during their Danse Macabre training. Then, shifting his foot, Leif took the hilt into his hand. Yet regret knocked him down a notch as his gloves combusted aflame.

The pain was exactly what he'd felt when the blade touched his leg at the party. It burnt through his flesh, tantamount to a scorching needle piercing skin. Refusing to let go of it, however, he staggered. Tears welled, and the palpitations of his heart made him wish to concede, but he hadn't. Reaching the smirking Empress and keyhole, his lip twitching as he cried in pain, Leif stabbed down; screaming in a want to be rid of it.

Pulling away, he collapsed to the ground. His hands were all but ruined before whatever gift coursed through him, ridded him of pain. Although the scars remained, as Isla affirmed, tracing them with her quivering finger while she chastised his heroism.

The similar mechanism that'd clicked earlier did so again and jolted them. The Empress stood to the side, adding more strands of hair to her lips that remained contorted into a smirk.

Quickly helping him stand, Isla and Leif scooted beside her.

Together, they'd watched the hardwood fold in on itself to reveal a circular and large room beneath their feet. It wasn't Ghulzar's home, but it housed something grand. The firmest boughs jutted out from a humungous trunk made of a striking wooden grain. Its leaves were greener than the highlands in winter, and its roots that'd twirled from amid stone and soil pulsated as if an artery.

A Searwood. *The* Searwood. The first to plant its roots.

"An unshattered crystal heart?" Leif leant over the edge that continued folding into the room's corners. "Still alive and thriving at the heart of Rimathea. I... I can't believe it. I'd only ever heard rumours of its demise."

"That's why there's no mana in the chateau," said Isla to the Empress. "If there was, you and your Searwood would've drained it entirely."

"Contrary to Falls Creek's," Leif said.

"Falls Creek's didn't drain anything because it was kept alive by the thaumaturgical soil, which, although magic, is too faint and isn't sentient to confirm itself as magic," said the Empress. "Mm, that's why you don't drain anything, Sir Leif. That's why the sword burns you."

The tree's height appeared to exceed even the modern edifices tightly erected in Coventry, and it'd seemed like The Horn had grown over it with time; further hidden by the chateau's construction thousands of years ago.

"I'm no Mystic." Leif stepped away, feeling the vibrations of the Searwood's aura. The same felt around Falls Creek's but far more intense and dangerous. "I'm not like Isla or yourself."

No matter how far he'd retreated from the aura, however, its intensity increased. Brushing by the two women, staggering against a bookshelf, Leif felt the weight of his armour for the first time since donning it. Felt constricted by it, as though it was choking him – tightening with every inbreath.

Wiping the sweat from his brow, he took deep breaths. When they didn't work, he ventured for shallow ones. And when those too failed to offer him succour, he'd floundered and sobbed.

"You're a Mystic, Leif Morrigan." the Empress held Isla's shoulder. "You're an equal to your sister, and you need to accept it. Mm, to stand in the Searwood's presence, you need to acknowledge that."

"I'm burning," he panted.

"Acknowledge what you are, and all will be fine," she said.

Isla approached, slapping away the Empress' hold. Leif searched her for support, and yet she nodded. She'd heartened him in favour of the Empress' goading.

Biting his dry lips that'd felt sunburnt and raw, he closed his eyes and looked deep within himself – searched quickly – for the recesses where he'd found Isla that night in Falls

Creek. Only he'd pursued himself in the dark. For a place in the void beyond reality where his conscious drifted.

There, he'd spotted a reflection of himself beneath the floating alphabets, runic or otherwise, and reached out. In reality, his skin boiled. He smelt his hairs burn; his beard being singed. But within that queer scape of mysterious occultism exotic to him, Leif appeared hearty and specially composed.

His mirror-image had accepted him, and he it.

The tawny-skinned hand Leif had held dissolved into a translucent stencil before shifting and twisting – melding with his own. They were one. Infused. A relief washed over him, but as he breathed a sigh of relief, a warmth reddened his raw cheeks. Though it wasn't the same intense heat he'd felt before.

He'd returned to them a new man.

Rising, he'd passed Isla and the Empress without acknowledgment and approached the rapier that'd remained in the keyhole. He then withdrew it with another mechanical click.

A sensation crept up his fingernails, into the crease of his palms, and seeped into the pores of his skin.

Leif absorbed it.

Something groped his heart – restricting any pulsation or secretion. Then, at the back of his mind, voices. A stirring in his stomach began, overwhelming the dread that'd sat there.

Leif looked down at himself, brushing his armour that covered his abdomen. Whatever was within him, whatever stirred, it was strange.

"The Calling." Isla shivered and cringed. "You feel it now."

The voices sounded a thousand in number and arrived sooner than Isla's had. They urged him to fulfil the prophecy – their want aligning with his own. His fear of sacrifice lessening as the voices encouraged it; they promised they'd be there every step of the way. They promised. They promised.

"Good." The Empress pointed at the Searwood, inhaling the scent of flora that'd permeated the still air. "Now, get to work."

Retreating across the empty space above the Searwood by way of invisible, floating tiles that'd highlighted rectangularly when her slender foot touched them, the Empress hadn't looked back at the Morrigans. Not once.

"Wait!" Leif held the rapier up to her. "Don't you want it?"

She shook her head, finally letting the strands of hair fall from her mouth, "My part in this tale is complete, Sir Leif Morrigan. I've done my duty, and now the two of you must do yours." She opened the door and peered out, lending an ear to the faint breeze that'd drifted through, "Sounds as though my varangian are missing me."

"But it's yours." He nodded to the black blade.

"No, it's not." She scoffed. "Sir, that's the sword of your forebearers. A sword of legend. And now that I think about it, I'd like to imagine your great-aunt foresaw this moment; knew that the day would come when I'd surrender it to you." She smiled at the Searwood, and not them. "So, keep it. It's yours, after all."

Grabbing at Isla's hand and eyeing the Searwood, Leif sheathed the rapier at his waist. Alone, they waited, and the door's hinges creaked and moaned. The Empress had left them.

With the aura's vibrations to remind them of their purpose, Leif felt the rapier's azurite convulse. Almost like it was rejecting him and wanting to flee.

He felt it pull in the direction of Isla's necklace.

Looking at her, at her once-red curls that'd become almost entirely ashen, he pondered the azurite's purpose and if Ghulzar still bore his own. If that was how he'd communicated through Isla's, Leif wondered why he'd yet to hear the dragon's voice.

Wondered if going to Ghulzar was the right choice.

It was the only choice.

"We've got this," he said, squeezing her fingers.

XIX

⚮

Scourge of The Horn

Descending to the ancient hill beneath the Archives, the Searwood's aura grew intense. Akin to what'd happened in Falls Creek, the tree rejected anyone on approach – Mystic and Laic alike – until it felt otherwise. Winking at Leif and gesturing onward, although her skin felt to be melting, Isla knew what they were in for when reaching the bark.

Leif stumbled, and Isla caught him by the arm before he'd collapsed. Beyond his helmet, glowing eyes searched Isla. As she held him, she felt a surge of power travel through their bodies – although separated by armour and clothing. She heard the voices of the Calling whispering to her brother; they encouraged his sacrifice.

Straightening him, patting down his surcoat, and fingering the sapphire crest she'd once coveted and longed to don, Isla pointed forward. The pain was becoming intense, yet neither of them chose to express that. Isla wanted to be Leif's pillar, and looking into his mystical eyes, she knew that he wanted the same for her.

However, she believed that she'd already failed him. Promising that he wouldn't die, that the sacrifice needn't happen, Isla had no idea how to circumnavigate it. The Conduit's purpose was to die as the Harbinger casts the spell. Thus, the pain from the aura's resistance served as penance in her mind, alongside the Calling's torturous cramps.

By the tree's remarkable bark, seeing the crystal heart rotate afloat in the perfect hole in the trunk, the heat didn't cease. The sweat blinded her, trickling into her eyes and stinging them.

What're we doing wrong? Isla hunched over, hands on her knees. *We've accepted what we are. We know what we've to do.*

"But are the Dyad whole?" said an implacable voice.

Leif, evidently hearing the same thing, closed his eyes, removed his helmet, and inhaled deeply. The half-smile that'd enriched his countenance said he knew something she didn't. It bugged her. However, unable to dwell on that annoyance, and as if struck by a mace to her chest, Isla fell backward, tumbling down the hill before a flood of emotion drowned her in a hefty deluge of pain, sadness, and all else.

The bond between them had been reopened, but it'd felt different. Better than before. After the initial hit, it no longer irritated the heart. Isla rose, ran to Leif, and hugged him.

A burst of energy shot through her, reaching her fingertips and toes, and tingling them. No longer feeling what her brother felt, instead feeling whole.

When the heat had expired, accepting the Morrigans as the Dyad, she cupped Leif's cheeks and asked him to click his fingers. He did, and they watched a flame come to life between forefinger and thumb. Doing the same, she joined it with her brother's and the flame grew brighter and stronger.

It reached up and billowed between their noses.

"A spell?" Leif gasped and dropped his helmet.

"No," she smiled and watched it tumble to the bottom of the small hill, "but we'll get there. Together."

Inches from the Searwood, Isla reached for its white bark – not blackened by rot. Her slender fingers being zapped by the current that ran through it, stronger than Falls Creek's. Leif's tawny-skinned fingers did the same, and together they drew that current into them.

Glaring at the rotating crystal heart which pulsed, a leaf sprouted between their hands; it'd grown into a twig, a branch, and soon a bough that'd separated them. Peeking beneath it, they reached for each other and held hands – their other still on the tree's current-filled bark.

"Get ready," said Isla. "This is it."

A saturation of colours took over everything, creating a vibrance unlike anything Isla had seen. It grew brighter, stronger, and she felt it. Felt the change in the environment, the difference in the air – stifling at first, and then humid.

Brightness became all, and white was all she could see.

She gasped, Leif squeezed her fingers, and rivulets of muted colours trickled down the obscenely bright white that had once been everything. Then the sepulchral darkness she'd been so used to amid spells of teleportation surmounted all else before a frigidness conquered her and robbed her of her senses until she heard... dripping.

Water dripped and the ripples of a still lake were disturbed by a heated and strong wind that'd whistled across the surface of whatever had surrounded them. Stones, she'd guessed as the rigid rock underfoot were icy and felt to burn her leathery soles.

Another breath, and the stones were warmer.

Ghulzar, she shivered and walked on, unable to see barely anything, but keeping a hold of her brother.

"We're inside The Horn," said Leif.

A strobing light attuned to the heated wind – a breath – then momentarily displayed the undercroft of sedimentary rock. Before them was a vast and black lake, hundreds of metres beneath the chateau – far grander and expansive than what Pelmora had offered. That light, however, died before returning brighter and warmer.

The Horn was hollow at its core. It bore no safe exits, save for a tunnel above which Isla barely made out when the light was at its brightest. Without magic, or Ghulzar, they were trapped.

Isla saw the canals created from the black lake leading their way in various directions to amplify the beauty of Coventry; and at the stygian expanse's centre were tall white trees. Their narrow trunks were warped and crooked, but straightened when nearing wherever the cavern's enshrouded ceiling was. Leafless and sporadic as they were, they were in abundance.

Sparking and spitting scars of lightning, they were familiar to Isla. Akin to the Searwood's white bark, they were its roots. Its recreation of nature ran deep and prevailed long after its race had faded into obscurity; remembered only in discarded history books that'd better served as coasters to a wayfaring mind.

The light had once again ebbed, momentarily enveloping them in tenebrosity; yet when it'd returned, they spotted a long and scaly tail shifting in the impenetrable shadows. It curled around itself and still had length enough to slither beside the rocky corner to their left. Sapphire and black scales served as tightly knitted armour, and blacker spikes of obsidian horns were its gilded applied latten.

"Niece? Is... is that you?" The dragon spoke aloud, its voice booming. Dust and particles shook free from the high ceiling. "Step into the light so I can see you."

Isla's knees buckled, and the cramping in her belly worsened on the request. Clasping at her abdomen, she did as she was told.

"Ghulzar Alpheniq," she spoke in earnest to the armoured tail, "we need your help!"

Rumbling from his belly, she felt him shift and slither through stone underfoot. Isla clasped her ears and huddled into a cold fissure with Leif, feeling that he'd repositioned to face them instead of fleeing – fearful of what that meant for either of the siblings when recalling the ferocity of the creature in her dream.

And she was right to do so. Loose stone from every inch of their immediate surroundings broke free and tumbled. Isla cringed into Leif's arms before he grabbed her head and brought her closer. She felt him shivering.

When the noise subsided, and she opened her eyes, however, Isla stepped out into the returning light to again confront Ghulzar.

Tongue-tied and dry-mouthed, she instead pointed towards the dragon that'd then faced them entirely in all his distinctions as an intellectual.

Dissimilar to her dream in Falls Creek, Ghulzar was regal and carried himself in a way that accentuated his age and wisdom – that savant she'd reverenced. Head held high, even when slithering it to a lower height, and a scaly brow that'd remained in a sage countenance even when he'd leered.

But it was his glowing belly that was the most contrasting to that amaranth beast of nightmares. With every inbreath it became brighter but was snuffed on a warm exhale through his enormous nostrils. It shared an azurite's colour.

"You're not my niece," said the sapphire-and-black dragon. "Unless my eyes have failed me in my years of captivity."

Ghulzar brought his head up. His wide, lengthy, and toothy grin steaming and smoking by the molten that bubbled within him and was secreted throughout his veins. Its faint glow visible in the pitch-blackness that would envelop them.

Then his reptilian eyes focused into slits when looking down at Isla. She felt for her azurite.

"Had you been taller, I could've confused you for her, sure enough. Had I not smelt the Calling in you – in you both – I would've." His grin widened, "Yet you're so alike in numerous regards." He gestured his head at the azurite she fingered. "And you bear her gemstone."

Isla pushed Leif behind her, planting her feet.

"Our story is long, and yours longer, so we'll not bore each other with pleasantries," said Isla. "What matters is our quest. We need to re-surface magic, and to do that we need your help."

Ghulzar nodded, his enormous talons flicking his chains.

"And why should I help you?" He inhaled mightily. "You wear my niece's azurite, you make demands, and yet you offer no decency. A please would suffice if nothing more."

"*Please.*" Isla felt Leif's breath on the nape of her neck as he pleaded. "Please, Mighty Ghulzar, for the good of the Realm... we need to get to Deacon. Without delay!"

Ghulzar rested on his haunches, his wings expanding widely before returning to his side after a curt flap. Leathery and old, they were riddled with holes likened to when a cloud of moths had taken to a cotton tunic in the night.

He didn't say much, but Isla knew by simply looking at him that he knew so much more than he'd let on. That sparkle in his spectacular eyes – like Velyn's – resonating with her.

Her feelings telling her that he knew who they were.

Again, he inhaled, and his chest inflated to unimaginable proportions. His veins glowed their brightest, and his throat became aglow with molten. Fearing a wave of dragon's breath, Isla quickly grabbed Leif and pushed him against the wall, wrapping herself around him. She shielded him.

Isla wanted to protect him, even when knowing that it'd do neither of them any good against an attack.

Anticipating the worst, she cringed into her brother's surcoat and dug her nails into the rockface. But when hearing nothing but the rustle of attire, Isla turned and beheld a robed man in the flesh.

No longer a dragon, but a male of equal height to Basem – almost a twin in appearance, too. A glow remained at his chest. A blue and familiar glow.

An azurite gemstone.

"Now, why would the Dyad need my help? Is it not I who should be propositioning you both to free me?" Ghulzar approached. The chains which confined his ankle restricted his movement whether a dragon or not.

Isla went to speak, but stopped when feeling that Leif knew her thoughts. Or, in a way, understood them.

They were one, but their thoughts were their own. They were one, but still acted independently.

"Because the woman who killed your brother and niece is in Deacon." Leif neared. "In order for the Dyad to do what's needed, and keep the Realm safe too, we need to take her life before she enacts—"

"Enough," said Ghulzar and waved away Leif's words with a dirty hand. "It was rhetorical. As stated earlier, a *please* sufficed. I'll take you to Deacon."

Ghulzar bore no hieroglyphic scars about his body and his black robes and violet eyes – when not reptilian – contrasted against her memory of Basem Alpheniq, who was a colourful man in amaranth.

Jerking back, Isla scoffed, "That easily? And without a word about your brother's death? I don't believe you. There's an ulterior motive here, I can feel it."

"Believe what you will," he sighed, "and I'll believe otherwise." Ghulzar kicked at his chains and waved over Leif in a short but stern motion.

Slapping an open palm against Leif's pauldron, Isla stopped him from going anywhere. Following Ghulzar's line of sight, she saw exactly what he was looking at. It wasn't Leif's armour, or his glowing eyes... it was the rapier at his waist.

The sword of the aenyr.

"Look, however you've managed to obtain my sister's sword, it's the only thing capable of breaking my bonds. Maker and destroyer." Isla kept her hand on Leif, and Ghulzar continued, "You want to get out of here, don't you? Deacon seemed rather urgent a few moments ago."

Leif brushed her off, kicked at the stone beneath them, and then went for the hilt. But Isla – quick as she was – drew it first and raised it above her head. She noted Ghulzar's reaction to it: awed, with his mouth in the shape of an O.

"I've got this," she said.

Spinning the hilt in her palm, Isla spat – disgusted at Ghulzar's dismissal of Basem's death.

She felt the tips of her ears warm in rage.

Clicking at the aenyr in the manner of a mother urging an unruly child to take her hand at a crossing, she aligned herself with the chains. Extending his foot out towards her, he turned away and faced the lake. He bit his thumb as Leif would.

Isla, focusing on those chains, brought down the blade with a mighty roar, creating a blast of light to illuminate the cavern. A force shook the ground and coursed through her body, like knocking on her bones with a chisel – painfully and continuously.

It'd reached her cramping and intensified it tenfold. It felt to bisect her! And then, at once, the sensation shot into her back – her bag, and the Codex – and ceased.

The rapier had cut through the thick, obsidian chains in a single attack. And as the panting Isla brought the hilt up, the blade disintegrated alongside the chains. Slowly, link after link, the massy constraints dissipated, the black blade liquified into deep-red blood, and Ghulzar bowed before Isla in the vein of a gentleman from one of the northern countries.

Another sword, another piece of art, destroyed in the pursuit of re-surfacing magic. Loving metallurgy as much as her blacksmith father had, Isla felt the strongest longing to see steel's preservation, and when looking at the pool of blood at her feet, the blood that'd forged the black-bladed rapier all those many years ago, she wanted to weep.

Approaching, free of his burden, Ghulzar took what remained of his sister's weapon and assessed it. With dirtied hands, he caressed the hilt's intricacies and fingered the pommel, the azurite, in particular.

Panting into her sleeve as she brushed the sweat from her lip, Isla saw him break the gem free like an awful twig from a stick.

Glancing over the hilt again, he then threw it somewhere into the vast and black lake without a grunt or saying.

"Here." Ghulzar extended the azurite towards Leif who was evidently wary, running his visibly clammy palms down his surcoat. "Don't be afraid, it won't harm you since I've told it who you are, and you'll affirm it by touching it with bodily fluid. Your sweat."

Bodily fluid, Isla nodded. *My tears in Falls Creek.*

"An azurite each," said Ghulzar, as Leif accepted the gift. "Without them, we'd be unable to hear one another in flight."

Again, he'd transformed, and before the Morrigans stood the imposing dragon. Spreading his wings mightily, he bowed his enormous head and allowed them both to climb atop it until reaching the nape of his neck. For Isla, it was *too* easy, and yet she mounted the spectacular creature all the same.

In an instant, Ghulzar had slithered up the tunnel overhead and breathed a wave of fire upward. Isla could feel the chateau's ground erupt – felt the rumbling through Ghulzar's body.

The dragon climbed, ordering the Morrigans to keep their heads down through the azurites. Shards of ancient rock and ironwood thrashed against Ghulzar's scales. Isla felt Leif hug her – shielding her from debris with his shiny armour that was dulling. Again, the dragon breathed fire.

Glimpsing the intense undercroft for a final time, and the roots that re-laid the foundations of nature, they ascended.

Reaching the throne room and slithering his large body to fit within it, Ghulzar released a shrilling shriek followed by an amazing roar that shattered all the surrounding glass. The audible gasping and squealing from outside echoing from every direction. Ghulzar turned, destroyed the surrounding archaic stonework in a single swing of his tail, and disintegrated the roof.

The parchment lanterns burnt, remains ascending into the smoky sky, and Ghulzar glimpsed the throne amid the rubble. Rays of light shone down on it and the trapdoor's scattered, broken ironwood. Again, Isla was awed by its beauty. A beauty destroyed as Ghulzar launched at it and obliterated the ancient seat beneath his enormous talons.

Flapping his mighty wings, Ghulzar burst upward to break through what'd remained of the vaulted ceiling.

"*Buuurn!*" she heard him say through her azurite. "For the years you've kept me here, *buuurn!*"

Perched on one of the many domes that made-up the chateau's rooftop, Ghulzar released another roar – this time accompanied by fire infused with magenta particles – and shattered all remaining glass from the city's blocky and tall edifices. Isla tightly clung to a scale as best she could, feeling her fingertips burn as the dragon breathed.

"Hold on, Leif!" She felt his nails dig into her clothes and skin. "Just hold on!"

Isla beheld the golden city; beheld its panic.

The people scurried, and the bells tolled. From the height they were, she could barely make out anybody in the city proper, but those on The Horn ran. They tripped over themselves, and they trampled their loved ones – all to escape the fierce beast that'd toppled the ancient chateau.

"What've we done?" Leif shrieked.

"Fly, Ghulzar!" Isla grabbed at her azurite, screaming into it. "To Deacon. Go! Leave this place before we're attacked."

But the dragon wouldn't budge, and instead he'd redirected his attention into the throne room from whence they'd came.

There, with her filigree mask glistening in the surrounding fire, stood the Empress. She didn't do anything, only stand there, as tall as she was, and watch the three of them above her.

"*Youuu!*" Ghulzar slithered his long, thick neck down into the room. "At last, you reveal yourself to me, snake of the east."

The Empress chortled, "Calm, old man, I only—"

A deafening snap erupted through the air like a thousand ship's firing their canons in unison. Isla felt her ears bleed; felt Ghulzar swallow his prey in a single gulp before shivering. The ulterior motive. She was the very reason he'd agreed to aid them so easily. Isla knew that. It had nothing to do with honour, manners, family, or duty.

"Devil of a woman." Ghulzar smacked his scaly lips together.

"You... killed the Empress. You ate her. Why would...? Are you mad?" Leif punched at Ghulzar's scales beside Isla's thigh. "In your stupidity, you've aided Keziah! She wanted her dead!"

Knights at Ghulzar's feet threw down their weapons and fled. Even the Varangian Guard didn't stick around for long after discovering their Empress' mask ahead of the destroyed throne.

"Dare not label me as stupid again, Conduit. Snakes can't be trusted, and their words less so," he declared, flapped his wings, and took flight into the billowing smoke above. "Now, I'll take you to your quarry in Deacon. Once she's dead, my assassination will seem trivial to you. Once she's dead, you won't even remember the Empress."

Isla dug her fingers into the scales again, cooler when he wasn't breathing fire, and looked behind. The chateau continued to burn, and soon the wildfire of dragon breath would spread over The Horn and into the city proper, if not somehow controlled.

Thousands would die, and Coventry would be no more.

We did this, her heart sank. *For the greater good.*

XX

The Painted Path

Amid the scent of the outdoors, the sound of warbling birds briefly flying in pace with Ghulzar, Leif sighed with a heavy heart. Through the smell of ash and cinder that bitterly lingered, he continued to glimpse the chateau's destruction at the back of his mind – devastating the beauty of Rimathea in his eyes.

Something he'd hoped would someday leave him as he'd grow to believe it was for the greater good.

Isla, however, didn't take her eyes off the Codex.

The intensity of her stare unnerved him. Resting his chin on her shoulder, Leif saw the passage she'd studied so intently. There were illustrations of humanoids becoming stone, and another below it depicted the reverse.

Folding the top-corner of the page, something Leif despised being done to books, Isla flicked to the next. What little was written in Common, although an older dialect, she found it and read it. Sometimes once, sometimes thrice.

"Preparing for the fight ahead?"

"Mm-hmm." She nodded. "You?"

"No." He inhaled through his gapped teeth. "No, I'm trying to justify what'd happened, actually."

Then the voices within, the Calling, reminded him of his sacrifice. A fate he couldn't escape.

I know what I must do, he shivered and spoke to them. *Just not if I've the strength to carry it through.*

"Relax, Leif. To topple Keziah, I'll need you at your best, yeah?" She ran a hand up and down his thigh. "You'll do great. I know you will."

He'd hoped, with all his heart, that that was true.

Looking beyond Ghulzar's enormous, holey wings, Leif drank-in all he could. Relished it dearly. He'd missed the rolling, grassy fields and the sound of natural running rivers, the abundance of flora and fauna that frolicked freely among the fresh, cool air. Humidity was behind them.

With Deacon on the horizon, his thoughts dwelled on the Enchantress. A Mystic he craved to exterminate. So close, yet so far. Taking his notebook from Isla's bag, he ran a hand down his collection of quarantine passes before spotting the monstrous obsidian chains that kept the floating islands at bay.

Ghulzar began his descent as the wind caught beneath the Codex and notebook's pages and flicked them to a close.

"Brace yourselves for landing," Ghulzar said through their azurites. "I'm a little rusty."

Having fled Deacon on worser terms than he had Falls Creek, Leif worried about re-entering the city. Looking down at himself, however, he imagined sentries and citizens alike wouldn't look beyond the multi-coloured armour and sapphire crest on his breastplate. The uniform is what mattered, and it'd allow them freedom in the streets.

Moreover, word wouldn't have reached the north concerning the chateau's destruction and Empress' death. Had it, though, then they'd experience neither freedom nor welcome, only a jailcell and three lukewarm meals a day. At best, they'd muck out the stables as civic duty, regardless of armour.

Following a less than stellar landing, Ghulzar let them off on the outskirts and away from vigilant bystanders, although the screams of terror said they'd been spotted, and took off without delay. Neither explaining where he'll go nor what he'll do, he flew en route for Enkhara.

Watching as he'd evanesced into nothing but a speck on the horizon Isla retrieved the transliterated spell from her bag and pocketed it, whispering to herself. Whispers concerning a promise and Falls Creek's Searwood, or so the little he'd heard pertained to. Taking her hand, he squeezed it. Returning that squeeze, she'd retreated from him and awaited their next move.

Leif looked at Deacon, fingered his sweaty and singed beard, and advanced on the city.

Arriving at the gates, Isla attempted to lead the charge but was overruled by Leif scooting between her and the flintlock-armed sentry. He felt her breath on the nape of his neck, as the sentry removed his barbute helm, unfolded a pair of octagonal, wooden spectacles and sat them at the tip of his red nose.

Carefully and methodically, he studied their faces.

"Hospices are overrun, find someplace else," he nasally said before his eyes found Leif's black-and-onyx armour. The sentry gasped and recoiled against Deacon's walls, pointing at the sapphire crest. "Heard whispers of a dragon, did you, sir?" he questioned in a new tone, but still nasally. "Said to be humungous and sapphire in colour, like that crest of yours."

Leif shook his head. "Rumours, all of it. Merely the sea's reflection, akin to the Emerald Eclipse."

"Nay!" He came closer, glaring into Leif's eyes and squinting at their intensity. "Dragons fly, it's true, and an Emerald Eclipse marks the imminent re-surfacing of magic, sir. My mother told me as much as a lad, and it's what I've passed on to my children. When an emerald aurora borealis dances amid sunlight, that's when we'll know the deed is done. Surely, a man of your stature—"

"An aurora borealis," Isla interrupted with a wave of her hand. "Flesh roasting beneath its emerald glare..."

Turning to face her, recalling the rumours overheard in the mushroom holt, Leif didn't know what to say to that.

"Sentry," he said instead and produced the quarantine passes from his notebook. "Take us to the café-theatre."

"Impossible, sir, I can't leave my post." The sentry pocketed the passes, surveyed the sky, and quivered. "But I can point you in the right direction."

Leif and Isla stalked intently through Deacon to reach the café-theatre. To reach Keziah.

Weaving through crowds panicked by whispers of a dragon, they descended a knoll before making two sharp lefts and a right and came to a crossroad. Taking another right after that, they found themselves beside the river Argolia.

From where they stood, Leif could barely perceive the snow-white manor where he'd stalked the commandant to.

Isla hollered for him and pointed at the river that flowed; sullied at a certain spot in the distance and beneath a building. Leif recognised it as the café-theatre. That's when they noticed the pluming smoke coming from beneath it too, its ash intermixing with the sewage.

"Keziah's doing?" Leif assayed a guess.

"Undoubtedly. As powerful as she is, she can sense our presence in the city. She knows we're here, and is drawing us in." Isla locked eyes with Leif. "Come on."

Advancing towards it, brushing shoulders with frenzied civilians, Leif held Isla close to him.

At the entrance to the sewers stood several sentries all attempting to see through the opaque clouds to no avail. Wherever the flames came from, they couldn't douse them. The building atop it, the café-theatre, untouched and with nobly dressed men with terrific moustaches pointing their canes and raising their brows. The aristocracy.

So, this this where you're hiding, Leif thought as he approached the sewers, and struggled to breathe amid the polluted and dreadful air. *Is this where we end your campaign of terror, Keziah?*

Looking back, he saw Isla clench the Codex close to her bosom. She smiled at him, yet Leif couldn't shake a horrible feeling that wreaked havoc on his soul. The voices still spoke to him, and the Calling still stirred. Giving her a half-smile in return, he gestured his head onward and through the smoke.

Acquiring a lantern and a wish of luck from a sentry that offered no argument to their entry, the Morrigans carried on. Following their entering of a second tunnel, however, it all appeared too similar. Infested with rats and a stench which reeked of dung and hot compost, smoke obscured Leif's vision, and a fear of the unknown unnerved him enough to perspire into the already putrid water beneath.

The miasma reached its uttermost foulness when nearing an unmoving lump. Three armoured husks, each possessing a stately vambrace, were tossed into a pile atop one another. The commandant and his lieutenants.

So, this is what loyalty to Keziah buys you in death? Immortality my arse.

Sidestepping them, guiding Isla behind him, Leif carried on.

Near enough to the maligned corpses, he'd ordered a halt before a crumbling brick wall and brought the light upward in a struggle to perceive what was ahead. Appearing plain and simple, before the smoke dissipated momentarily, the wall revealed a set of glyphs which would highlight one-by-one and then extinguish.

Aside the glyphs, a set of spear-wielding statues.

"I've seen these before," he said. "In Father's smithy."

"Good. That means we're in the right place."

Leif nodded, reaching out towards the wall.

Then a light akin to a new dawn – had the dawn been magenta – washed over the Morrigans and highlighted the tunnel. It came from the glyphs; from his hand nearing them. Examining closer, Leif saw the Sandscript runes all bunched together. Exactly like his father's smithy.

Retrieving the plain tome from Isla's bag, he skimmed over many a page, and then aligned exactly which rune correlated to which glyph. Hastily, and excitedly, he translated them and spoke those glyphs aloud. Although in Common, the wall acknowledged him with a distant ding.

"You did it!" Isla clapped.

The water at their shins drained, gushing in the direction of the wall, as the smoke had also been vacuumed into it and the lantern died. The cacophony of gushing water intensified with the churning of granite against clay as the old, mossy statues turned to one another and touched spear-tips, creating an arch over the magenta glyphs.

A rippling image of another world was then revealed.

"A pocket dimension," said Leif, discarding the lantern and placing a foot within the magical world. "A well-dressed hobgoblin peddling pocket dimensions," he recalled in whisper.

It felt peculiar, like breaking through the skin that'd form on milk; keeping that gelatinous feel on you no matter how often you shook free of it. But keeping his foot within, as he helped the cramping Isla through, it'd felt natural. Like when your body would adjust to a cool pool of water's temperature in the summer.

The stirring within him had then felt calmer, and the voices were pleased – or so it'd seemed to Leif.

Be it spell, or a prayer, whatever it was he said had revealed something that wasn't more tunnels and stale water. An estate with a bizarrely eldritch alcazar sat beyond an enormous, foggy, granite maze. A world within a world. A painted world.

V-shaped, sketched birds swooped overhead and flew off, heading towards Deacon's streets.

"Over there." He pointed and regarded the smoke pluming from its windows. "That alcazar is where we need to go; that Enkharan castle."

The eldritch atrocity sat atop rocky terrain that shot upward on its outskirts, before plummeting downward so deep it'd reach the Hells. Its grounds appeared to bear neither grass nor soil fertile enough to sprout decretive blossoms, or anything edible.

For every tower there was a balcony, and for every balcony there was a gargoyle, crouching over balustrades and above the doorways with an intense scowl that'd fluster the fearless.

A sense of gothic pride permeated from the painted house, even to Leif at a distance; it oozed from every spire that sprouted from the top of a belfry and steeple. And with every flying buttress that inclined on a half arch, there was a pointed pinnacle displaying an inverted pentagram.

Glimpsing the long and oval stained-glass windows which dimly glimmered with yonder candlelight, Leif knew that's where she hid. That was where Keziah plotted and schemed.

Wholly entering the painted world, they reached a greensward dell by way of a brushstroke hillock; the portal behind reforming into brick and fading into the strange blue sky.

Looking up, and where a sun should be at midday, Leif spotted a moon instead with two celestial bodies behind coloured red and purple.

"Look." Isla pointed to the numerous paths that all led to one point before folding in on herself and crying aloud.

"You're in pain. We can stop and—"

"No! The Calling will be sated soon enough. I can do this." Isla forced herself upright with short exhales. "We've no other choice, but to go inside."

All paths were en route for the grotesque maze, no matter which avenue Leif thought to take. So, they entered it.

Birdsong didn't exist in there, nor did a sycamore's subtle rustling, or the whistle of long grass. In there – in the maze – all that was heard was a heartbeat. A continuous thrum, thrum, thrum that'd echoed in the mind.

Leif heard it; he felt it. And judging by Isla's reaction to clasp at her ears and seethe, he didn't doubt she had, too.

A step forward, and the thrum intensified, a step back and it'd lessened. The maze was a death-trap, and it was plain to see for Leif. But still, he moved in.

Three steps in, and a wall shot up from behind to cut off his retreat; to cut him off from Isla. In a panic, he bashed against the wall, kicked at it, and threw himself at it. And he tried that over and over until he was battered and bruised.

When hearing only the voices in his head urging him on, however, Leif looked to the murky sky.

"*Brother.*" There was a hum beneath his breastplate. The azurite. He pulled it out and glared into it, glimpsing his reflection. "*Carry on. Find me on the other side.*"

"Isla?" he shouted at the blue gemstone but received nothing in return. No acknowledgement, no well-wishing... nothing.

Unlike how Ghulzar's voice was projected through it, Isla's was through the mind. Like a whisper. Adhering her wish, he moved away and continued deeper into the painted horror.

The maze's greyness was sickening and dark; Leif swore the plain walls grew faces and sniggered, mocking him. Attempting to glimpse it, his head would snap towards them, yet when glancing at the ordinary granite he saw nothing but greyness.

That greyness endured, far beyond however long his legs could take him before exhausting.

Peering into deep shadow, rounding every corner, Leif hoped to glimpse Isla's pale skin and ashen hair. Almost resorting to prayer. The voices needed him to find her, the Dyad couldn't fail so close to their goal; they urged him to carry on walking, and to never stop.

Their wants aligned with his, thus he walked and walked.

Losing track of time, a bell atop the alcazar tolled and he stopped to shuffle his feet. Then, silently and without noise, a marble statuette emerged from beneath the hard, cold ground. Surveying the thing, focused solely on the finer details and how it captured a human's likeness magnificently, Leif pictured Isla.

Longingly, he'd looked within those marble-grey eyes, expecting to see something, even a smidgen of emerald. But nothing. Was it his sister? He couldn't tell. Not even with his glowing eyes could Leif discern anything other than the plainness that was the statuette.

Is that you in there, Isla? He bit his thumb and pondered.

Addled, and following a small fit of yanking on his coily hair, he decided to wait. He stopped walking. Pounding on the maze's walls, and succumbing to despair, Leif tried pleading to them; he begged them to let him pass and return his sister.

The statuette leapt up with life and took off.

Leif pursued, ducking and weaving, splashing through inky-puddles, and grazing his elbows against the thinner, twisting corridors which'd evolved into his old home. If it was Isla, he wouldn't risk losing her.

The statuette leapt up, broke through the roof, and exposed Leif to the midday moon's brightness in a murky sky.

It continued by running on the rooftop, but as Leif started to sprint after it again, something else had caught his eye.

Encircled in a ray of light was a familiar mandolin being strummed by a yellow-skinned hand. The rest of his body was shaded, but when seeing the outline of furry wings and devil horns, Leif knew who it was. What it was.

"That mandolin was broken."

"It was made anew." The alsheytan strummed the taught strings. "Come now, don't scowl. You got what you wanted, didn't you? My donkey – sorry, horse – helped. I helped. You got to Coventry."

"Helped? You didn't help me, creature. Keziah planted you in our path, knowing we'd walk it. Because of that, my friend was murdered."

The alsheytan chortled, spun the mandolin in his hands, balanced it on his foot, and then kicked it back into his lap and played a bleak tune.

"Say what you will," he massaged the strings with sharp and black fingernails, "I helped."

Leif was getting jittery, and he could feel his hands twitch for something – anything – so he could defend himself. But he carried no weapon and had no idea how to cast magic.

"So, first you *helped* me, and now you're here to stop me?"

The alsheytan rapped his yellow knuckles on the instrument's body, "No. I'm here to guide you. You stopped walking, see? Had I not caught your attention, and you followed that statuette... well..."

"Oh." Leif cringed. "So, you've done your part, and now I need to do mine?"

"Right on." The alsheytan clicked his tongue.

Leif turned around, wary of presenting his back to the trickster, and stopped. "Is this a dream?" he spoke to the painted image of his old home. "Am I dreaming?"

"Well, it's hard to say." He appeared at Leif's side. Clicking his fingers, the mandolin turned into a toy – so small in his hand you could barely see it in the darkness surrounding them. He pocketed it. "Dreams are oft confused for reality, and vice versa."

An archway rose and shattered the twisted reality into shards of muted colours and brushstrokes from a paintbrush. All became black. Stepping through the archway that shot directly into the abyss, the ground returned to a dirt-like texture before evolving into cobblestone, and Leif arrived at the eldritch alcazar.

Ahead was a locked door, smoke sifting from beneath it, and an addled Isla. Leif hugged her tightly. Pulling away, Isla nodded at the lock, not wanting to discuss their separate forays. She revealed the Codex to him. Opening it to a page near Isla's corner fold, was a list with small sketches beside each Sandscript phrase or spell. She pointed to the one that bore a key next to it.

"Not a man of six-foot-three?" He half-smiled and Isla massaged her abdomen. "Give me a moment to transliterate it."

Tearing a page from his notebook with the transliteration, Isla read it. The lock glowed a striking cyan and dissipated like the chains that'd bound Ghulzar. A click, a sigh, and the hinges squealed as the ornate rosewood door eerily opened.

Stepping within the alcazar constructed of a pale-green brick, Leif led the charge into the bedazzling interior of purple and greens as far as the eye could see. The wood had been painted in a vivid, royal purple whilst the leathers of chairs, the carpets, and sometimes the candelabrums were all a muted pale green.

Each identical to brushstrokes on an artist's canvas.

Awed by the peculiar, Leif was directed towards a bookshelf enshrouded in the thick smoke that'd plumed out into Deacon by Isla. Assessing it from afar first, he noticed no scraping marks against the purple flagstones, nor anything to indicate it was a noteworthy or false bookshelf. Thus, like the novellas of his youth, Leif mimicked the fictional inspectors and ran a finger along its timbered sides feeling for a lever, a button, or even a wind from beyond – the smoke had to be carried on something.

On the right-hand side, he felt something tickle his clammy fingertip and be caught beneath his nail. A breath, it seemed, a wind, more likely. A secret entrance.

"Now to find the secret lock."

Real-world books lined the shelves, some with stray leaflets or parchment jutting out from the top or folded beneath them. Leif caressed their covers, enjoying the feel of the leather-bound treasures.

Leif couldn't say that he'd read any of the works, each with names of various authors he'd never known. Mystic authors. All of them were alien to him, and he wondered which he'd enjoy reading – which bore secrets that a raised Laic would covet. And then, near the end of the knee-high fourth shelf was a book he was familiar with.

"Well, well." He reached for it and ran a finger down the spine, feeling the indented title. "*The Enthronement of Daeva.* What's the bet that it's a first edition, too?"

Pulling on it, it slipped out of his fingertips and remained on a lean. A click sounded, followed by the laborious and loud churning of gears, like an old clock that was nearing the end of its lifespan. Jumping back beside Isla, he hugged her close to his breastplate and felt a current course through her akin to the Searwood's bark.

Her pale skin was paler, and her eyes were sunken.

"It's the Calling," she said, pointing to the shelf sinking into the flagstones. "It needs to be sated."

Gradually, a loudness swelled; the sound vibrating his ears and piercing his brain. Louder and louder, it grew more intense. The pale-green stonework beyond the bookshelf turned in on itself and parted to create a passageway. A way forward to a path of darkness. In that darkness, Leif perceived nothing, even with his glowing eyes.

On approach, rows of thin stairs were made apparent – torches that lined the descending handrails combusting aflame when proceeding towards them.

"Right. But how do we sate it?"

Pushing away and leading their way down into wherever the darkened passage led, she said, "I don't know, not for certain. Basem never really explained it to me. So, I'm hoping that re-surfacing magic will do the trick."

"You're hoping?" He scoffed. "What if it doesn't?"

"Guess we'll find out, brother. Come on."

Descending, cyan flames lurched from the torches and into trenches at their feet; they swirled, spat, and gurgled like molten lava. In the fashion of two brooks, that painted fire ran down each stair in unison.

At the landing, rooms and corridors were created before their eyes – confusing them at the behest of the alcazar's owner. Keziah toyed with them in her pocket dimension.

Walls shifted at the knock of knuckles, and flames spread and recoiled at the clap of hands.

The echo of dripping water played on Leif's mind. A relentless drip accompanied by a baritone, whistling wind which made no sense given how deep underground they were. And then the wind found them, kissing their skin with freezing lips; it'd forced Isla to shiver and sniffle, but Leif welcomed it.

A heat was within him, creating beads of sweat to appear on his brow; vengeance was near.

Three linear paths were made apparent before them, diverging like a trident from their feet. Each bore a torch. Between the paths were oily columns of a material unfamiliar to the Realm. Almost an oily alloy that Father would've disregarded as alien waste. Yet it appeared sturdy from the offset, with no hallmarks that'd say otherwise.

At the centre of them, a symbol. One, a pentagram; two, a phoenix; three, water. With no indication on which path to take, Leif looked to an aching Isla for help.

"For someone who wants to be found, she doesn't make it easy," she said, striking a pose, manipulating a hand over her other, and clicking her fingers. "Shield your eyes, Leif."

Doing as he was told, and stepping away from her, Isla cast an encircled pentagram accompanied by the scent of singed flesh and hair. The light from the spell sparked and discharged; rogue flares and molten flying from the exterior ring and sometimes the pentagram itself.

Then, and beneath their feet, an inverted pentagram grossly emerged out from the flagstones in the same pale green of the alcazar itself. It glowed, it spat molten, and it erupted a single line out from its core. Aflame, the line travelled to their left and down the passage.

"The ring has weakened her," said Leif before he'd even thought about taking a step. "Remember that."

"Right. But also remember who we're dealing with." Isla winced, a droplet of blood dangling from the tip of her nose. "Keziah isn't somebody to be trifled with, weakened or not. Be on your guard."

Brushing her nose with the back of her hand, Isla nodded onward only to stumble and be caught by Leif who'd then attempted to use his healing hands on her cramps to no avail.

Apologising for his failure in curing the suffering that'd waylaid her, he led their way down the path towards a candlelit room, and towards an enthroned and leering Keziah.

XXI

Vengeance in Basalt

Chortling at their approach, Keziah ran her salivating tongue up and down her basalt. Her leg was thrown over the chair's arm, and her leather balmoral tapped against the multi-coloured, vivid throne as she swung it back and forth. Unlike the muted pale-green and purple, Leif knew that Keziah wanted to stand out; to draw the eye of any beholder.

Her leer remained, wrinkling her cheeks beneath her beguiling hazel eyes. She would've been beautiful, had her deeds not sullied her visage.

"At last, the Conduit arrives to fulfil his duty." She pouted her lips and saluted him, speaking softly and sweetly, but growling at the tail-end of her sentence. "Tell me, after all your journeying to find little ol' me, are you prepared to die? Prepared to sacrifice yourself?"

Leif snarled, wildly baring his teeth. The voices ceased, the stirring in him intensified. He felt his fingernails dig into his clammy palms. It hurt, and that's what he wanted. This is what he'd wanted. To be in front of the murderous hag that'd stolen so much from him. Kill Keziah, re-surface magic. Die... if that's what it took, and if that's what was needed of him.

Fear of death was fleeting, as were the Calling's voices that'd abandoned him. The voices that helped him come to terms with the long sleep. However, like an unsuspecting wave, that fear would rear its ugly head and nip at his heels. Eternal darkness. Eternal nothingness.

Leif shuddered, shaking his head to be rid of the thought.

A gold goblet sat by her side, the beverage inside tipping over the rubied rim with every swing of her leg. Enkharan wine, judging by the burgundy colour. It'd stained her attire, droplets strewn across her chest and legs. She'd been drinking.

"The Calling stirs. I feel it in you both." She snatched the goblet and sipped. "Poor little itty-bitty Morrigans."

"Murderous bitch, tell me why!" Isla snarled. "Basem said yours was sated once you understood yourself and what you are. I do. So does Leif. So, why?"

Running her tongue along the rim, suckling each ruby until ridding them of the burgundy alcohol entirely, Keziah swung around in her painted throne and tossed the goblet. The clash of metal against flagstone was non-existent, instead sounding identical to a knife scraping against canvas.

"Oh, what a fool." The Enchantress massaged a droplet of wine between her forefinger and thumb, and then licked it. "You know what you are, but you still don't understand. Not fully. Neither of you comprehend your power."

A break in her façade caused Keziah to shudder, her ring finger – darker and more shrivelled than the rest of her hand that'd devolved into deformity – jittering madly. Grabbing at her thin wrist, she squeezed it, focusing intently on the dying finger.

Leif moved forward and half-smiled.

"Magic's taking a toll, isn't it?" he said, peeling his nails out of his palm. "Your stone skin. Your ring. It's killing you."

Keziah leapt from her seat, stumbling down a short dais. Barely able to keep her head straight, she fell back against the vivid-coloured throne and punched it with her jittering hand. The basalt moaned. Straightening herself, she ran the source along her forehead and down her nose. Letting it catch her bottom lip.

She kissed it longingly.

Hair falling in wet hanks around her, moistened by sweat and wine, she queerly quivered and felt for her breasts.

"Death is unbecoming of me, so I'll not die. Not today. But you... you're here to fulfil your duties as the Conduit." She weakly pointed towards Leif, and he noted her aversion to glance at his sister. "Together, we'll do this."

Inches from the dais, Leif felt for the azurite tucked away snugly behind his breastplate. Fingering its design helped him feel grounded. Confident.

As if he'd still bore the rapier at his waist.

Unknowing of their plan, if they even had one that didn't involve the bare necessities, Leif held his hand behind his back and waited for Isla to take it. She did, and they advanced. A foot on the first narrow step, however, and they halted.

Glaring at his boot, drunk on wine, pain, and presumed power, Keziah blew a kiss at Leif and fell back into her seat. The ripples of paint that'd created the room wobbling with the force. Its alien geometry hitherto unseen by Leif, with proportions entirely obscure and claustrophobic, yet vast and wide.

The dripping he'd heard earlier continued alongside other ghoulish noises that would've ceased the beating of a weaker heart.

"For all your scheming, Keziah, your men are dead," he said, "and your plan has failed. You've lost."

"Failed? I brought you here, didn't I? By my calculations," she wiggled her fingers in the air, "that means I've won."

Feeling Isla's hand shift from his, around his surcoat, and against his chest, she moved him back down from the step. Watching his sister's every gesture, Leif readied himself for a fight. Unable to cast – not knowing how – he relied on Isla and her might. She raised the Codex between themselves and Keziah, who simply giggled at the act.

Remembering what she'd said about using the Codex as a shield when battling the Enchantress on the island, Leif moved behind Isla and it, lowering her arm slightly to keep a watch of their enemy. Grasping the basalt so tightly, Keziah's fingers were white with strain; knuckles purple and fingernails pink.

"Is that an offering to me?" She held out her shivering, black hand near the Codex. "And not even gift-wrapped? I'm shocked."

"The only gift you'll receive is the mercy of a quick death," said Isla, her arms quivering with the Codex's weight.

On those words, Keziah leapt to her feet and pointed her blackened hand towards the ceiling. With a blast of purplish-blue light, a thread of lightning tore through the air and collided with the brushstrokes overhead. Swirling, the colours loosened and became watery, before unifying and loosening again.

"By my will, your empress is dead," she said, "I feel it in my blood. Yet you threaten me still in the hope to unnerve me? You can't contest the will of Keziah and Daeva."

Leif crossed his arms ahead of his crest. "Oh, she's dead. But not by your hand or will. Your assassin failed, as did your lieutenants."

The lightning withered to thin slithers in the air as her eyebrows fluttered and bottom lip wobbled. Keziah frowned, glaring up and into the swirling and evolving colours overhead.

"Regardless, the throne is free for the taking. After her return, Daeva can sit the throne uncontested. A Mystic ruling, as it should be."

"A Mystic *had* ruled." Isla scoffed. "You were just too blind to see it. The Empress was one of our own, Keziah."

The raging branches of lightning then devolved into something miniscule. The ceiling solidified into the pale-green and purples, and Keziah faltered in her spell.

"*Keep her talking*," Leif heard whispered through his azurite, although echoing in his mind. It was Isla. "*Talk about her blackened hand. Distract her so I've a chance to strike.*"

Recalling all he'd learnt about Keziah and her quest; he brought it to the forefront of his thoughts. Everything from Daeva, her manipulation of the aristocracy, to her delusions and false identity as the Harbinger to the Dyadic Prophecy.

"Do you know what I think?" Leif ran his hands up Isla's back and stopped at her shoulders, guiding her footfalls as they side-stepped the ghastly throne. "You used your stone skin to inflict fear into your inner-circle – the commandant and his lieutenants. You'd only shown them that form because you needed to keep them in line."

Leif caught Isla's gaze as she turned and looked at him, her hand moving to retrieve the transliterated spell from her pocket. Handing him the Codex and indicating to open it, Leif accepted. Stepping ahead of his sister, he'd opened the book and came to a halt at the marker where Isla had previously folded the page's top-corner – on those illustrations.

Keziah did nothing but watch. Unnerving Leif, she was unmoving; yet the tension in the room was thick.

"You feared a coup because the men that'd served you weren't your own. They belonged to Daeva." Leif paused to gauge the fury in Keziah's hazel eyes. He continued, "Of course, the noblemen needed to see the beauty; drawn in by their desire for immortality and lust of such a *divine* Mystic. But you couldn't risk them seeing you perform your foul deeds in service of Daeva, right? So, you'd done so as a stone-skinned enchantress, that way they'd never know it was you, had they seen you. The beautiful Mystic that promised them so much.

"But you couldn't deliver what you'd promised on your own, could you, Keziah? No, of course not. Instead, you've killed yourself to serve another."

Unspeaking, his quarry stood as still as a mountain; she didn't even blink. Hair wetter than before, almost greasy beneath the room's limited light, and with bags beneath her eyes so dark and wrinkled that she'd appeared ten times her age.

Isla reached over his shoulder and pointed at the illustration of humanoids turning into stone. A paramount spell.

"*When I attack, I need you to transliterate that,*" Isla whispered into his mind. "*And then you need to cast it, Leif. You, not me. Whatever you do, don't let go of the Codex. Channel your magic through it. Make me proud.*"

"Me?" he blurted and lowered the Codex below his chest.

Another blueish-purple blast lit up the room.

Lightning coursed through the air again, and this time en route for the Morrigans. Diving to the ground, they huddled behind the Codex and caught the spell in its ornate cover.

Keziah held the basalt above her head, slithering her tongue around her lips like a headless snake.

Leif peered around the book, and Keziah fired at him.

"I may die to serve another," she'd admitted in a different tone of voice – one less playful and more sober, "but I'm okay with it. Hells, I'd do it all again if it meant bringing back my beloved. Now, burn! Acidic chaos, smokeless flames, drink deep the soul of my enemy!"

Green lights now shot over the Codex and melted the floor beneath them. The paint had liquified again and drew their prone bodies into it. They needed to move, and quick, before it solidified. Crawling, Leif dragged his breastplate through the sludge of colours – still fighting off Keziah's assault.

"Do you honestly believe that? Keziah, Daeva lied to you," Leif screamed over the sound of magic. "She lied because it's what she's best at. She manipulated you, as you manipulated the aristocracy into thinking you could make them Mystics and immortals – that once Daeva had returned, she'd fulfil your promise to them. But you couldn't. Even with Daeva's help, you'd never be able to."

"Silence, traitor!" Leif glimpsed her cave in on herself momentarily as she continued to cast with her blackened hand. "You and I were meant to change everything. Not you and Isla!"

"You and I are nothing together!" Leif pushed the Codex forward, angling it to reflect the spell but instead only further liquified the paint. "Keziah, you were never the Harbinger. Daeva wanted you to let Isla live that night in the forest because she knew what she was... what she'll do. She lied! Your beloved lied, and now you'll die!"

Isla jumped up from behind their shield, clicking her fingers and conjuring a ball of fire above her forefinger. That small ball caught the green, acidic skulls fired at them, and, in a spin, she returned the magic towards the Enchantress. She attempted an attack to evolve out of her staunch defence.

But instead, Leif watched her jolt as her left hand trembled on her abdomen. The cramps were ruining her. Keziah, laughing at the display, kicked her foot up and placed the sole of her balmoral on her inner thigh. Clapping her hands, and creating a queer symbol with her fingers, she unleashed a shield of fire that'd evolved into a deluge of acid droplets.

The miasma of noxious fumes beset the rancid air as the painted room melted.

"This wasn't all for nothing, it can't be! Daeva will return!" Keziah's voice broke. "She'll return in your body, and there's nothing you can do about it!"

The acidic attack burnt through the flagstones, and Isla fell against Leif, at the mercy of the Codex's shielding. That same current still coursed through her. Searching her tearful eyes, and seeing his sister in such a state, Leif knew what he had to do.

Isla needs me to cast the paramount spell. There's no place for want. She needs to reserve her strength to re-surface magic. Keziah's spell waned. My sister needs me.

Eyes trained on Isla, Leif took a deep breath and said, "You've lost, Enchantress! And Daeva won't have my body!" Helping Isla to her feet as his heart fought the break free of his chest, they stood together. "This is for Mother, Estrid, Aivor, and everyone else you've hurt in your quest for power!"

Advancing, Codex in hand, Leif pushed Isla out of the way and threw a fist forward that connected dully with the Enchantress' cheek. Keziah, chuckling, opened her palm and sent a magical yet invisible hand to grab hold of Leif's face; she lifted him up with a crook of her black finger, drew back her other hand that still held the basalt, and thrusted it – shattering the sapphire crest.

A force shot through Leif's body, grabbing hold of his bones and – with what felt like powerful hands flexing them to test pliancy – tried to break every bone in his body. Yet as the sapphires rained down around them, Leif's hardened bones, from drinking the silver blood, saved him.

Smiling a full gap-toothed smile at Keziah, she screamed in Leif's face and tossed him aside into the pale-green wall that wobbled and bowed on impact. Rapping her knuckles against the throne, the room transformed with the sound of old, grinding cogs, and its exit vanished.

With the aid of a wall as soft as canvas, Leif quickly got to his feet and readied himself for another run. But Isla held up a finger to him, her focus entirely on Keziah. She then moved in the same manner as when she'd practice the Danse Macabre. The same watered-down and barbaric take on a Poirdelais' technique.

Although weapon-less, Isla took off her bag, tossed it at Leif's feet, and struck a familiar pose. Mystic against Mystic, Harbinger against Enchantress. Leif wanted nothing more than to help, but physically he couldn't. Mentally, however...

Elemental spells brightly coruscated before him as their foray into the endgame began. Shuffling backward to where the exit once was, Leif leant against the new wall and dove into the bag. Retrieving the plain tome, he aligned it with the Codex and his notebook; he glared at the extravagant and haunting illustration of humanoids becoming stone.

Green flame combusted against Isla's red; lightning then fought against it, and then water. The fracas' odour was ghastly. Like sulphur mixing with the stench of wet dog.

Screeching, Keziah sent forth a curse that overcame the painted room; a curse that'd shrunk Isla on approach and enlarged her on retreat. Countering it, Leif watched his sister cast at the throne and explode it! Sounding more like a tear in material in lieu of an explosion, painted shards flew everywhere and liquified on their descent. Keziah's focus was broken.

Charging at her dazed opponent, Isla kicked at Keziah's visage, but she blocked it without touching her. She attempted a round-house kick, and Keziah punched at her foot.

Hobbling back, Isla caught Leif's gaze and nodded at him.

Whipping out his pencil, he fell forward and crushed the lead against his notebook with such force that he'd almost snapped the pencil in half. Gathering himself with quick in-breaths, he focused on the Sandscript runes. Solely on them, and nothing else. He couldn't focus on anything else. He tried. Needing to check his notebook, he gestured his head; he waved a hand in front of his face – nothing.

Leif had become immovable.

Then the light from his eyes intensified, shining down on the spell. The light shifted to his notebook, and like sifting sand through fingers, the Common letters fell in grains on the page and took shape. Leif, at a loss, discarded the pencil as the light transliterated the spell. A homogenous feeling to the sensation in the Archives, yet in reverse.

When the last letter formed through the grains of light, and the sensation had ceased, he held a finger to his eye. The brightness was gone, his vision unhindered.

The spell was transliterated.

"Give that to me!" Keziah fired at him. Leif rolled away, ripping the page from his notebook, and dragging the Codex along with him. "Don't be a fool, Conduit. You can't beat me!"

Forcing Isla back, and to her knees, Keziah manipulated a hand around the other and clicked her fingers. Like what Isla had cast earlier, a duo of fiery rings were conjured and expanded before her with inverted, pink pentagrams occupying the space between the two rings.

From the centre of them, she again fired at Leif as he shielded himself with the Codex. Stronger and harsher than her earlier attack, the fireballs sought Leif with the intent to kill. Smelling the hair on his hands burn, he felt his skin boil.

At the corner of his eye, Leif glimpsed Isla rise, stagger, and brush her nose with the back of her hand.

"This is for Basem," she said, and manipulated her fingers theatrically before Keziah had the chance to face her and focus her attack, "*aqua pila!*"

Spheres of water projected from Isla's hands, casting a blue glow to overrun the room that oozed muted colours. Hitting Keziah, her conjured pentagrams flickered with whatever strength remained until she'd faltered and collapsed with nothing left to give. It didn't take long for the screams and pleading to begin after that... a pandemonium Leif abhorred.

However, relentlessly, Isla blasted the downed Enchantress.

Keziah squealed until she'd lost her voice and deformed her countenance by digging her fingernails into it. Rivulets of blood streamed from her fresh wounds and down her moist cheeks to intermix with Isla's spell.

Leif watched as the blue water turned crimson.

In a burst of light, Isla relented, and Leif took up the page, tightly clasping the Codex. He looked to Isla, on her knees and hugging her abdomen tightly, panting with exhaustion; and then to Keziah, rolling on her back with pieces of flesh bestrewn about her head; remains beneath her nails, too.

"Cast it, Leif! Feel the words as you say them," Isla groaned, spittle dribbling down her chin. "Words are magical and the closest thing Laics get to magic. I know you know this."

Nodding, he closed his eyes and placed his fingertips on the transliterated spell. In his mind's eye, he envisioned what he'd written. He felt the spell course through his flesh and into his veins. Inhaling, he'd recalled each syllable and shuddered when feeling a coolness run up and down his spine before expelling from his extremities. Opening his eyes, he felt invigorated.

With his skinny fingers pointed at Keziah, Leif's aim was true and complete. Legs not too close together – shoulder-width apart – back straight and strengthened, and a cool in-breath followed by a steady exhale.

He said, "*Asmae hajar!*" And the room grumbled.

As if a street being paved in rapid succession, using magic instead of mortar, cobbles were laid across the air from his fingertip towards his drenched target. They slithered like a viper and groaned like a kyojin. They found their quarry.

Leif clutched the Codex to his shattered crest as the stirring in his belly became a faint glimmer in the dark.

The Morrigans approached the architect of their pain as she lay there helplessly transforming, ironically, into stone as the paramount spell overtook her flesh. Soon enough, the stone-skinned Enchantress would be solidified in her elected façade; confined to the same stone that'd entrapped the magi of Spellforge.

However, unlike those magi, she'd not endure.

Through raspy breaths, Keziah didn't resist. Her arms fell by her side amid the destroyed throne, yet she never released her basalt. Glaring up at the ceiling, she'd wept.

"I don't fear death," she uttered through strings of saliva – the stone reaching her breasts. "No, I weep because I'll never again see the face of my beloved; that I'll not see an aurora borealis dance amid the sunlight. Magic re-surfaced... what a beautiful dream." And then her hazel eyes found the Morrigans as Leif held Isla's hand. "Farewell, Dyad."

The spell crept up her neck, over her lips, into her mouth, and spread to the furthest strand of hair. It overtook her basalt, and whatever pulse of magic remained in it was snuffed.

Preserved in stone, Leif helped Isla to Keziah's side where they both lay a hand on her abdomen. Opening the Codex, they recited a spell in unison. Doing so, Leif felt the magic course through Isla alongside the current and disintegrate the stone statue of their enemy.

Keziah Gaunt was reduced to nothing more than debris and rubble. Her basalt, too.

They'd avenged their fallen.

XXII

The Sough of Wind

All around them, the alcazar declined into ruination. The walls flaked away and tore in half as the floors and ceilings liquified. Leif knew they needed to get out of there, and quick, because like all pocket dimensions the painted world was tied to its owner: Keziah. And like all pocket dimensions, once that owner died, so did that world.

Trying to help Isla to her feet, to again try and ease her pain with healing, Leif was pushed away as she pulled free from his hold. Slamming the transliterated spell down against the Codex, she pounded an open hand against it and wheezed.

The Calling was killing her.

"Your hands don't work on this, Leif; not on magic this powerful. Not on the Calling. So, we see this through as we are. We make do with the hand dealt to us." She cried out in pain as she clawed at her abdomen, drawing blood. "We re-surface magic here and now!"

The ceiling's paint was a pool at their feet, coalescing with the pale-green and purple that'd already reached Leif's knees.

"Isla, why don't you let me cast—"

"No!" she snapped, spittle flying from her lips. "No, Leif. Our duties are our own. You know yours, and I know mine."

Promises were lost in that moment, and Leif bore no hope that what Isla had said about saving him from sacrifice bore fruit. The Conduit must willingly sacrifice themselves as the Harbinger casts the spell. He knew no other way, and neither did Isla. However, it bothered him not. Coming to terms with his task at hand, Leif was ready. The knowledge that his dead body wouldn't be possessed by Daeva helped.

When that little, insignificant fear of the long blackness crept up on him, he'd flinched and bit his thumb. The alcazar groaned and the leaking intensified – the exit opened. Thumb in mouth, it crept up again, and he bit down so hard that he broke skin and drew a mouthful of blood.

You're no coward, Leif, he said to himself. *You can do this.*

Grabbing at him, Isla clapped a clammy hand against the nape of his warm neck and brought his forehead against hers. He watched as her eyes listlessly drifted from his own and down to the transliteration; heard her rapid heartbeat through her thin wrist against his ear.

"*Aeud...*" a blood-flecked and phlegmy cough stopped her. Wiping the crimson from her chin, Leif lifted the parchment and her hand. With bloodied lips, she smiled at him. "*Aeud basahr!*"

A blast burst upward, dividing the siblings, and forcing Leif into the murky depths of pale-green and purple paint. It went up his nose and into his eyes, it burnt his throat as he swallowed. Armour weighing him down beneath the wavelets created from the spell, he struggled on his back and flailed his arms wildly enough to surface his head.

Barely able to make out a sphere of light that tore through the ceiling and transcended beyond the pocket dimension, Leif vomited into the wavelets and rolled onto his stomach and then his knees. Rising to see Isla – Codex in hand – ascend into the sphere, the spell still being cast, he ran towards it only to be flung backward and against the throne's debris and Keziah's scattered remains in an agonising assault on his consciousness.

Attempting to breathe steadily and stay awake – to not pass out   muted, liquifying colours were forgotten and only a blackness remained.

It wasn't death. It didn't feel like death.

Bursting out of the pool and gasping for air, Leif glimpsed the sphere's intensity grow. Its width expanded by the second, and it sparked with every whir it'd exuded. Finding his feet below the paint, the room had devolved into nothing but the distant stars of a handcrafted dimension.

All that'd remained was the exit, and beyond.

As quick as he could, he made his way to it as the floor gave way. The paint gushed into that great void of space, and as it did, he saw it disintegrate into stardust. Drifting and glittering.

Sprinting through the alcazar and out into the open planes, they too were liquifying. The sphere had transcended the dimension and was nowhere to be seen, but the archway remained before him, and then another shot up in the distance on the brushstroke hillock; where the sky parted and opened to the sewers. There, he saw the yellow-skinned al-sheytan wave to him and disappear through the opening.

Jumping through the archway, and up the brushstroke hillock, Leif reached the exit. Glimpsing the pocket dimension diminish into nothing more than a void of space and stardust, he leapt through the exit and into the world he knew.

Leaving the painted world, Leif was once more overwhelmed with the putridness of sewerage and decomposition. What'd accompanied them, however, wasn't the bellowing and squeals pertaining to the smoke that'd once plumed from there... but promises of the end times.

The rumbling that'd accompanied such proclamation's briefly convincing him of their veracity.

Looking over his shoulder, at the closing portal that locked him out of the pocket dimension, Leif heard Isla through the azurite. Not a coherent sentence, or a plea for help. Just her.

Sprinting through the muck that was infused with rubble, Leif felt the ground quake. Overhead, the ceiling collapsed – leaping to avoid falling bricks, he sprinted onward towards the light at the tunnel's end. Towards magic's re-surfacing.

Able to see all that was before him without a lantern's aid, Leif feared the ominous emerald glow that highlighted his path and guided him. He cast his mind back to words concerning an aurora borealis – feared them.

Hugging the curved wall at the exit to the river Argolia, Leif caught his breath as the reflection of emerald light practically blinded him. It projected across his vision, comparable to green lightning tearing through his sight.

The buzz of mana, absent in the presence of such power.

At surface-level, after having crawled out on his hands and knees, Leif gazed at an aurora borealis dancing amid the sunlight – wriggling akin to the dragons depicted in eastern cultures. A phenomenon that disturbed the Natural Order; something usually sought to be done by foul Mystics but was necessary to fulfil the Dyadic Prophecy. The hypocrisy not lost on him.

At the centre, enveloped in the sparking sphere akin to the current that'd coursed through the Searwood and Isla, was his ashen-haired sister. Barefoot, she held a hand upward – irradiating a steady stream of lightning overhead and into swirling, thick clouds – with the Codex hovering at her other. The tome was opened, and, from what Leif could scarcely make out, his transliteration was hovering above it.

Read aloud and cast, the spell wasn't complete.

"Isla!" he called to her, but his voice was lost amid the spell's overbearing din. He grabbed for his azurite and spoke into it. He repeated, "Isla!"

She was unresponsive.

Thus, Leif approached the swelling sphere and noticed that the same hieroglyphs he'd seen on Basem – hieroglyphs that Isla bore on her hand – were making their way across her flesh and reaching her toes. Carving and ruining the alabaster-white, they burnt and seared.

Leif jumped and shouted into the azurite, he pleaded with her to hear him, but she couldn't. Isla was in a trance. Eyes entirely white – either rolled back or overwhelmed by magic.

About them, buildings collapsed and advertisements exploded. A quarter of the town had been reduced to rubble already, and the cracks in the ground that gradually opened with every passing minute suggested that Deacon would soon be nothing but ruins. The snow-white manor was among the fallen, and a break in the river's banks caused the water to flow throughout the ruination.

The stink of sulphur and ash permeated the wild air; the river's watery breeze coalescing with them and the raw sewerage.

People screamed and wailed – they lamented their sins to their respective divines. They bashed into Leif as he stood his ground and watched his sister, fighting with himself on whether to fulfil his duty or to abandon it and save Isla's life.

He'd happily die; he'd happily sacrifice himself, tenfold, if it meant securing a future for her.

Sentries readied their flintlocks, and before Leif could say or act, they were commanded to fire simultaneously at Isla whose curly hair had become entirely ashen.

The bullets rebounded from the sphere and shot back at the shooters. Piercing their barbute helmets as simply as a knife to butter, they collapsed. Dead. One fell off his horse: a battle-hardened mare that reared at the noise but stood her ground as firmly as Leif had.

Shakily, Leif caressed her snout.

Gaze fixated on Isla; he could hardly breathe.

More shots were fired by cowering sentries and old veterans, whom both feared and relished the fight, and those bullets rebounded, too. However, with no targets to fire back at, they burst outward in a spray and found whichever surface they could. Standing still, and without a moment to hide, a bullet tore through Leif's surcoat but barely made a dent in the armour.

The same couldn't be said of the mare that'd collapsed with a wound to her chest. Looking to his nails, broken and dirtied, Leif reached out for the steed – her eyes wide and black. Calmly shushing her, diverting his gaze between the horse and his sister, Leif lay a healing hand on the puncture. And like poison from a wound, he drew the round, lead ball from the mare's flesh.

Arising with the steed, Leif then slapped her rump with the tips of his fingers and sent her away from the destruction around them. To flee with the civilians. Unwilling to abandon him, though, she trotted away and rounded a close corner, knocking away anyone that'd tried to mount her.

Jeu de Café was destroyed by the sphere above it, and the men inside crushed beneath the rubble. Their canes visibly broken as blood drenched the steps leading up to the once ornate doors. The building opposite it, however, which bore the neolyt gentleman that'd doff his hat, still stood. Although barely. The neolyt no longer fizzed with colour or life, and all that'd remained other than it was the façade.

Back then, the jump seemed so daunting. Its distance to the café-theatre too great for Leif. Yet Isla's sphere appeared closer, if not by an inch, then by something less. Closing his eyes, imagining how he'd do it, Leif instead pictured Mother, Estrid, and Aivor. He pictured the way Isla once smiled at him.

Feeling a stony agitation from the azurite that'd glowed and hummed, Leif peered up at its twin that hung from Isla's neck and recognised the same effect in it.

Holding it to his ear, he heard murmuring.

"*Aeud basahr!*" In her trance, she spoke into the azurite, yet her lips were unmoving. "*Aeud basahr! Aeud basahr!*"

Kicking out a brick from the façade and reaching up to a crumbly windowsill, Leif ignored what he'd seen of Isla – of what she'd become – and instead kept that happy image of her in mind. It was, after all, such a pleasant thing.

Resigning to fate, Leif knew what needed to be done. For the greater good, but mostly for Isla. He'd jump. Whether preordained, or a choice of his own, he didn't care. Not in that moment. Leif Morrigan had decided to save his sister, no matter the cost. No matter what happened to him.

Climbing towards the collapsed roof, Leif's fingers sweated on the bricks. Shoes finding an awning's tiles, he kicked at them furiously, traction keeping as they ramped him upward. Reaching the top, he stood tall on the roof's remains and destroyed what little eaves prevailed. Leif neared the end of his road.

The gap was still too wide to reach what'd remained of the café-theatre, but Isla's toes were in reach. Only just.

Edging closer, the crumbling windowsills fell to the road below in a magnificent cloud of dust and debris. They crushed the dead and pulverised what'd remained of civilisation.

Be it life or death, you must do this, he told himself and went to bite his thumb, but stopped himself. *For her, you must!*

With a quick inbreath – an inbreath that he held – he jumped.

Mid-air, Leif projected that image of a smiling Isla on the ashen-haired wraith that floated barefoot ahead of him. With that image in mind, he smiled a full gap-toothed smile.

The sphere neared – his fingers inches from its surface.

Leif searched her visage, but Isla in her trance didn't even raise a brow; however, her hand above the Codex shifted ever so slightly. Magenta ripples corkscrewed around it, shooting from the tips of her forefinger and ring finger. A cantrip.

A crack then rang through every bone, organ, and vein.

Feeling it at first in his head, it ran the length of his body before expelling out of his extremities. He felt weightless – unable to even feel his heartbeat. All fear had left him; extinguished, finally.

Recollection overwhelmed.

Images of his adventure outside of Falls Creek flashed before his eyes. Memories then failed him, but a notion persisted in his dwindling subconscious. Content with his efforts, Leif had convinced himself that he'd done all he could. But he'd lost that image of Isla... her smile. It felt like death.

A final thought before rumination ceased.

What'd remained in finality was the sough of wind and the plash of a distant wave rolling in on sandy shores of far-off lands. Pebbles knocked together, seaweed wreathed driftwood... and an awoken Isla shrieked the grim melody of lamentation.

XXIII

Penance Beneath the

Waves

Isla's consciousness returned to her, and she screamed. Suspended mid-air, she'd flailed wildly and punched at the Codex – the tome that'd caused her grief, pain, and fear – unable to even shift an inch from where the sphere held her. Heartbeat pounding against her scarred and ruined chest, she peered at her once alabaster-white hands and sobbed at the burgundy hieroglyphs that were carved into her skin.

What've I done? She lamented as the burgundy turned to a glowing golden amid the pungent scent of magic.

Leif's body drifted around the sphere, displaying her atrocities to her. Showing her what they'd achieved together. Although unconscious, she felt the magic course through her – the cantrip cast to kill her own brother. Through their connection, heightened by the paramount spell perhaps, she felt his intentions, thoughts, and feelings as clear as when the bond first opened. He'd tried to save her.

She felt the very moment when she took his life.

Frantically, Isla looked around her, above her, and saw that the emerald aurora borealis had danced no more. The scent of magic, however, permeated the air stronger than she'd ever known. The Dyadic Prophecy was fulfilled. The prophecy which Leif had willingly sacrificed himself to save her from fulfilling.

In the end, neither of them could escape their fate.

Water flooded into Deacon; most buildings were razed; and the roads had become rocky chasms that led deep into parts unknown, as the river Argolia flowed into them to create waterfalls. The buzz of mana was absent, as was the screams from the people.

In the distance, beyond Leif's floating corpse, a handful of survivors fled en route for the islands that'd remained chained and undamaged.

Leif's body fell.

Head bashing against a crumbling façade, a neolyt sign fell with him, destroyed his azurite, and buried his remains beneath the razed building's bricks and mortar.

Roaring, Isla punched at the Codex and sent it spiralling away and opened her hand – spreading her fingers – to command the sphere downward. It whirred and shifted, but it didn't move. Bricks tumbled and rolled. Leif's armour was being ruined. Tasting the blood in her squeals from a hoarse throat, as she wailed and flailed, the sphere relented, and she descended to the watery floor of a destroyed city.

Dragging Leif's body out from beneath the rubble, manually and without magic, Isla hugged him into her chest and cried.

She couldn't recall for how long, nor when day had become night, yet endless tears fell and mingled with the blood of her most beloved brother.

Come midnight, when the moons were at their highest, a warm snout had nudged Isla's arm. Unmoved, it did so again. Relenting and looking up from Leif's broken face, she locked eyes with a beautiful yet wounded mare. Isla focused, squinting beneath the combined moons' brightness, and noticed: not wounded, but healed.

Finding Leif's tawny-skinned, healing hands, covered in a blue dust from the shattered azurite, Isla kissed them both longingly and the mare gently nudged his armoured body.

When seeing the Codex, however, the horse reared and trotted backward.

The Codex. The book that was coveted by Mystics – the book that'd saved her life one day and took her brother's the next. A powerful tome that should've never seen the light of day; that should've never left the darkness of Pelmora.

It floated, dry amid the wavelets.

Like the mare, Isla flinched from its cover. She feared it.

"It needs to be hidden." Isla kicked it behind her back as it coruscated with magic. "Buried deep and far, away from passers-by and ahigh the clouds... It needs to be lost again.

But where?" The mare came closer again, drinking the river Argolia's waters that lapped at Leif's corpse. "Spellforge."

On horseback, with Leif behind her and the Codex atop him, Isla and the mare made their way southward. They passed signboards with dead mana-lamps and neolyt, refugees that pleaded with her for help, and a kind yellow-skinned alsheytan that gave her a cloak to hide her scars.

Before moving on, however, that same alsheytan placed a long, black nail against Leif's scarred temple and closed his eyes. Waving a hand, he produced coloured wisps of dust to form a misty rainbow. In it, was then materialised a cloth sheet that enveloped the deceased.

With a half-smile, similar to her brother's which she'd missed, the alsheytan handed her a toy mandolin and carried on his way – an oaken kit beneath his arm.

This can't be... Isla quickly looked about but couldn't spot the devil-horned alsheytan anywhere. *Aivor's mandolin. But how? When? Oh, Aivor!*

All around her, in every direction and zephyr, Isla felt the magic she'd re-surfaced.

On the breeze that smelt of burning timber freshly doused by drizzling rain with a strong scent of cinnamon, through the mare, and through the sycamore boughs she brushed against when entering a strange mushroom holt.

Beneath the glowing gills of looming mushrooms, Isla reached for her abdomen. The cramping had ceased, but faintly, like a glimmer in the darkness, she felt the Calling still stir. She ran her scarred hand up and down the scratches she'd given herself; feared that stirring to grow and return to what it was.

Feared the pain it'd again cause.

Isla needed Spellforge to both bury the Codex and her brother. To learn the wisdom of Mystics. What'd happened to her – the blackouts and trances – was the unsated Calling's fault. She knew that. Fused with her lack of understanding, it'd ruined her and those around her.

Death followed where instead it could've been salvation.

So, she'd learn all that she could – further herself, better herself. She'd become great. Isla would hide herself away from the world until the day she felt ready to face it again.

When she'd never again feel the Call of Magic.

Deep into the holt, she dismounted aside a gypsy caravan full of wonderful creatures and races throughout Rimathea that'd celebrated and danced. They sniffed the cinnamon-scented air like seeking hounds and joyfully quaffed as if it was their last day – yet to many it was the beginning. The start of a new era for magic; the start of a new life for Mystics.

They brazenly cast cantrips and spells in the manner of party tricks, they spoke candidly about Spellforge and returning there for studies. Passing a group of teenagers, they even plainly mentioned Basem Alpheniq and hoped that he was still willing to teach and share his sage wisdom.

The Mystics sung the Dyad's praises – the Harbinger and Conduit's. They drank to latter's willing sacrifice, and they swore to worship the Harbinger for the rest of their lives. Although not a single person there raised the question of all the innocents killed in the accomplishment of magic's re-surfacing.

They were too happy to care.

Yet all Isla felt, and all she thought about, was dread.

Dread over the numerous lives she'd indirectly taken; over the fact that she'd promised him – promised Leif – that he wouldn't need to die.

I promised him... I promised. She cried again.

Fae from the south danced around her head, they dried her tears with silken handkerchiefs of embellished designs, and they told her to rejoice – to revel in magic. But she couldn't. She couldn't even talk to them, although their beauty wasn't lost on her. Reminding her of Velyn, she waved them away and carried on through the increasingly dense crowd.

Passing a circular mirror hung by a caravan's door, Isla tilted her head back to let the torchlight shine beneath her low-hanging hood. An action she'd rued. Wincing at what'd become of her mien and the burgundy scarring that'd covered her entirely from forehead to chin, to her neck, to her chest, and so on.

It was deep, ugly, and it glowed when a spell was cast nearby, or she advanced towards channelled magic.

The fae, however, hadn't cared. In fact, they welcomed her.

Moreover, akin to Leif's eyes after he'd ingested the silver blood of the first men, Isla's irises emitted an emerald glow.

Although not as bright as what Leif's silver-greys had become, they were bright enough to be seen in the pitch black.

Like a feline in the night.

Pulling the hood beyond her brow and scraggly, ashen hair, Isla tied the mare's reins to a log and retired beside a campfire bringing the Codex beneath her cloak and hugging it tightly. She feared it falling into the hands of another; feared ever using its power again. Sated Calling, or not.

Come daybreak, as the Mystics still danced in circles and linked arms, Isla left the mushroom holt's magnificent glow without so much as a word to the celebrators. The fae wept at her departure, and they'd braided the mare's tail in the night. Thanking them with a small nod, Isla carried on.

Though unknowing of her path, the holt guided her through without hinderance or cloud of fog.

On exiting, the mare brought her to the fallen monuments of Hotham Heights highlighted by both the holt's light and the sun. Although crumbled and darkened with lichen, the craftsmanship wasn't lost on a weary Isla. Wild cows wandered and parted so they could pass, chewing mouthfuls of grass, shaggy pelts contrasting against the environment.

Brought to the grandest monument of all, the mare bowed her head so Isla could see why. Beneath it, beneath the monument of Basem Alpheniq, and where the sunlight shone the brightest, was a gravesite marked by nothing but raised dirt, and a set of rocks in the shape of an E.

Dismounting, Isla spent the better half of the morning with Estrid Alberg's grave. Together, they'd cried and laughed; and at the end of it, Isla revealed the toy mandolin handed to her by the alsheytan. Brushing its intricate designs with her rough, scarred thumb, she kissed it and buried it in a small hole beneath the E.

If only in spirit alone, she'd united the Albergs.

Standing at the foot of the mountain, and on the opposite side of where she needed to be, Isla turned to the mare and hugged her snout dearly. The horse's large, beady pupils glaring deeply into her soul as they locked eyes. They'd reached the end of their journey together.

Reaching for the healed wound, Isla instead took Leif's corpse. Weighted and heavy by death and his armour, he fell at her feet in a swirl of dust and a hefty thud. The mare reared at the sound, and Isla slapped her rump, but she didn't budge from Isla's side.

Spellforge was no place for a horse.

Reaching for the vibrating Codex which'd visibly jiggled with magic from beneath Leif's cloth, Isla held it up before the mare – pushed it closer to its face.

Petrified of it, and with an awful neigh, she fled in an opaque cloud and towards the south. Towards a freedom that Spellforge could've never provided her.

"Thank you." Isla watched the muscles at work as she galloped over hillocks and into dells. "And I'm sorry."

A sickness then stirred in her belly. From the moment she'd touched the fabled tome, until then... it'd evolved into malady. So, she hid it in the cloth once more and shuddered.

Arms akimbo, Isla's head became lighter, and the world spun. Exhaling shortly, and inhaling deeply to counter the effect, she regarded the ranges from north to south... and vomited.

Blood and bile coalesced at her feet.

I've killed so many, she chastised herself. *All because of this... thing. I need to be rid of it. I will be rid of it.*

Readying herself to drag Leif's corpse the rest of the way, Isla was halted by a grumble over her shoulder. A grumble which'd spread up through stone and fern. At the foot of the mountain a crack had appeared, and with an inbreath from Isla it opened like floodgates and exposed her to a familiar and pleasant breeze that'd once welcomed her.

Its abnormal humidity a surprising excitement.

Through it, she'd entered the same magical and exclusive realm within the mountains. Her heart skipped a beat when noticing the wispy hand offering her guidance into the cave she'd once walked away from.

This time accepting it, Isla dragged Leif's body up the numerous steps leading to Spellforge, and without so much as a complaint. Penance. Her feet sweated, and slipped on the mossy granite, but still she endured. Penance. Step-by-step she carried ever upward, and when reaching the top, collapsed on the Codex and Leif's unmoving chest.

Looking up at the seven magi's faces, she'd made it.

"We're home," she said, running her clammy palm up and down the cloth covering Leif.

The Codex then burst through and opened; its parchment rapidly flicking to the fold she'd made in a page's corner. The page that bore the paramount spell Leif had cast. Tracing it with her eyes, she looked back up to the seven magi. She weighed up her options – if she could even cast it without Leif's transliteration, merely remembering the words he said.

Would the same spell reverse the effects? She pondered. *Will this serve as penance for the wrongs I've committed? Awaken the magi from stone. Do what Basem couldn't... or wouldn't. Use the Codex one last time.*

Proceeding without answer, she entered the mountain.

Within, Spellforge was brighter than when she'd left it – the crystals still throbbing but attune a different heartbeat. Feeling for her chest, she took a moment to breathe and see. It was attuned to her own. Although broken, Isla's heart had beat strongly for magic and that strength painted Spellforge in a brightness only seen in its heyday.

Days had passed and Leif's corpse grew colder. His tawny skin lost to the dreary greys of death, and his silver-grey eyes nothing more than hoary, white spheres of horror. Undressed and prepared for burial, Isla displayed his battered armour in the library beside Basem's dented diadem. Armour she'd once desired in simpler times of yore.

Taking up the Codex that she'd come to fear, Isla entered the ziggurat and the Chamber of Wisdom to look on the stone magi and Basem's old seat. Dustier than she recalled, the dais had grown new fungi and the steps' cracks grew as the mushrooms thrived in the room's darkness. Although wanting to go to her grandfather's seat, she instead approached his stone comrades.

Kneeling at their feet, she lowered her head and placed down the Codex. Days had indeed passed her by, and in those days, she tackled the idea of using the Codex again – to awaken Basem's friends he'd frozen to protect from the Purge. Isla had again wondered if performing the selfless act, and once more placing herself in danger, would serve as true penance; that then she could forgive herself for taking so many innocent lives.

Feeling lightheaded again, and wrinkling her nose at the paramount spell, she realised that nothing ever could. Not really. She'd live with that grief and guilt until her death. Forever a kin slayer; forever a murderer. There was no penance for that, only a deep-seated penitence which'd eternally torment her.

Apologising to the magi, to Basem, and Leif, Isla wearily took the Codex, bowed towards the phoenix crest, and retreated out into Spellforge where she'd bury the Codex and its power. Bury it deep underground where nobody could find it.

She'd bury it beneath the water.

Thus, that night, Isla revealed her scarring to the bright, magic crystals and let them glow. And at the centre of the dried-out lake, she dug a six-foot deep hole. At the centre of the dried-out lake, Isla Morrigan would bury her brother in nothing more than the cloth that the alsheytan had wrapped him in.

In the hole, abreast Leif, lay Isla. Atop him, with his wonderful hands wrapped around the ornate cover, was the Codex. It thrashed and shook, as though it was sentient and wanted to break free. Glaring up at the jutting crystals, however, Isla ignored it; feeling her heartbeat, she watched them glow.

She didn't say anything. She couldn't say anything. Although simply being next to him, and knowing that she was making the right decision, felt like it was enough.

The Codex was too dangerous, even in her hands, and it needed to be lost on the world forevermore.

Thus, planting a kiss on Leif's cold, grey cheek, Isla retreated from her brother's sepulchre.

In retreat, she neither wept nor spoke. Isla didn't want to say goodbye. Goodbye was too final. A nail in the coffin, so to speak. So, with her hands held out before her, she instead said, "*aqua pila*" and cast a torrent of water to fill the once-dried lake until clear wavelets drenched her toes and the grass around it.

Dive beneath the waters – draw it entirely – but you'll need to dig after, too. Dig deep to find the Codex and the Conduit.

Returning to the library, attention on Leif's armour, Isla ran her hands up and down it until stopping at the shattered crest.

The sapphire blue had been lost, but the dust of his shattered azurite remained. Brushing it, feeling it between her fingers, Isla felt for her own around her neck. She waited and listened, hoping to hear Ghulzar or somebody, but received nothing.

With a sigh, she grabbed at the old book that'd been marked by Basem. A book, she'd felt, that he either intended for her to read or foresaw her needing. She read its title: *The Twenty-Four Proficiencies of Magic* and dropped it back onto the desk in a coiling cloud of white dust.

The desk beside the diadem and Leif's varangian armour.

"You couldn't get me to read much in life." She side-eyed the black-and-onyx breastplate and felt the stirring faintly in the pits of her stomach. "But in death, you've won me over."

Seated where Basem had once drowned his sorrows, Isla took up her grandfather's dented diadem. Glaring at the empty prong setting and fingering her mother's necklace that'd brightened over the marked book, she held it against her forehead and closed her eyes.

It'd still smelt of Basem: a mixture of alcohol and an almond-esque fragrance. And that scent that'd once disgusted her, had brought her comfort.

Placing it by her side, and caressing its design, Isla opened *The Twenty-Four Proficiencies of Magic* to the first page.

By the second paragraph concerning the Recommendation of Two, she paused on a quote attributed to Basem, and written in his own hand. A quote made visible by her azurite's light. Scribed on an angle and along the margins, she tilted her head and focused the azurite's blue on it.

"A secret message," she said in awe. "So, you weren't lying after all, Grandfather."

Tracing her nail along his handwriting, Isla read: "*Death is but the pathway to newer, grander adventures. Adventures that put even the most terrific knight's tales to shame. So, do not weep for the dead. Rejoice, for they're living like kings and queens in far-off lands.*"

Either a message to his grieving self, or to the future Isla, a weight had been eased. A weight that would've ruined her if left untouched. All she'd needed was a slither of reassurance.

Reading over it again, she smiled.

With the Codex buried and drowned, hidden from one and all, Isla Morrigan began her long and arduous study of magic to sate the Calling and become the powerful magi she was destined to become. Sometimes, she'd visit the lake and read to the waves – to her brother beneath them. Other days, she'd read Basem's quote from dusk to dawn.

And as the years passed her by, Isla never again left the comfort and safety of Spellforge until the day she passed from the world and reunited with Leif in death.

In far-off lands.